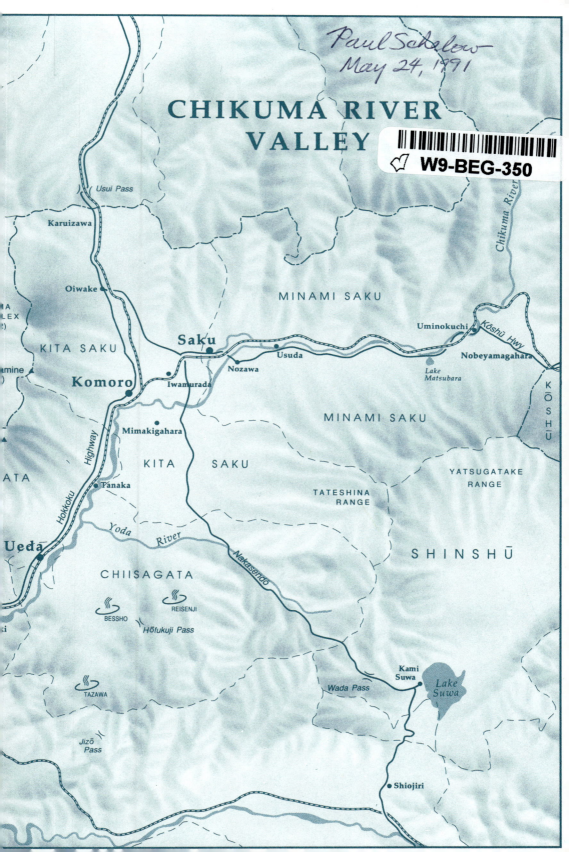

CHIKUMA RIVER VALLEY

Usui Pass

Karuizawa

Oiwake

MINAMI SAKU

Uminokuchi

Kōshū Hwy

Chikuma River

KITA SAKU

Saku

Nobeyamagahara

Komoro

Usuda

Nozawa

Iwamurada

Lake Matsubara

KŌSHŪ

Mimakigahara

MINAMI SAKU

KITA   SAKU

YATSUGATAKE RANGE

Tanaka

TATESHINA RANGE

Hokkoku

Highway

Yoda   River

SHINSHŪ

Ueda

Nakasendō

CHIISAGATA

REISENJI

BESSHO

Hōfukuji Pass

Kami Suwa

Lake Suwa

TAZAWA

Wada Pass

Jizō Pass

Shiojiri

Chikuma River
Sketches

A publication of the
SCHOOL OF HAWAIIAN
ASIAN & PACIFIC STUDIES
University of Hawaii

Shimazaki Tōson

Chikuma River Sketches

Translated by
William E. Naff

SHAPS Library of Translations

University of Hawaii Press

Honolulu

To
Hsieh Chih-hsien

Chikuma River Sketchbooks originally published as
Chikumagawa no Suketchi by Sakura Shobō
© 1912 Shimazaki Tōson
© 1967 Shimazaki Ohske

Additional texts by Shimazaki Tōson
© 1966, 1967 Shimazaki Ohske

English translation
© 1991 School of Hawaiian, Asian & Pacific Studies

Library of Congress Cataloging-in-Publication Data
Shimazaki, Tōson, 1872–1943.
[Chikumagawa no suketchi. English]
Chikuma River sketches / Shimazaki Tōson ;
translated by William E. Naff.
p.   cm. — (SHAPS library of translations)
Translation of: Chikumagawa no suketchi.
ISBN 0-8248-1314-6
I. Title.   II. Series.
PL816.H55C413   1991
895.6'84203—dc20
[B]   90-26474
                                           CIP

Publication of this book has been assisted by
a grant from the Japan Foundation

University of Hawaii Press books are printed
on acid-free paper and meet the guidelines
for permanence and durability of the Council
on Library Resources

Contents

Maps

Acknowledgments

I wish to express my gratitude to President Kansaku Kōichi of Tōyō University and President Muramatsu Tomotsugu of Tōyō Tanki College, and to the staffs of those twin institutions, particularly Itō Kazuo, professor emeritus at Tōyō University, and Professor Kanda Shigeyuki of Tōyō Tanki College, whose guided tour through the Komoro and environs he knows so thoroughly brought this crucial stage of Tōson's career to life for me as never before. The members of the Shimazaki Tōson Gakkai have been unfailingly and without exception generous in their assistance.

To Professor Morimoto Ryōichi of Tokyo University and Mrs. Morimoto I am more indebted than words can express. Professor Hayasaka Raigo, recently president of Miyagi Gakuin in Sendai, was most generous in every way. Mr. Mamada Goichi of the Tōson Memorial in Komoro not only provided invaluable personal consultations but was instrumental in arranging for permission to reproduce many of the illustrations and maps in this volume.

Mr. Komiyama Matsuyoshi of Kita Mimakimura was most generous in making a copy of the painting *Shinano no Sanga* (A Shinano Landscape) available for reproduction on the cover of this volume. Mr. Tsuchiya Kazuo of the Saku Kyōiku Iinkai gave permission to adapt several maps from *Shimazaki Tōson to Saku* (Saku: Saku Kyōiku Iinkai, 1978). Mr. Takezawa Kōji gave permission to reproduce the profile of Mt. Asama, which originally appeared in Hayashi Isamu, *Asamayama to Chikumagawa to Komoro* (Komoro: Takezawa Shoten, 1968). Mr. Ishimori Hiroki, president of Sōkyūshorin, granted permission to use photographs from *Komoro: Tōson Kinenkan* (Tokyo: Sōkyūshorin, 1982). Mr. Shibata Kōji of Shinchōsha was instrumental in forwarding my request to Mr. Fujita Mitsuo, president of Kobikisha, who granted permission to use photographs from *Shimazaki Tōson* (Tokyo: Shinchōsha, 1986).

Again thanks to my wife, Hsieh Chih-hsien, and my editor, Stuart Kiang, for their unfailing support and invaluable advice. Their enthusiasm, generosity, and understanding lie behind whatever virtues this translation may possess. Its shortcomings are entirely my own.

WILLIAM E. NAFF

Translator's Introduction

"I went out as a teacher; I came back as a student." Those are the words with which Shimazaki Tōson[1] summed up the six years he spent in a private school in the old castle town of Komoro at the foot of Mt. Asama, a huge and ever-threatening volcano on the eastern edge of the great landlocked province of Shinano.[2] Komoro is about a hundred airline miles northwest of Tokyo and about half again that distance to the northeast of Tōson's birthplace in the village of Magome in the extreme southwest of the same province.

When Tōson arrived in Komoro in 1899, he was already famous. Two years earlier this hitherto obscure twenty-five-year-old had brought a painful and often demoralizing youth to a brilliant climax with the publication of his first volume of poetry, *Fresh Greens*.[3] These poems captivated (no other word will quite do) the Japanese reading public, initiating a new epoch in the history of Japanese letters. When Donald Keene writes that "Tōson may fairly be called the creator of modern Japanese poetry," he is endorsing an overwhelming popular and critical consensus that still stands unchallenged nearly a century later.[4] For Tōson this poetry was a celebration of the breaking of a dark winter of the soul that had persisted for more than a decade. In an interview of 1910 he reflected on the hackneyed use of the four seasons as metaphors of childhood, youth, maturity, and old age, and noted that for him it had been different. Youth had been the wintertime of his life and spring had broken only with the writing of *Fresh Greens*.[5]

Upon his return to Tokyo from Sendai, where he had written *Fresh Greens*, Tōson found that the role of passionate young genius of romantic poetry which public adulation tried to force on him brought neither personal tranquility nor economic security. In "Among the Boulders," Tōson speaks of the revulsion with which he came to look upon urban life during that interval and of the "futile resistance and fatigue" that it entailed. This was itself a radically new feeling that would not begin to become widespread until the next decade. For all the ambivalence with which many viewed the capital in those days every ambitious young man in the provinces still dreamed of going to Tokyo, while everyone already there was firmly convinced that he was at the center of things. One of the most important constituents of Tōson's large and faithful audience consisted of readers who found a reflection either of their dreams or of their actual experience in this country boy who had gone to Tokyo and made good through hard work and strength of character after years of bitter struggle.[6]

After turning down a more comfortable and lucrative position in a middle school in Nara, Tōson accepted an invitation from Kimura Kumaji, his old teacher, pastor, and benefactor, to teach English and Japanese at Komoro Gijuku, beginning in April 1899. The motives for this retreat to Komoro were diverse but the immediate cause seems to have been a brutal joint review of the novella *The Nap* by a group of critics that included Mori Ōgai,[7] an elder whom Tōson revered. *The Nap* was his first serious attempt at prose fiction. He would not try again for some time. The charges of pretentious obscurity and mannerism, regularly raised not only by readers of his earliest published writing but by many of his schoolmates long before he had been published, had not been altogether stilled even by the triumph of *Fresh Greens,* and now they were being leveled more devastatingly than ever against his prose fiction.

Yet poetry was not where he saw his future. For all the popular and critical success of the first volume of poetry and the lesser but still solid successes enjoyed by the three subsequent ones,[8] Tōson was already committed to prose. This is made obliquely clear in the awkward and self-conscious little anecdote about an apocryphal Japanese student of portrait painting in St. Petersburg that introduces *The Nap.* When the student decides to return home by way of western Europe his teacher pleads with him not to gaze upon the scenery along the Rhine. He does so anyway and is immediately converted to landscape painting, explaining that "he had gazed upon the Rhine." This declaration of his intent to abandon poetry for prose is a partial explanation of a changeover that still continues to arouse speculation. But what Tōson wanted to say in the future may have been more appropriate to the medium of prose rather than that of poetry.

The circumstances under which Tōson made the change from poet to novelist would seem to remove whatever might be left of the mystery. His survival as a writer was still very much in question. It may well be, as some have suggested, that he found his poetic inspir-

ation running thin, or even that he might have felt the sheer timeli-
ness of *Fresh Greens* had almost as much to do with its reception as
had its quality, but he was above all aware that his knowledge of literature and of the world was not yet sufficient to serve as the basis
for the kind of literary career he envisioned for himself. Moreover,
the financial demands resulting from the seemingly endless permu-
tations of misfortune and mismanagement achieved by his siblings
were a steady drain on his extremely limited resources. While it was
at least theoretically possible for novelists to support themselves
through their writing, there was no prospect that poets would ever
be able to do so. If he failed to establish himself as a novelist he
would at best spend the rest of his life as a provincial schoolteacher,
an honorable and useful profession but one that was several orders of
magnitude below the scale of his ambition.

Whatever the hopes for professional improvement that he might
have brought with him, his gratitude and sense of relief in escaping
from the inner and outer turmoil of the previous twenty months in
Tokyo are plainly reflected in his repeated descriptions of a near
epiphany on the morning after his arrival in Komoro. The description of this scene in the "Afterword to the *Chikuma River Sketchbooks*"
serves also as as a reminder that he had recently read Tolstoy's *The
Cossacks:*[9]

> In truth, from the time on that first morning in Komoro when I gazed
> out upon the mountains like a famished traveler—those distant, snow-
> capped peaks—Mt. Asama, and the range shaped like fangs, the
> deep-shadowed valleys, the ruins of the old castle, the clouds clustered
> like wisps of smoke over the mountain peaks—from the time I first
> caught sight of them bathed in morning light, I felt that I was no
> longer the same person as before. It was as though something some-
> how different had begun in me.

Once Tōson was in Komoro, it seemed obvious to everyone that
finding a wife was the absolutely indispensable next step for a young
country schoolteacher, and appropriate arrangements were made.
Tōson's choice was Hata Fuyuko, an 1898 graduate of Meiji
Jogakkō, then considered to be the most advanced institution of
women's education in the country. Iwamoto Yoshiharu, headmaster
of the school and Tōson's former employer, successfully undertook
the delicate negotiations required of a go-between in this suit by an

impoverished, though promising, young man for the hand of the daughter of a wealthy Hakodate family of advanced and liberal views.[10]

The marriage was under tension from the beginning. Foremost among the many problems confronting the new couple was the cultural conflict inherent in a marriage of the daughter of a newly established frontier family with the son of a history-obsessed old mainland family whose catastrophic decline in fortune had tended to make it cling even more rigidly to its sense of itself. Fuyuko had been brought up to take it for granted that women would occupy a strong and vital role in the household. Her father's business required him to spend much of his time away from home and during his protracted absences her mother had routinely taken over the management of all aspects of the family enterprises. In the strongest possible contrast to the traditions of Tōson's family, Fuyuko had grown up in a socially and intellectually adventurous atmosphere, one that included a fondness for nice clothes and valued comfortable, though highly disciplined, living. Her father shared the common belief of the self-made man that, beyond a certain, very quickly reached point, indulgence of the chronically unsuccessful was not merely foolish but immoral.

It was ultimately the strength of her own desires that convinced her father to allow Fuyuko to become the wife of Tōson, whom she had not known at school but whose reputation had been that of a quiet and gentle young man. She had read his poetry and his early essays about the partnership involved in divine love—surely he would instinctively understand her wishes and her goals in life.[11] The reality proved to be otherwise; her husband was from the beginning obsessed with what he saw as his duty to support his extended family. Hideo, Tōson's eldest brother, had sold the family holdings in Magome and gone to Tokyo, where he quickly dissipated what little remained of the Shimazaki family fortune in ill-advised business ventures, two of which netted prison terms for him (naiveté, not evil intent, seems to have been the cause). The second brother was neglecting home and family to engage in a long and ultimately successful political fight for the interests of his former neighbors in the Kiso, while the long-missing third brother soon turned up at Hideo's Tokyo residence, disabled by disease and totally dependent for the rest of his life. Tōson was usually the prime, and not infrequently the sole, support of all. His salary—forty yen in 1899 and shrinking to twenty-five by 1905 as he reduced his teaching load in order to write —could not be stretched to cover these demands and the disposition of the money that her father had given to them to assist in the launching of their new household became a source of contention that constantly exacerbated the strains resulting from their poverty.[12]

In the following years, Tōson and Fuyuko would find themselves bringing up three little daughters in circumstances the extreme austerity of which are for the most part only hinted at in these sketches. Their lives were further complicated by Tōson's discovery that Fuyuko had come to their marriage with still unresolved feelings about the head clerk back in Hakodate to whom she had originally been affianced. Chancing upon a particularly despairing letter from Fuyuko to her former fiancé, he read it in the worst possible light. The marriage came close to breaking up. At the same time Tōson's continuing friendship with Tachibana Itoe, his former piano teacher during his brief interlude as a student at the Tokyo School of Music in 1898, caused further complications. She even visited him once in Komoro while staying at the nearby summer resort of Karuizawa.

The marriage eventually settled into a pattern of mutual tolerance that seemed to be progressing toward something more by August 1910 when Fuyuko died from a hemorrhage following the birth of her seventh child. Brought up in wealth, comfort, and bright prospects for the future, Fuyuko had experienced little but poverty, hardship, and disappointment during the eleven and a half years of her marriage. It is difficult to know how much of the shadowy character of Fuyuko's presence in the *Sketchbooks* and the related stories derives from Tōson's well-known reticence and how much from a guilty conscience, although both must have been operative. More about their marriage comes out in the novel *The Family,* and still more in two ostensibly non-autobiographical novellas from the Komoro period, but much remains unexplored in his writings. The brief glimpses of this woman grubbing in the vegetable garden and hauling water from the well a block away from their dilapidated little Komoro home, and of an old Tokyo friend finding her shabbily dressed and hard at the grimmest domestic drudgery, are heart-rending. It is not at all surprising that she is quoted as telling her older sister, "There is no connection between the 'I' that lived in Hakodate, the 'I' that went to Meiji Jogakkō, and the 'I' since my marriage."[13]

Tōson has been harshly judged for his apparent selfishness during these years. The evidence for this judgment, while strong, is circumstantial and inconclusive, but at the very least this is a period in Tōson's life about which there are more questions than there are ready answers. At best he seems to have been self-centered to a degree that is indefensible in human terms. It is only a slight mitigation to note that he also seems to have been free of the deliberate cruelty that characterizes the careers of so many other young men, in Japan or elsewhere, who shared his romantic notions about the necessity of sacrificing all those around them to the demands of art.

Throughout the Komoro years Tōson gave the highest priority to his own program of study and self-improvement. Relying upon friends, particularly Tayama Katai, and his connections with Tokyo and Yokohama dealers to keep himself supplied with books, he became acquainted with, or deepened his knowledge of, the works of writers such as Tolstoy, Turgeniev, Dostoevsky, Ibsen, Merejkowski, Goethe, Nietzsche, Hauptmann, Stendhal, Flaubert, Maupassant, Balzac, Zola, Darwin, and Lombrozo, all of whom he read in English translation. As his knowledge of European culture and literature increased, he was also gaining a new appreciation of the classics of Japanese literature and of their immediate relevance to those seeking to define the course of contemporary Japanese literature. He returned once again to Bashō's travel diaries, works which had always been important to this writer from a family that had for generations operated a post station on one of the great highways. Bashō was the writer most frequently quoted in his juvenilia, and echoes of Bashō's works are to be found on almost every page of the travel portions of the *Sketchbooks*. Equally important was his discovery, in the course of teaching Sei Shōnagon's *Pillow Book,* that her attitudes and techniques were immediately relevant to what he was trying to do. She is a constant and creative presence in the *Sketchbooks* and in the numerous collections of short pieces that he published later. While the conventions and demands of contemporary journalism lie behind these collections, most of which were originally published in magazines and newspapers, so also does the long and honorable tradition of the personal miscellany in Japanese literature, and the overt echoes of that tradition come most frequently from its first and arguably greatest practitioner.[14]

In short, the Komoro experience shaped Tōson's entire career, for it was in Komoro that he sought and found a renewed sense of connection with the Japanese soil and the people who live on it. This rediscovery of both the high culture and the lives of ordinary people in traditional Japan informed everything he did during the rest of his life and it plays a particularly vital role in the success of *Before the Dawn,* the masterpiece of his mature years.[15]

The title of the *Chikuma River Sketchbooks*[16] defines both their character and their immediate purpose with precision and economy. In Komoro, Tōson set about to retrain and reeducate himself for a career in prose. This program of self-improvement was made up of conversation, reflection, experience of country life, wide ranging but carefully selected reading, and what he called "practice in seeing" *(mono o miru keiko).* This discipline reminds us not only of Tōson's discovery while in Sendai of Ruskin's *Modern Painters* but of how consistent the English writer's famous dictum on speaking, thinking, and seeing was with Bashō's values. Indeed, the contemporary debate surrounding the development of realism in modern Japanese literature centered around parallels between literature and painting, for the most part pursued through comparisons between Japanese and European painting that were invariably to the advantage of the latter. *Shaseibun,* "writing that draws from nature," the term used to describe realistic writing, came from the vocabulary of painting. There was then, of course, little awareness in Japan that European painting was at that very time being revitalized by its discovery of Japanese painting and woodblocks, and that the effect of European art on Japanese painting would be much more ambiguous. The irony is now being brought full circle with the belated recognition that some traditional Japanese narrative strategies are comparable with the most advanced practices of European literary modernism.[17]

Between 1900 and 1902, Tōson began the practice of depicting in words the life he saw around him. This "practice in seeing" produced a number of notebooks filled with short prose descriptions in much the same way that a painter might essay practice sketches of the same scenes. It was not, however, until a decade later, when his career in prose was already firmly established, that he selected the most promising parts of their contents for revision and publication.

The metaphor of the sketchbook came naturally to Tōson. As a child he had dreamed of becoming a painter and he retained a deep interest in painting throughout his life, an interest that is reflected throughout the *Sketchbooks*. Now, under the influence of his friend the watercolor artist Maruyama Banka (the B—— of the *Sketchbooks*), he took up once again the artist's brush and easel to supplement his verbal sketches with pictorial ones. Only the verbal sketches have survived, but it is not surprising that two of his sons would grow up to become painters in the European style.

These depictions of life in and around Komoro took on an added dimension through Tōson's friendship with Yanagita Kunio, the great pioneer of Japanese ethnology and ethnography. The *Sketchbooks* have obvious affinities with Yanagita's extremely influential *Legends of Tōno*,[18] published in 1910. At the same time, it is already consistent with Tōson's character, as it is with the Tolstoy of *The Cossacks*, that the *Sketchbooks* should go beyond the merely picturesque or the merely entertaining to make an attempt to record objectively the way of life that he found in his new home, but Yanagita's influence may be seen in the comparative rigor and sophistication of Tōson's method as well as in his choice of subjects. Tōson and his friend Tayama Katai were among the first Japanese writers to take the stance of the serious and respectful student of folkways, although they did so in strongly contrasting ways.

This acceptance of the full validity of contemporary provincial life is a dimension that is missing from the works of Natsume Sōseki (1867–1916) and Mori Ōgai (1862–1922), those two great elders of Tōson's who filled out the dominant triumvirate of late Meiji letters. Their interests lay elsewhere for completely valid reasons, but all too often the very determination of their contemporaries to be cosmopolitan and up-to-date rendered them too provincial to treat the kinds of people that Tōson describes here with anything but condescension. This shallow mid-Meiji snobbery grew out of the emulation of unfortunate European models and through too respectful attention to those who claimed to have "scientific" explanations for any and all "backwardness" as they chose to define it; it would have seemed utterly alien to Bashō or Saikaku (1642–1693), and it would be alien to many Japanese writers of succeeding generations. Thus, although a narrow focus upon metropolitan experience has characterized one pole of Japanese literature from its very beginnings, it is in large part balanced by the exhaustive cataloging of the Japanese hinterlands in the travel literature and military tales that established the opposite pole.

Through his general acceptance of the givens of the society in which he found himself (although his honesty ensured that the strain would show occasionally), Tōson achieves a universality that very few of his striving contemporaries could approach with their inadequately informed cosmopolitanism. Tōson observes the life of the soil and of the mountains with a clear and unsentimental eye that gives the same careful attention to its grinding poverty and toil as to its touches of often startling grandeur. He perceives its paradoxical blend of excitement and stimulation with deadly monotony, isolation, and hardship; of a frequent sense of exhilarating richness in the midst of poverty. In doing so he creates a picture of rare balance. The reader comes away from these sketches with vivid impressions of the flavor and quality of life in this turn-of-the-century provincial Japanese town; he will know what he would have liked and not liked there; what he would have admired and what he would have found deplorable. Such a picture is not only capable of showing why so many of those throughout the world who were born into such a life have left it, an easy enough thing to do, but it is also capable of performing the far more difficult task of showing why so many of those who have left it are likely to feel forever diminished, however satisfying their subsequent lives might prove to be.

The austere vision that lies behind these sketches may skirt some issues and evade others, but it never fails to see that the apparent certainties with which the past may seem to have been blessed were usually anything but certain to those actually living among them and that even the most desirable changes often exact a seemingly unbearable cost. If the *Sketchbooks* are illuminated by a lyrical sensibility, they are also driven by a vision of life as a harsh and painful struggle. When, a few years later, Tōson's request to go to the front as a war correspondent in the Russo-Japanese war was turned down, he consoled himself with the observation that "life is a vast battlefield. The writer is a war correspondent."[19]

Stylistically, Tōson's sketches reflect his determination to correct his most egregious shortcomings as a writer by forcing himself to make his points clearly and simply. This is never an easy hurdle and even less so for those, like Tōson, with a tendency to overwrite, but the problem was especially formidable in the Japan of ninety years ago. Such prose standards as had survived the turmoil of the previous generation favored a written style that was ornate and complex, stiff with classical allusion, and far removed from the spoken language. The addition of yet another layer of allusion, to European history and culture, kept an already overburdened style perpetually at the edge of dysfunction. Tōson's early versions were made still more tortuous and convoluted by the remaining traces of the schoolboy showoff he had been not so very long ago.

But the job that he set for himself went far beyond the correction of his own grave faults. In order to create a viable prose style, he had first to create a new literary language. That he succeeded in this creation was, like his earlier creation of a poetic voice for the new age, an achievement that was nothing less than revolutionary. It makes him one of the handful of writers who played a major role in creating the language in which modern Japanese prose is written and lends a special authority to his survey of the process of creating that language in his "Afterword."

The state of literary Japanese around the turn of the century was one of flux bordering on chaos. The shattering of faith in traditional literary forms and conventions occasioned by the discovery of modern European literature was just beginning to mend, in part through a rediscovery of earlier writers such as Ihara Saikaku, but the new norm had yet to define itself. A renewed appreciation of Saikaku stood behind the works of Ozaki Kōyō (1867–1903), the most renowned author at the turn of the century, whose successes did not, however, long outlive his death. Similar influences were behind Higuchi Ichiyō (1872–1896), briefly a member of the same literary circle as Tōson, who had begun to achieve a remarkable reconciliation of Edo-style narrative with contemporary subject matter but whose career was cut short too soon for her to leave a lasting impression on the language.[20] A number of others had already pointed the way. The most notable was Futabatei Shimei (1864–1909),[21] who was producing a very creditable version of Russian realism in Japanese as early as the late 1880s but whose achievement was not fully appreciated until after his death. By then others, including Tōson, had already made their contributions to setting the course of the subsequent development of the literary language.[22]

In his "Afterword to the *Chikuma River Sketchbooks,*" Tōson notes the importance to his own thinking of Mori Ōgai's 1900 essay on the language problem, "Cloth of Many Colors."[23] Aside from its cogent and closely reasoned argument, which Tōson accurately summarizes, the very existence of such an essay from the hand of this brilliant, German-trained physician demonstrates how much of the problem remained to be resolved. Tōson's discussion focuses on what was perhaps the most fatal objection to traditional styles: their inescapable tendency, despite all their real charms, to let their intricacy and their arcane conventions exhaust the writer with extraneous concerns and to distract him from what he was trying to say.

Tōson's awareness of the problem was based on firsthand experience. The prose of his earliest works, published between 1892 and 1896, although immature and even more pretentious than the norm, was otherwise very much like most other ambitious things being written at the time. That is to say, it was clotted with allusions to Japanese, Chinese, English, and continental literature, the more arcane the better. Rhetorical flourish was piled upon rhetorical flourish and the thread of argument was forever on the verge of vanishing into thickets of pretentious and overblown syntax. Realistic portrayal of everyday life was out of the question.

Even at its best such writing presented the reader with most of the philological problems of the best of Edo writing while offering few of its rewards. The affirmation of shared cultural values that had been one of its greatest strengths no longer obtained in a literary world seemingly cut adrift from its foundations. Written Japanese based on traditional styles was coming to seem inescapably *passé* but there was as yet nothing to take its place. The influence of those whose literary tastes were wholly informed by nostalgia for earlier times was clearly on the wane while a new reading public was rapidly losing patience with literary archaism. Something better had to be found and it was in the *Sketchbooks* that Tōson found his version of something better. In them he began to perfect the lean, straightforward, apparently artless style that would characterize his mature works. After the material later to be compiled as the *Sketchbooks* was completed, he published a number of short works of fiction, including "Among the Boulders" and "An Impoverished Bachelor of Science," that also reflect what he had learned.

The first published work to display something approaching full control of Tōson's newly acquired linguistic and narrative skills, and the first to attract widespread attention, was *The Broken Commandment*, published in 1906.[24] Mostly written in Komoro, *The Broken Commandment* draws heavily on the *Sketchbooks* in both style and content, and it occupies a position almost as pivotal in the history of modern Japanese prose as that of *Fresh Greens* in modern Japanese poetry.[25] From a historical point of view, what Tōson achieved in the *Sketchbooks* tells us much about what he would achieve in *The Broken Commandment* at the same time that the mastery achieved in *The Broken Commandment* was brought to bear on the later revisions of the *Sketchbooks*, a text the original versions of which predated it. The interrelationship is complex and interlocking and it is further complicated by the fact that only the edited versions of the *Sketchbooks* have survived.

There were a few false steps (some of them in these pieces) before Tōson had completely assimilated his newly augmented erudition but his mature approach was one of restraint. While many of his contemporaries gloried in displays of new-found learning—his close friend and colleague Tayama Katai is a notable example—anything remotely suggestive of a vulgar display of erudition became repugnant to Tōson. Understatement was his way and this understatement makes it easy to overlook the breadth and richness of Tōson's range of reference and his masterful handling of resonance and allusion, particularly in those of his works which may seem almost dry and commonplace to the superficial reader.

Tōson's long quest in search of his mature voice is worth pursuing. To begin with, he was the earliest major Japanese writer to have an education oriented to Europe and America almost from the beginning. He started reading English in early adolescence, well before he began to think about a literary career. His cosmopolitanism was less immediately conspicuous than that of Mori Ōgai and Natsume Sōseki because it existed at an even more basic level of his thought processes. While Ōgai and Sōseki had also begun learning European languages at an early age, the greater part of their education had been in traditional Chinese and Japanese learning. Tōson had a fair grounding in the Chinese classics and a somewhat better one in traditional Japanese literature, but the resonances of the great tradition of Chinese writing both in China and Japan that appear in Ōgai's works and Sōseki's outstanding accomplishments in Chinese verse, not to mention the latter's prominence in the development of the modern haiku, were simply not accessible to one of Tōson's background. Given the relative depths of their immersion in traditional East Asian culture, it is an interesting paradox that Tōson should so often be viewed by general readers as the more "traditional" of the three. The resolution of this paradox is to be found in Tōson's lifelong search for a way home, a search that never lost its urgency even while he was living in Japan, since for most of his life he was far more cut off from his roots than Ōgai and Sōseki ever were when living abroad.

At its best Tōson's poetry had come out of an utterly fresh blending of the stance and subject matter of the English romantics with the manner and diction of a millennium of Japanese literature. Even after his studies in Komoro had provided him with an exceptionally broad range of reference in European literature, the allusions and quotations in both his poetry and his prose still tended to come from Wordsworth, Shakespeare, Milton, Byron, and Dante and from the parallels to their concerns that he found in Saigyō, Bashō, and Chikamatsu. Embarrassingly ostentatious and flamboyant in his juvenilia, these references would recede into the background in his mature works, where their constant presence subtly informs virtually every line.

The success of his poetry ensured that for a long time Tōson's readers would go to his books quite simply because they wanted to learn everything they possibly could about the poet who had created *Fresh Greens.* In one sense Tōson honored this expectation faithfully; the reader does indeed learn about the incidents and ambience of his day-to-day life in sometimes almost excruciating detail. Although he always retained control of the revelations, ensuring that much would remain hidden, he often lets us see things about his own personality and character that are both puzzling and disturbing.

The character of these revelations is reflected in the three different approaches that lie behind the overall stance of these pieces. In the *Chikuma River Sketchbooks,* figures and events are treated as archetypes of mountain life. Characters are referred to only by their initials; their full names are known with considerable certainty, but to supply them in the text would violate the nature of these sketches.[26] Works of fiction such as "Among the Boulders" and "An Impoverished Bachelor of Science" demonstrate a second approach. Here the story lines are still very close to the actual occurrences, but the names of the characters are changed to show that these are not literal portraits of their models: Tōson becomes Takase, Kimura Kumaji becomes Sakurai, and Ide Shizuka, the business manager of the Komoro Gijuku, becomes Captain Masaki, while Samejima Shin, the bachelor of science, is Hirooka in the first story and Saitō-sensei in the second. The essays—the "Afterword" and the two pieces entitled "At the Foot of Mt. Asama"—seem to represent Tōson's best understanding of his subject matter, and real names are used. Yet there is fiction in the essays while much of the value of the *Sketchbooks* lies in their reportage.

Although Tōson never falsified the overall character of the real-life story he was telling, he was a literary artist, not an annalist. He regularly selected and rearranged details. In these closely related works some incidents appear in more than one context as Tōson, still experimenting with the depiction of reality, returns to his sources again and again, trying to understand them fully and to exhaust their possibilities. The sketches and stories are, however, brought to life through Tōson's intense personal engagement with his subject matter, an engagement that, at this stage of his development, could become fixation. The incident in which the bachelor of science demonstrates the properties of carbon dioxide before an enthralled class of students appears in the *Sketchbooks* and is repeated in the two stories; its invariant presence in three successive works reflects a personal obsession with the wasted promise of the old man's life that perhaps reflects more favorably on Tōson's character than on his maturity as a writer. The missing half of the ring finger on the bachelor of science's left hand is somewhat more thoroughly assimilated, being attributed to an incongruously up-to-date baseball injury or, in other, more likely versions, to his participation in the civil war that followed the Meiji Restoration of 1868. Tōson's pleading of this man's cause when Kimura wanted to discharge him was one of the reasons for a growing estrangement between the two. His preoccupation with this unfortunate man also mirrored Tōson's apprehensions concerning his own very uncertain future. As still another surrogate father, the bachelor of science prefigures Aoyama Hanzō, the protagonist of *Before the Dawn*.

These anecdotes are clearly based on real-life incidents and the way in which each one is adjusted and adapted for each new context reveals much about the way in which Tōson dealt with reality. They remind us that fiction and reportage are two separate things, so that questions about which, if any, of the versions of a particular incident "really" took place are not only unanswerable but irrelevant to any judgment about the validity of Tōson's depictions of life in turn-of-the-century Komoro.

The original readers of these sketches would have had many ready associations to time and place that are not necessarily present for most readers of English. Tōson summed up the special qualities of the physical setting of Komoro in his essay entitled "Clouds":

> The location of Komoro on the Chikuma River in Kita Saku county affords five advantages for the observation of clouds: there is little rainfall from spring through fall; the elevation is three thousand feet, or the same as that of the summit of Mt. Tsukuba; its site is on the southwestern slope of Mt. Asama; the air is pure and clear; and the skies over the plateaus are vast and spacious.[27]

Komoro was, however, a fine vantage point from which to reflect on far more than the endlessly changing clouds in its spectacular skies. Like Tōson's hometown of Magome at the other extremity of the province, it was sufficiently remote from the turmoil and distraction of metropolitan life to provide a perspective on national and world-wide trends, while sufficiently tied to those areas by history and its function as a trading center on a major avenue of communications to keep from falling into a wholly self-involved isolation.

Much has been said about the spiritual stresses suffered by Japanese intellectuals of the Meiji period and later in their struggle to assimilate European culture. Victory in that struggle came earlier than is often believed. It was already possible in turn-of-the-century Komoro for Tōson to discuss Millet and Corot with the painter Miyake Katsumi, a man who had direct experience of the originals, or to have the classification of clouds in Ruskin's *Modern Painters* come up in conversations with a technician at the Nagano weather station. Among the many things that Tōson has to teach us about the Japan in which he lived is the extent to which, even in the midst of cultural conflict, everyday life was then already colored by a harmonious and productive coexistence and interaction of native and European cultural elements. The frequency with which English words and phrases, usually reproduced in jarringly exotic Roman letters, appear in the text reflects a lingering immaturity but also shows that Tōson could expect most of his readers to know enough English to follow him.

"Civilization and enlightenment" was the watchword of the Meiji Restoration. In practice this tended to be interpreted as wholesale importation of all aspects of European culture, both material and immaterial. It is easy to condescend to this policy from the safe distance of a century and a quarter, but there were very good reasons why it should have seemed an urgent necessity in Meiji Japan. The ambiguities of such a course and the conflicts it engendered were, aside from their national and international significance, also part of the flavoring of local life at the most intimate level, even down to questions of diet. The slaughterhouse scenes that Tōson describes in Sketchbook IX carry deep resonances of intercultural tension.

The traditional Japanese diet being one of the world's most austere made the relative richness of the European diet seem in the eyes of Japanese observers through four centuries of contact to be one of the most conspicuous of the cultural differences between the two civilizations.[28] Most notable in that richness was the importance of meat in the European diet. When, during Meiji, the need was felt to bring Japan up to the allegedly superior levels of vigor manifested by the Europeans, foreign arguments, both scientific and pseudo-scientific, for the introduction of meat into the Japanese diet seemed to carry great authority. That there was room for improvement in the diet remains beyond question even after most of the nineteenth-century certainties have evaporated, but like all adoptions of alien practices everywhere, the introduction of meat into the diet incorporated a broad range of issues, some of which are only now beginning to come to the fore.

Japan, of course, presents an interesting perspective from which to consider the dietary and other aspects of such problems. Dairy products were not used and the sources of animal flesh had traditionally been limited to seafood, eggs, and the occasional chicken. The only four-footed domestic animals common in Japan were horses, cattle, dogs, and cats, all four of which were equally beyond the pale for consideration as sources of food. The relative scarcity of large animals in Japan may have had something to do with the exclusion of their flesh from the diet, but any such tendencies were reinforced by Buddhist teachings concerning the interrelatedness of all life. For centuries the eating of large animals had seemed, to those few who thought of it at all, to be an aberration bordering on cannibalism. For those who were disposed to see Europeans as cold-blooded, rapacious barbarians, few facts about them afforded such ready invitations to the drawing of invidious comparisons as did their fondness for meat. Yet improvement of the diet through the inclusion of animal products came to seem such an urgent part of the program of national self-preservation that traditional repugnances were for the most part overwhelmed.[29]

The presence of the slaughterhouse in Japan embodies the ambiguities of civilization and enlightenment. It was completely alien to the provincial Japanese scene, not simply in its purpose but in the very style and shape of the buildings and in the tools of the trade. Yet the enlightened and civilized role of the veterinarian, who assures that the animals to be slaughtered are in fact in good health and that their corpses are handled in strict accordance with the requirements of elementary sanitation, would make it seem that the enterprise conformed in all respects to the best standards of European and American practice of the time.

The sympathies that underlie Tōson's rather dour exterior are rarely expressed openly, but his moving and disturbing depiction of the individuality of the animals awaiting their turn in the slaughterhouse and their apparent awareness of the approach of death make this episode an exception. His straightforward presentation of his own reactions, which eventually arrive at an acceptance of the process of transforming living animals into beef and pork that becomes shocking only in afterthought, together with his refusal to pass easy moral judgments on the people who work in the slaughterhouse, provide a rare unguarded glimpse of the man.

An aspect of the slaughterhouse scene that could easily go unrecognized outside Japan is that the herding and slaughtering of animals and the handling of meat and leather goods was a sphere of activity reserved for the outcasts. Tōson makes no overt allusion to the fact that his visit to such a place had been enough to set tongues wagging in Komoro because it would have been only too obvious to the Japanese reader. His perception of the conditions of outcast life is brought to the foreground in *The Broken Commandment*. Although his depictions did not meet with universal enthusiasm in the outcast communities the fact remains that he was the first major Japanese writer to depict their plight openly.[30]

The pleasures and the insights offered in these sketches make them an ideal introduction to those reading Tōson for the first time.

For those who already know him from other works, they may also help to moderate the intense ambivalence with which he is often viewed even in Japan, an ambivalence which has impeded his recognition in the rest of the world.

Many years of affection and admiration for the originals lie behind these translations of the *Chikuma River Sketchbooks*. Shimazaki Tōson's portrayals of Japanese provincial life at the turn of the century are rewarding at whatever level they may be approached. Delightful as *belles lettres,* they are also informative as history and ethnography. In these sketches from life in Komoro and the surrounding countryside, Tōson has provided vivid and lasting impressions of the way in which the timeless and universal human questions manifested themselves at this stage of the history of this once-remote mountain town. At the same time, he has documented some of the assets and liabilities not only of Japanese rural life at the beginning of this century, but also of rural life anywhere at any time.

Notes

1. The pen name Tōson was not adopted until 1894 (his given name was Haruki), but common practice uses it even in contexts where it is anachronistic.

2. Also called Shinshū, the province corresponds to the modern Nagano prefecture. The explosive eruption of Mt. Asama in 1783 was one of the worst natural catastrophes in Japanese history. The main blast seems to have been toward the east, and contemporary reports describe the lower stretches of the Tone River, which runs just to the northeast of Edo (modern Tokyo), as being choked with wreckage and the bodies of people and animals washed down into the lowlands more than a hundred miles away by the waters of a tributary stream on the north side of the mountain. This was the beginning of years of terrible famine which may have been at least in part a result of the explosion.

3. *Wakanashū;* the title carries associations with the joys of the world's rebirth in spring as exemplified by the picking of the first young wild greens of the season after a winter of living on dried and pickled foods. *Wakana* and related words, e.g., *wakakusa* (young herbs), are also long-established metaphors for the lush sensuousness of nubile young women. Its translation as "Seedlings" by Donald Keene and other authorities, though more graceful and succinct, may convey images of a neatly domesticated kitchen garden while *wakana* are for the most part the new growth of wild perennials.

4. Donald Keene, *Dawn to the West: Japanese Literature in the Modern Era— Poetry, Drama, Criticism* (New York: Holt, Rinehart & Winston, 1984), p. 204.

5. "Waga Shōgai no Fuyu" [The Winter of My Life], *Tōson Zenshū* [Tōson Collected Works] (Tokyo: Chikuma Shobō, 1967), vol. 6, pp. 497–502. Origi-

nally published in the March 1910 issue of *Chūgaku Sekai* [Middle School World], the interview contains a number of controversial assertions about certain details of Tōson's youth but its main thrust seems to be beyond cavil. I am indebted to the discussions in Hayashi Isamu, *Shimazaki Tōson, Tsuioku no Komoro Gijuku* [Shimazaki Tōson, In Memoriam: Komoro Gijuku] (Tokyo: Tōshishotenshinsha, n.d.), pp. 105–106, and Yoshimura Yoshio, *Tōson no Seishin* [The Spirit of Tōson] (Tokyo: Chikuma Shobō, 1979), pp. 13–15.

6. See William E. Naff, "Shimazaki Tōson: Life History as Archetype and as Commodity," in Edmund Leites, ed., *Life Histories as Civilizational Texts*, International Society for the Comparative Study of Civilizations (U.S.) Occasional Papers, no. 1 (1977), pp. 25–39.

7. The massive scale and magisterial quality of Ōgai's contribution to modern Japanese letters has been taken up in a number of excellent English-language studies. See Richard John Bowring, *Mori Ōgai and the Modernization of Japan* (Cambridge: Cambridge University Press, 1979) and J. Thomas Rimer, *Mori Ōgai* (Boston: Twayne Publishers, 1975). Tōson's contribution has as yet been much less thoroughly examined outside Japan.

8. *A Leaf Boat* (*Hitohabune*, June 1898), *Summer Grasses* (*Natsugusa*, October 1898), and *Fallen Plum Blossoms* (*Rakubaishū*, August 1901), all of which included prose pieces as well as poetry.

9. *The Cossacks* echoes throughout these pieces in the expressions of disgust with city life, in descriptions of the roughness of local life and the strength and vigor of the farm women, and in the hints of Olénin in the persona which Tōson gives himself, while touches of Eróshka's earthy wisdom and Lukáshka's vigorous simplicity are present in the portrayals of the townsmen and country folk. These influences do not in any way compromise the validity of Tōson's observations; they provided him with a powerful model through which to assist the reader in experiencing this life.

10. This discussion of Fuyuko is indebted to Morimoto Teiko, *Fuyu no Ie* [Fuyu's Family] (Tokyo: Bungei Shunjū, 1987), an illuminating study of the life of Hata Fuyuko and of her family and cultural background. Morimoto, the granddaughter of a niece of Fuyuko, gives a moving depiction of an interesting and significant life hitherto almost completely unknown to the public and in the process casts important new light on Tōson's early career.

11. The gloriously idealistic, if somewhat confused, vaporings of Tōson's "Jinsei no Fūryū o Omou" [On Sensibility in Human Life], an immature reworking of Kitamura Tōkoku's 1892 "Ensei Shika to Josei" [The Pessimist Poet and Womanhood] that appeared in *Bungakkai* [Literary World] in April 1893, must have contributed to her illusions about Tōson.

12. The tensions in the marriage and the repeated demands for assistance from his two oldest brothers that lie behind the *Sketchbooks* come to the foreground in the novel *Ie* (1910–1911), which has been translated by Cecile Segawa Siegle as *The Family* (Tokyo: University of Tokyo Press, 1976). They are examined from another perspective in Morimoto, *Fuyu no Ie.*

13. Morimoto, *Fuyu no Ie*, p. 99.

14. See the "Afterword to the *Chikuma River Sketchbooks*," p. 124.

15. *Yo-ake Mae* was originally published as a magazine serial between 1929 and 1935 and then revised and issued in book form in various editions. See my introduction to Shimazaki Tōson, *Before the Dawn,* trans. William E. Naff (Honolulu: University of Hawaii Press, 1987).

16. The *Chikuma River Sketchbooks* appeared in the magazine *Bunshō Sekai* [The World of Letters] in twelve installments between June 1911 and August 1912, and were issued as a single volume by Sakura Shobō in December 1912. The text on which the present translation is based is in *Tōson Zenshū,* vol. 5, pp. 3–152 (hereafter *Zenshū*). *Bunshō Sekai* was a literary journal issued by the publisher Hakubunkan from March 1906 through December 1920 before reappearing under the new title *Shinbungaku* through 1921, when it ceased publication.

17. Ivan Morris takes up the "modernity" of *Genji* in a number of places in *The World of the Shining Prince* (New York: Knopf, 1964) but most particularly on pages 268–269. Norma Field, in *The Splendor of Longing in The Tale of Genji* (Princeton: Princeton University Press, 1987), reminds us on page 8 that it was the European comparisons of Murasaki Shikibu with Virginia Woolf and Marcel Proust that inspired avant-garde Japanese writers to take a new look at her work. For a review of Tōson's connection with the *shasei* movement, see Janet Walker, *The Japanese Novel of the Meiji Period and the Ideal of Individualism* (Princeton: Princeton University Press, 1979), pp. 160–170.

18. *Tōno Monogatari,* or "Tales from Tōno," a compilation of folklore from the countryside around the village of Tōno in Iwate prefecture, may be counted as the first masterpiece of modern Japanese folklore studies, equally admired for its literary qualities and for its ethnography. See *The Legends of Tōno,* trans. Ronald Morse (Tokyo: Japan Foundation, 1975).

19. Preface to *The Greenleaf Collection* (*Ryokuyōshū,* 1916), *Zenshū* 2:304. *The Greenleaf Collection,* mentioned in the preface to the *Sketchbooks,* consists of eight stories from the Komoro period, some of which had been published individually at an earlier date.

20. For a study of Higuchi Ichiyō and translations of selected works, see Robert Lyons Danly, *In the Shade of Spring Leaves* (New Haven: Yale University Press, 1981).

21. For the contribution of Futabatei Shimei, see Marleigh Ryan, *Ukigumo: Japan's First Modern Novel* (New York: Columbia University Press, 1965), particularly "A Modern Language for Literature," pp. 80–95. The nature of the language problem is masterfully stated and the early efforts to deal with it clearly outlined in Masao Miyoshi, *Accomplices of Silence: The Modern Japanese Novel* (Berkeley: University of California Press, 1974), chap. 1, "The New Language," pp. 3–37. Important new ground has been broken in the vexed problem of creating a viable English-language criticism of the modern Japanese "I-novel" by Edward Fowler, *The Rhetoric of Confession* (Berkeley: University of California Press, 1988). The account given by Fowler on pages 16–18 is invaluable for the clarity and succinctness with which it places the question in its historical context as well as for the further questions it raises.

22. Tōson made no secret of his debt to Futabatei Shimei. See, for example, "Hasegawa Futabateishi o awaremu" [Mourning for Hasegawa Futabatei] in

Shinkatamachi yori [From Shinkatamachi], *Zenshū* 6:88–91, where, on the occasion of Futabatei's death, he recalls the impact that Futabatei's translations from Turgeniev and his *Drifting Cloud* had upon him in his youth.

23. For a complementary reading of "Cloth of Many Colors" *(Somechigae)*, see Rimer, *Mori Ōgai*, pp. 27–28.

24. For a fine translation with an informative and stimulating introduction, see Shimazaki Tōson, *The Broken Commandment*, trans. Kenneth Strong (Tokyo: University of Tokyo Press, 1974).

25. Sōseki was among the first to recognize Tōson's achievement. In a letter to Morita Sōhei dated April 3, 1906, just ten days after the novel was published, he wrote, "I have read *The Broken Commandment*. It is an outstanding work that will be passed down to later generations as the novel of the Meiji era. Such works as [Ozaki Kōyō's] *The Gold Demon* will be forgotten in twenty or thirty years. *The Broken Commandment* will not. I don't read many novels, but if a novel worthy of the name has been produced during the Meiji era, I think it is *The Broken Commandment*. You should make a strong introduction of Tōson in this month's issue of *Geien*."

See also the discussions in Edwin McClellan, *Two Japanese Novelists* (Chicago: University of Chicago Press, 1969), pp. 79–93, and Donald Keene, *Dawn to the West: Fiction* (New York: Holt, Rinehart & Winston, 1984), pp. 256–257.

26. See Saku Kyōikukai Tōson Iinkai, ed., *Shimazaki Tōson to Saku* [Shimazaki Tōson and Saku], 2nd printing (Saku, Nagano prefecture: Saku Kyōikukai, 1978), pp. 76–110.

27. "Kumo," Tōson's first published prose piece from Komoro, appeared in the periodical *Tenchijin* [Heaven, Earth, and Man], vol. 40 (August 1900), and was later included in *Fallen Plum Blossoms, Zenshū* 1:252–264 (the quoted passage appears on p. 252). It was inspired by Ruskin's treatment of the subject in his *Modern Painters*, vol. 1, chap. 3.

28. See William E. Naff, "Some Reflections on the Food Habits of China, Japan, and Rural America," *Comparative Civilizations Review*, no. 5 (Fall 1980): 70–95.

29. For some of the more facile assimilators of European traits, real and imaginary, the eating of beef became almost a hallowed undertaking. For a satire of such manifestations of "civilization and enlightenment," see the excerpt from Kanagaki Robun, "The Beef Eater," in Donald Keene, ed., *Modern Japanese Literature* (New York: Grove Press, 1956), pp. 31–33.

30. The best general introduction to the problem of the racially indistinguishable outcast group is still *Japan's Invisible Race* by George A. De Vos and Wagatsuma Hiroshi, revised ed. (Berkeley: University of California Press, 1972). The term *burakumin*, meaning "people [of the special] hamlets," is the currently preferred designation among the euphemisms and evasions that reflect the extreme discomfort the subject can still arouse in Japanese society.

A Note on Prefecture and Province Names

Since the prefectures, established during the 1870s, were still new at the turn of the century, people usually felt more comfortable with the names of the old provinces that had formerly occupied the same areas. The present and historic names of the four prefectures with which these stories are primarily concerned are as below:

Prefecture		*Province*
Nagano		Shinano, Shinshū
	To the east:	
Gumma		Kōzuke, Jōshū
	To the south:	
Yamanashi		Kai, Kōshū
	To the north:	
Niigata		Echigo

Shimazaki Tōson, November 1903.

The house in which Tōson lived in Baba'ura (now restored on another site).

Tōson's sister Sono (standing), his wife Fuyuko (seated), and his daughters Midori (left), Takako (center), and Nuiko (right). Photo taken in late 1904.

Tōson (right rear), his father-in-law Hata Keiji (center rear), Fuyuko (left front), and her sister Hata Takiko.

Samejima Shin, model for Saito-sensei in "An Impoverished Bachelor of Science."

Kimura Kumaji, headmaster of Komoro Gijuku.

Faculty of Komoro Gijuku and the graduating class of 1904. Back row, left to right: Tsuchiya Shichirō (natural history), Tōson, Kimura Kumaji, and Ōi Shōtarō (physical education). Second row, left to right: Akata Gorō (English), Maruyama Banka (painting), and, skipping two, Watanabe Hisashi (history and geography, "W——" in the *Sketchbooks*), and Samejima Shin (mathematics, physics, chemistry).

Suimeiro, Kimura Kumaji's study and villa in Nakadana.

Tōson (lower center, dark robe) and Komoro Gijuku students standing on the snowy lower levels of the Komoro castle walls. Memorial picture on the occasion of Tōson's departure from Komoro in April 1905.

Former main building of Komoro Gijuku, now moved to the site of the Tamura hospital.

Post memorializing the former site of Komoro Gijuku on what is now part of the grounds of the Komoro railway station.

Memorial stone on the former site of Tōson's home in
Baba'ura with an inscription by Arishima Ikuma,
artist and lifelong friend of Tōson.

View of Komoro from Ōkubo.

Third Gate of Komoro castle and the entrance to the Kaikoen.

Calligraphic copy in Tōson's hand of the
"Chikuma River Travel Song."

Chikumagawa Ryojō no Uta

1

Komoro naru kojō no hotori
Kumo shiroku yūshi kanashimu
Midori nasu hakobe wa moezu
Wakakusa mo shiku ni wa yoshinashi
Shirogane no fusuma no okabe
Hi ni tokete usuyuki nagaru.

Atatakaki hikari wa aredo
No ni mitsuru kaori mo shirazu
Asaku nomi haru wa kasumite
Mugi no iro wazuka ni aoshi
Tabibito no mure wa ikutsu ka
Hatakenaka no michi o isoginu.

Kure-yukeba Asama mo miezu
Uta kanashi saku no kusabue
Chikumagawa izayou nami no
Kishi chikaki ni noboritsu
Nigori-zake nigoreru ṇomite
Kusamakura shibashi nagusamu.

2

Kinō mata kaku arikeri
Kyō mata kaku arinamu
Kono inochi nani wo akuseku
Asu o nomi omoi-wazurau.

Ikutabi ka eiko no yume no
Kie-nokoru tani ni orite
Kawanami no izayou mireba
Suna majiri mizu maki-kaeru.

Aa kojō nani o ka kotau
Kishi no nami nani o ka kotau
Sugishi yo o shizuka ni omoe
Momotose mo kinō no gotoshi.

Chikumagawa yanagi kasumite
Haru asaku mizu nagaretari
Tada hitori iwa o megurite
Kono kishi ni uree o tsunagu.

Chikuma River Travel Song

1

By the old castle of Komoro
Beneath white clouds a wanderer grieves
Green chickweed not yet grown lush
Young grasses not yet burgeoning.
From silver-paneled hillsides
The thin, sun-struck snows melt away.

Warm though the light may be
The land's fragrance goes unheeded,
Spring still bears but shallow mists—
The barley fields turning to green
As scattered bands of travelers
Hasten past on roads amid the fields.

Asama lies hidden in thickening dusk,
Sad notes from grass flutes of Saku;
Motionless Chikuma River waves
Stand firm along the banks.
Drain the murky wine, lees and all;
Brief solace for a traveler's pillow.

2

Thus it was in days gone by
Thus shall it yet be today
Why pass this life in turmoil
Thinking only about the morrow?

How often do dreams of life and death
Vanish as down in the valley
The unmoving river waves
Roll back the sand-laden waters?

Ah, what does the old castle answer;
What do the riverbank waves reply?
Reflect in tranquility on ages past
A hundred years is but another yesterday.

Misty among the Chikuma River willows
Waters flowing through earliest spring
Solitarily circling around the boulders
To moor their grief at these banks.

Originally appearing as two separate poems in *Fallen Plum Blossoms* (*Rakubaishū*, 1901), "Komoro naru Kojō no Hotori" (*Zenshū* 1:237) and "Chikumagawa Ryojō no Uta" (*Zenshū* 1:292), they were combined under the title of the second in *A Tōson Anthology* (*Tōson Shishū*, 1904; *Zenshū* 1:457–459), and have been treated as a single work ever since.

Memorial stone in the Kaikoen with a bronze tablet on which is inscribed Tōson's "Chikuma River Travel Song."

Chikuma River
Sketchbooks

Preface

My dear Yoshimura (or better, Shigeru):[1]
 As I write this preface in the form of a letter addressed to you, I find that I naturally fall into the familiar forms of address that we have always used. I have at last been able to put together the chronicle of life in those mountains that I have for so long been wanting to send you. The ties between us are old and deep, Shigeru. I came to your home before you were born. Later I held you in my arms and carried you around on my back. You were attending grade school in Hisamatsu-chō in Nihonbashi when I was going to the Meiji Gakuin at Shirogane-chō. We grew up almost as brothers. I took you along when I spent a summer with my sister in the Kiso country. As I remember, that was your first time away from home. After I came to have a family of my own there in Komoro in Shinano province, my wife and I had the pleasure of your company during two summers. At that time you were already a fine young man about to graduate from middle school. One summer you came with your father and another summer you came alone. I am certain that the old Komoro castle and its surroundings, the slopes around the foot of Mt. Asama, and the Nakadana hot springs are places that are firmly fixed in your memory. I am not simply writing this letter to you in place of a preface; I am dedicating the entire book to you—from the me still living in the mountains to the you still wearing your middle-school uniform. It is very natural for me to do this, and I feel it will make the best memoir of our lives at that time.
 Isn't there some way to make myself more fresh and pure—more simple? It was with that thought that I left the air of the city behind me and went to those mountains. Of course, I learned many things by going out among the farmers of Shinano province. My job as a country teacher in the Komoro Gijuku was to teach the sons of the merchants, former samurai, and farmers of the town, but in a sense it was I who learned from those people—from the school janitor and the families of the students. In the end I put in seven long years in those mountains and during that time I ceased to be a poet and became a novelist. This book is rooted in the impressions of the first three or four years of that period, when I lived there in silence.

3

Your father is no longer with us, Shigeru, nor is my wife. My way of life and yours have changed since the time I came down from the mountains. Yet I will never be able to forget the seven years I spent in Komoro as long as I live. Even now I can see the entire course of the Chikuma River before my eyes. I feel I could put myself right down on that vast stony slope at the foot of Mt. Asama. I feel I can actually smell that soil. Since you have been kind enough to read such of my works as *The Broken Commandment, The Greenleaf Collection,* the first part of *The Family,* and my recent volume of short stories,[2] I am certain that you understand how deeply I feel about those mountains. I regret that I failed to introduce you to the mountain-village home of my friend Kōzu Takeshi, who appears in these sketches. Up to now I have done nothing directed especially to young readers, but I have written this work with that aim somewhat in mind. It is also my wish that this book might bring some solace to those who live in the lonely countryside.

In the winter of 1912, the first year of Taishō.

TŌSON

Sketchbook I

A Student's Home

It is the empress's birthday when a few colleagues and I go on an outing up toward Mimakigahara. We stalk through the pine forests like hunters and on top of a hill heavily covered with young pines we gather a great many fiddleheads. Afterwards we go on to a village called Tokikubo to pass half a day in surroundings that, even here in the country, feel extremely rural.

I am presently teaching students about your age in a school near the ruins of Komoro castle. Try to imagine how we await the spring in these mountains and just how short it always proves to be. The cherries never bloom before the twentieth of April and winter plums, cherries, and spring plums all flower at about the same time. At the Kaikoen, the park in the old castle grounds, there is a festival each year on the twenty-fifth of April when the cherry blossoms are at their height. Then each year, as if on schedule, a storm comes up and strips the blossoms from the trees all at once. Our classrooms are surrounded by double cherries and the trees outside the class- room windows were in bloom about three weeks ago, looking just like huge bouquets. When we went out to enjoy them during recess we could see the pink tints of the densely packed flowers reflected on our faces. Students frolicked beneath the trees, especially the younger ones who had only recently come over from the grade school. They flew about like little birds, now hiding behind this tree, now grasping that branch.

And now it's already early summer. One noon a week ago, as soon as I had finished with my lunch box, I went out with several students to have a look around the Kaikoen. The high, crumbling stone walls were buried in fresh greenery.

Not all the students are from Komoro; they also come from Hira- hara, Kohara, Yamaura, Ōkubo, Nishihara, Shigeno and other vil- lages around Komoro. Some walk as much as four or five miles each way. They are mostly from farm families and when the day's lessons are over each seeks out his own path, returning home through the

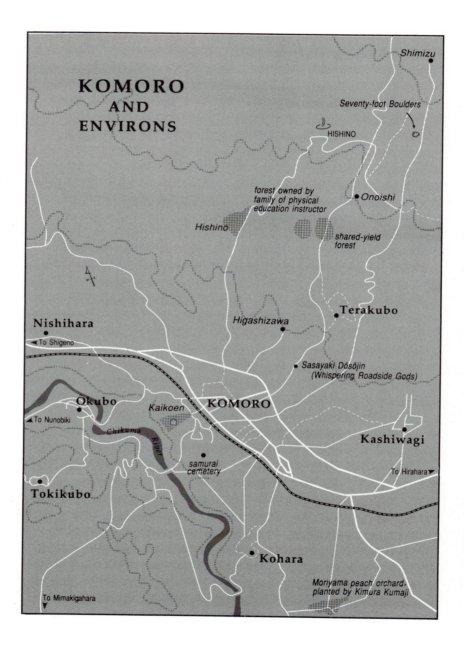

KOMORO
AND
ENVIRONS

Shimizu

Seventy-foot Boulders

HISHINO

forest owned by
family of physical
education instructor

Hishino

Onoishi

shared-yield
forest

Nishihara

◄To Shigeno

Higashizawa

Terakubo

Sasayaki Dōsōjin
(Whispering Roadside Gods)

Okubo

Kaikoen

KOMORO

◄To Nunobiki

Chikuma River

Kashiwagi

samurai
cemetery

To Hirahara►

Tokikubo

Kohara

To Mimakigahara
▼

Moriyama peach orchard,
planted by Kimura Kumaji

pine forests or along the railroad tracks or beside the banks of the Chikuma River, listening to the voices of the frogs along the way. Yamaura and Ōkubo are on the opposite bank of the river where the soil is good for root vegetables such as carrots and burdock. Shigeno is not in Kita Saku county; it is a farm village on the slope of Chiisagata county. Many students come from the villages thereabouts.

Both men and women work very hard here. Since you go to school in the city you probably do not know about such things as letting school out during the silkworm season. I seem to recall something about farm children in other countries also being let out of school to harvest wheat and the like; I must have read about it in some book or other. Our silkworm-tending vacation is something like that; when the busy time comes the children must help at home. They become accustomed to such work at a very early age.

The student S—— comes from Kohara and today I have promised to visit his home. I am fond of villages like Kohara because they have plenty of fresh green shade. I also like the level road that passes through the fields between Kohara and Komoro.

I set out with the scent of the vigorously growing grain in my nostrils. Barley fields lie to the left and right; their green waves seem to come alive with each puff of wind. Between the waves I can make out the pale gleam of the young barley heads. As I walk along this country road, listening to the voices of the frogs rising up from the deep valley below, I begin to feel oppressed by the disquieting sounds of growth and increase. Sometimes, when our senses are particularly keen, the mysterious, unknown world of living things is communicated directly to our hearts.

S——'s family has recently taken up dairying. They are rather prominent farmers and both the father and the older son are well thought of in the neighborhood. Here in the country, households of seven or eight people are not in the least uncommon and households of ten or even fifteen are to be found here and there. Everyone in S——'s family seems very attractive to me; all of them, from the old people right down to the children, have fine country manners.

Have you ever visited a farm? The front yard here is broad and spacious so that you can go directly around to the back door by passing alongside the kitchen. It is a special characteristic of farmhouses to have a large earthen-floored room directly in front. At this house this room opens onto grape arbors and the cow shed is off to one side. They have three milk cows.

The older brother comes out of the cow shed carrying a large bucket, while at the door the mother and sister are bent over their preparations for bottling the milk. I stand and watch for a while.

Later, out by the cow shed, I talk with the older brother. It appears that some cows take kindly to being milked while others do not. Some are wild, some quiet; there are all kinds. Cows have very sensitive ears and can recognize their master's footsteps. I learn too that they have established a pasture for these cows in Nishinoiri at the foot of Mt. Eboshi.

When it comes time to deliver the evening milk, the older son sets out for Komoro.

Rifle Bugs

At the top of the hill I meet a young girl with dull brownish hair. Come to think of it, some is very close to being gray. To see such girls standing before straw huts or beside the stone walls of the mulberry fields makes one aware of the harshness of life here.

"These farmers work straight through from spring to fall and when winter comes there is nothing to do but eat it all up. They're just a bunch of rifle bugs—eat and let fly, eat and let fly . . ."

The school janitor told me this.

The Pasture at the Foot of Mt. Eboshi

Following his return from his travels in Europe and America, the watercolor artist B—— built a new studio in his hometown of Nezumura. A watercolor artist by the name of M—— had previously taught in our school but he returned to Tokyo after a year, carrying with him a great store of Shinano landscapes. B—— succeeded him as art teacher. He takes time off from his painting to come in from Nezumura to Komoro once each week.

It is a Saturday and I take the train from Komoro to Tanaka. From there I climb up a slope in Chiisagata for a couple of miles.

A young man named O——, a graduate of our school, lives in Nezumura. He is hoping to take the examination for the military academy but in the meantime he is practically a full-time farmer. I drop in on him at his home and meet his mother and older sister. O——'s mother is a large plump woman whose glowing red cheeks give her an air of simple cheerfulness. The women along the Chikuma River work very hard and this makes them strong-willed. This is probably something which you, accustomed to seeing only city women, are unable to imagine. I have met women in this country who seem downright savage, but O——'s mother does not have that kind of coarseness. She just gives an impression of astonishing physical strength. The sister also has the hands of a woman accustomed to hard labor.

I walk around Nezumura at the invitation of B—— and his neighbor. The neighbor says that he has been a friend of B—— since elementary school. There is a panoramic view of the surrounding area from this vast, open hillside. We can even see the flowing waters of the Chikuma River at the bottom of the distant valley. After passing along the road through the fields at the edge of the village, we come to a place shaded by the young leaves of the white ash. There is a lush growth of devil's parsley and other poisonous plants in the streambed. The three of us sprawl out on the grass near the foot of a small hill and break out the rice brandy that B——'s friend has provided. Groups of young girls on their way out to cut grass occasionally pass before this scene of outdoor revelry.

B——'s friend now takes a tone of reminiscence.

"I came out here to go hunting with you once and we ended up drinking half the day away."

B—— replies in the same tone of voice, apparently recalling this incident before he went abroad.

"That's already five years ago . . ."

B—— takes out his sketchbook and continues talking as he begins to sketch the gray trunks of the ash trees and the young leaves moving in the wind. He is never without his sketchbook, even on the shortest stroll.

On the next day, B—— and I set out for the foot of Mt. Eboshi. We talk about how I might go over to see the pasture and how B——

could make sketches, and in the end I impose on him for a night's lodging. The pasture is another three or four miles' climb from this village and I could not possibly go without a guide. Summer mountains—mountain wagtails—the very words will probably evoke for you the mountain paths we are walking over. The earth is dry as ashes. As we walk along the narrow path through the forest we meet a traveling peddler there in the cool, yellowish green shade of the young leaves.

We go even deeper into the mountains, where the doves are singing. B—— starts telling me about a trip he once made to Hida and how lonely the voice of the "eleven bird" or *jūichi-no-tori* sounded. He imitates the cry it makes as it flies across the valleys, his voice growing gradually fainter: "JŪ-ICHI . . . JŪ-ICHI . . . jū-ichi." As he speaks, we come out onto the top of a small rise.

Try to imagine a hilltop bathed in the light of early spring and covered with thousands of flowers like little hanging white bells. We never dreamed that the fragrant lily of the valley—"bell-orchid" in Japanese—could bloom in such profusion. B—— had heard of this flower while he was abroad and we knew that it also grew in Hokkaido and in the Asama range, but there are so many here that we soon lose interest in picking them. The two of us stretch out on the ground, lying in a veritable bed of flowers. B——, who is fond of flowers, tells me that another name for lily of the valley is "love's likeness" and that it stands for good fortune.

There is not a dull moment as I walk up to the pasture with this fascinating artist. Azaleas are in bloom everywhere. I understand that they grow here so profusely because the cattle will not touch them.

A part of the vast highlands, an area more than five miles in circumference, now meets our eyes. We can see whole herds of cattle. Some suddenly look up and take a step or two in our direction as though they are trying to figure us out. Not being used to this sort of thing, I am quite uncomfortable as we pass among these cattle running loose on the range.

We hurry on to the herdsman's hut at the bottom of the valley. On our way, we see a calf drinking out of a stream in the meadow and a child out gathering fiddleheads. There is a fence around the hut, apparently to keep the cattle from smashing it. An elderly herdsman lives here and the wretched little vegetable garden at one side appears to be his handiwork. He heats water and makes tea for us beneath his sagging, leaky roof.

A pack of the type known as a "wildcat" is leaning against the wall. It is hung with saw, hatchet, sickle, and other implements. The herdsman is obviously pleased to have company. He tells us about his experiences in tending cattle, that he is given a stipend of ten yen a month by the manager of the pasture, and of how he had come here from another pasture. He also explains that the horns of the cattle sometimes itch, that they will tear things up trying to scratch them for relief, and that the cattle are moving quite rapidly as they graze since the grass is still short this time of year.

The herdsman reflects for a while and then begins to talk about a cow that has recently strayed. Has it possibly left that deep mountain pasture and headed off toward Yamanoyu? Then he thinks it over again.

"But how could it have got clear down to that swamp at the foot of the mountain? It's got to be livin' on willow leaves."

The herdsman soon leads us out of the hut. Carrying a bag of salt with the air of one who has a great many cattle waiting for him, he takes us this way and that, telling us, "This pasture is all grass so it's good for the cows," or "The trees are low here now, so it's hot in the summer and there's no breeze."

I am struck by the way in which the lives of human beings and of cattle are all blended together. This old man believes that any disease can be healed if only the cattle get salt and plenty of fresh water to drink. His ear can even recognize the peculiar bawling of the cows in heat.

Crossing a valley where the purple akebi vines are in bloom, we come out near a herd of cattle. A black calf that twitches his ears as he walks is the first to arrive when the herdsman puts out the salt. Next comes a broad-faced red cow with gentle eyes, and then a long-necked spotted one. Both advance, switch their tails, and gratefully start licking the salt. The herdsman tells us that when the cows first come up here they get homesick but they get used to it in a day or two. The strong cows keep with the other strong ones and the weak ones also keep to themselves. There is another herd of cattle on the opposite slope, some lying down, some standing up . . .

Each cow cared for costs its owner fifty sen per month. Fifty cows and one bull are presently being pastured here. The herdsman's main responsibility is to oversee the breeding of the cattle. We say our farewells and leave.

Sketchbook II

When the Barley Ripens

The school janitor is an interesting man. I learn all sorts of things from him. In addition to all the odd jobs and errands around school, he also works as a tenant farmer. His aged father and younger brother handle most of the work, but his is a real tenant family. Sometimes when school is out for the day and the janitor is cleaning the classrooms, his red-cheeked wife comes by with the baby on her back to lend a hand. He even goes to the homes of the teachers to help out with their vegetable gardens. At the headmaster's home they raise vegetables every year almost like a farm family. They also raise oats. I always hunt up the janitor during recesses to ask him questions about tenant farming.

From our faculty room, which looks out over the old samurai residences, we can hear the sound of the Chikuma River far down in the bottom of the deep valley beyond the pine grove. This room, on a corner of the second floor between the offices of the business manager and the headmaster, is situated directly over a classroom on the first floor. It has four windows. From one side you can see the pine grove and the thatched roof of the headmaster's home, and from the other a succession of shallow valleys, mulberry fields, and bamboo groves. You can even see a bit of the distant mountains.

As I lean against the windows of this room, so poor and simple yet possessing such splendid views, I learn from the janitor about the work of planting beans in June. It is usually done in teams of four: one to spade up the ground, one to plant the beans, one to add the fertilizer, and one to smooth out the ground. The soil gets hot as fire. It is impossible to do the work barefooted but it is just barely tolerable in straw sandals. Next the janitor tells me about growing grain.

For one *shō* of barley—ninety *tsubo* of land—a *shō* of bran is needed as fertilizer.[3] He says that this is mixed with barley hulls and with well-rotted grass previously cut and brought in from the hills. Barley goes into the payments in kind to the landowner while the tenant gets to keep the summer beans and buckwheat.

12

"When the south wind blows, the snow melts on Mt. Asama; when the west wind blows, the barley ripens in the fields." This is what the janitor tells me. As he speaks, a warm gentle west wind caresses our faces. It is now the season for going out beyond the windows.

A Group of Children

On the way home from school I meet a group of children playing beneath the stone wall just beyond the railroad crossing. Some have a pair of black wooden swords hanging from their waists, some are wearing straw sandals, and some are barefoot. They are playing at sumō, pitting "this guy" against "that guy."

All children are actors. As soon as they notice that I am watching, they start playing a little harder. Some show off by climbing up to the top of a dangerous-looking wall, and others stand at the bottom and shout, "Look out! You'll get hurt!" I ask one of the smaller ones how old he is.

"Me? I'm five!" comes the reply.

The voices of another group of children can now be heard over by the mill. One of the group I have been watching runs over toward them as soon as he notices.

"Are you coming? Oh, what a dope! —Here! Take my hand!" He takes the younger one by the hand, playing his role of older brother to the hilt.

"Hey, have some rice!" shouts one of the others, pulling up a handful of grass and stuffing it into his friend's mouth.

The other does not take this quietly. He fails to say that he'll get even but he does yell "Damn you!" at the top of his lungs.

His playmate shifts to insult.

"Bastard!"

"What? Take that!" the first one says, picking up a rock and throwing it at him.

The first child runs off laughing and shouts, "Stop it! Stop it!" while his playmate picks up a stick and runs after him. Another child with a tiny baby on his back runs along behind them.

I see this sort of scene every day around the school. An adult will pick up a rock and pretend he is going to throw it at a child, playfully shouting, "You little bum! I'm going to kill you!" You must understand that these words are completely innocent and are exchanged between laughing adults and laughing children.

You've been raised in the atmosphere of downtown Tokyo. I wonder just what you would say if you saw such a thing. I'm sure you would say they were savages. But I'll tell you that these savages are of the sort that bring interest and stimulation to the senses of the weary traveler.

Barley Fields

The sun drenches the fields in boiling heat. The trees scattered along the edges of the fields are full of life in their new foliage. The piercing notes of the oriole rise over the chattering of the sparrows and the song of the lark.

These fields on the slopes around the foot of the great volcano are separated by stone walls. In this season the walls are themselves festooned with new vegetation. There are lots of persimmon trees along the stone walls and it is pleasant to walk in the shade of their yellowish, translucent young leaves.

The long, narrow town of Komoro follows this slope along both sides of the rail line. Honmachi and Aramachi are wedged in on the left and right and they are bounded in back by the grounds of the local temple, the Kōgakuji. This is the main shopping district; Ichimachi and Yoramachi lie in front of them on either side. I cut across the road running from the back of Honmachi to the station at Aioichō, pass through Fukuromachi with its old samurai residences, and come out on a narrow road through the rice paddies. From here there is a view out over the rooftops of Aramachi and Yoramachi. The white stucco walls and the earthen embankment are all awash in fresh greenery.

A man is sleeping flat on his back with his dirt-stained legs stretched out on the grass at the edge of a rice paddy, apparently exhausted from his labors. The ripening heads of the barley are showing yellow and the small white flowers of the daikon are at their height. I walk along the rocky road between a stone wall and a grassy bank which soon brings me out into a barley field next to Yoramachi.

A young hawk is wheeling overhead. I select a grassy spot and stretch out on my stomach, the smell of the earth rich in my nostrils. A moist breeze comes up and the barley heads begin to rub against each other with a whispering sound. From nearby comes the thump of a farmer's mattock as he breaks the clods in a field—I can just barely hear the sound of a thin trickle of water making its way toward the bottom of the valley and I try to picture the sand that is being washed along within that sound. I lie down and listen for a long time, but unlike the field mouse I cannot stay here alone in the grass forever. The sky, which has turned milky but is still brilliant nevertheless, begins to oppress me. I find that nature is something that cannot be stared at for a long time—I soon want to run home.

I get up. The soft warm wind over the barley fields blows my hair around my face. I put my hat back on and start walking again.

Children are playing between the fields. There is also a woman hard at work. She is wearing hand covers and her sleeves are tied up with pale yellow cords that leave her arms bare. Her baby has been sleeping on the bank at the end of the field but now it suddenly wakes up and begins crying. The young mother puts her hoe down and runs to the baby. She clasps it to her heavy breast right there in the field. With the feeling that I am witnessing a spontaneous tableau, I stand still for a while to watch mother and child. An old woman passes by, carrying a great packload of grass that she has cut from the embankments.

In back of Yoramachi I meet K—— out working in his field. K—— is a small cheerful man, just married, one of those in the prime of life who is building the new Komoro. The people hereabouts have high expectations of him and it is pleasing to think that men of his quality are also tilling the soil.

An old man with salt-and-pepper hair, deep-set eyes, and great, knotted hands greets us as he passes by. At his waist is a large tobacco container with a horn netsuke. K—— points him out to me as the oldest farmer in the region. Just then the old man seems to have thought of something and he suddenly turns back toward us, displaying his white beard.

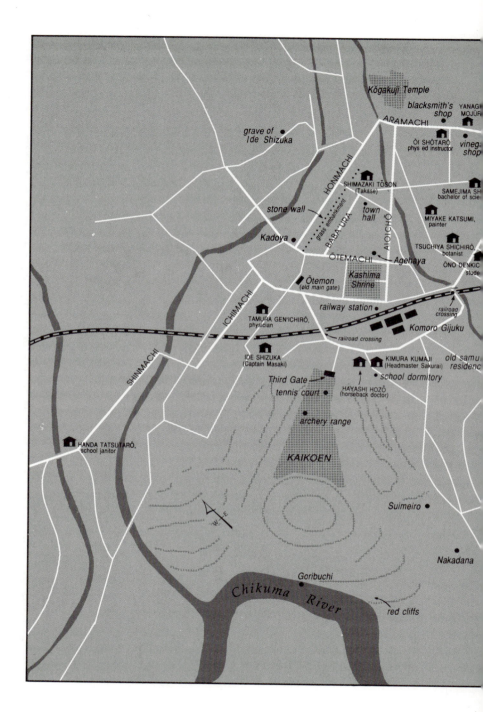

Kōgakuji Temple

blacksmith's shop

YANAGI MOJŪR

ARAMACHI

grave of Ide Shizuka

ŌI SHŌTARŌ phys ed instructor

vineg shop

HONMACHI

SHIMAZAKI TŌSON (Takase)

SAMEJIMA SH bachelor of scie

stone wall

grass embankment

town hall

MIYAKE KATSUMI, painter

BABA-URA

AIOICHŌ

TSUCHIYA SHICHIRŌ, botanist

Kadoya

ŌTEMACHI

Agehaya

ŌNO DENKIC stude

Ōtemon (old main gate)

Kashima Shrine

ICHIMACHI

railway station

railroad crossing

TAMURA GEN'ICHIRŌ, physician

railroad crossing

Komoro Gijuku

SHINMACHI

IDE SHIZUKA (Captain Masaki)

KIMURA KUMAJI (Headmaster Sakurai)

old samu residenc

school dormitory

Third Gate

HAYASHI HOZŌ (horseback doctor)

tennis court

archery range

HANDA TATSUTARŌ, school janitor

KAIKOEN

Suimeiro

Nakadana

Goribuchi

Chikuma River

red cliffs

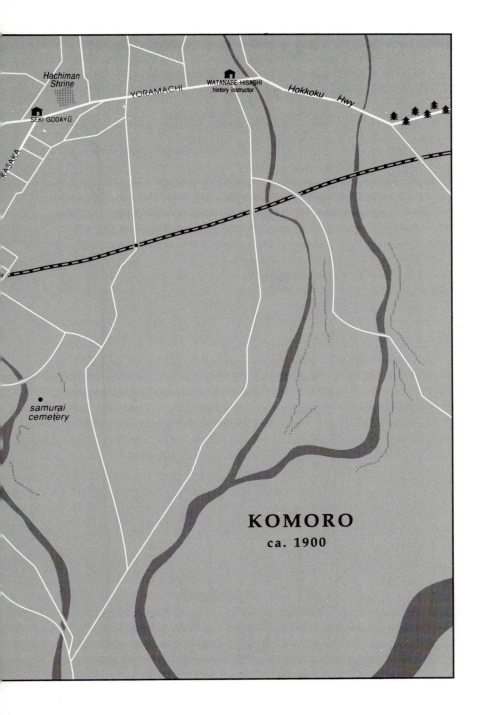

Hachiman
Shrine

SEKI GODAYŪ

YORAMACHI

WATANABE HISASHI
history instructor

Hokkoku Hwy

KASAKA

● samurai
cemetery

KOMORO
ca. 1900

Another man passes by on the far side of the field, carrying two buckets of night soil fertilizer on a pole. K—— also draws my attention to him, saying with a laugh that there is certain to be a bunch of onions or something else that has been stolen at the bottom of each of those buckets. Next I meet a farmer with reddish white hair whose eyes have taken on a grayish cast and who has the ruddy complexion of a good drinker.

Early Summer in the Old Castle Grounds

There is a bachelor of science at my school who teaches physics and chemistry. I happen to be passing by the classroom of this old gentleman at the end of the day. I watch from the door as he stands before his desk, finishing up a demonstration for the students. On the desk are a bottle of hydrochloric acid, some marble chips, a drinking glass with a glass cover, glass tubing, and various other objects. There is also a lighted candle. The teacher picks up the glass and tilts it a bit, releasing carbon dioxide from under the cover. The candle goes out just as if he had poured water over it.

The students gather wide-eyed around his desk, some smiling, some standing with arms folded, and some with their chins cupped in their hands. When they are told that a mouse or a bird would die if placed in the glass, one student immediately pipes up.

"Wouldn't a bug do, sir?"

"No, bugs don't have quite the same need for oxygen as birds and mammals."

The student who asked the question suddenly vanishes from the classroom only to reappear beside the peach tree just outside the window. One of the other students looks out and says, "Oh! He's going to get a bug!" The boy in the garden searches under the cherry trees, picks something up, and comes back. He hands it to the teacher.

"A bee?" says the teacher, with some alarm.

"Hey! He's really mad! Look out! He'll sting you!"

The excited students chatter on as the teacher bends himself backward as far out of danger as possible. As the bee goes into the drinking glass the students laugh nervously.

"It's dying! Its dying!" one of them cries, while another observes that it must be a weakling. As if to prove his point, the bee buzzes around inside the drinking glass, writhes a bit, and dies.

"Well, I guess he's a goner all right," the teacher says, joining in the laughter.

Later, on the same day, the other teachers are taken by the head-master over to the Kaikoen to practice archery. A thirty-yard arch-ery range has been built in the cool shade. The science teacher invites me along and I decide to go straight over to the castle grounds after school.

When I first met the science teacher I thought of him only as another old scholar who had hidden himself away in the country. I had no particular interest in getting to know him any better. All but three of us teachers are no more than birds of passage, but even in this group the science teacher looks like one who has come a hard way. Completely indifferent to his appearance but passion-ately involved in his teaching, always wearing a nondescript old suit covered with chalk dust, he makes such a poor impression that at first even the townspeople kept their distance from him, since most people base their judgments of character on a man's salary and clothing. However, it was impossible for the families of the students not to become gradually aware of his kindly, honest, and quite admirable character. I have never seen a man so open about all his affairs and I eventually became close friends with this old scholar. His uncontrollable sighs and deeply buried resent-ments have come to echo within me as if they were those of a blood relative.

We set out together. From time to time the science teacher breaks into light and fluent French. The sound of it makes me reflect on the brilliant past he must have had. He is the sort of man who still pre-serves traces of a former refinement beneath his seedy, rundown appearance. His necktie is always elegantly knotted and sometimes an unusual collarpin gleams from beneath it. The first time I noticed it, I almost burst out laughing like a child.

The yellowish white persimmon blossoms are falling everywhere, filling the air with their perfume. The science teacher begins to talk as he walks along beside me, carrying a bow wrapped in a long bag and a small pouch of rosin.

"Really, that's the way it is. Our second son is pretty good at sumō. Just the other day he won a bowstring. The sumō names they give everyone are pretty funny, too. Just listen to this—they call him 'Oki-no-same,' the offshore shark!''

I cannot help laughing. The science teacher, unable to repress his own smile, continues.

"The oldest boy has also taken a sumō name. What do you suppose it is? Since I am fond of archery he calls himself 'Ya-atari,' 'arrow strike' or bull's-eye, in the hope it will help him to do better in sumō. 'Ya-atari' indeed! Children are really funny!''

He is still carrying on this fatherly discourse as we reach the old castle gate. A physician on horseback greets us as he passes by.

The science teacher gazes after him.

"That doctor will try raising anything—chickens, herbs, birds, morning glories. When chrysanthemums are in season, he tries chrysanthemums. You'll always find a doctor like him in a country town. He's quite opinionated, too. 'Those other guys,' he'll say, 'they're no doctors! They're just a bunch of medicine peddlers!' But he's a good sort. He'll go way out to farms in nearby villages and if they have no money to pay him, he'll say that any produce they have on hand will do. 'Just give me a few leeks when they're ready,' he'll say. The farmers think highly of him."

He is not the only odd character around these parts. You may see a certain former samurai who has become a recluse, trying to fill out his empty days by fishing in the Chikuma River, or another who lives with his older sister and carries water to the Kaikoen and helps out at the town hall. There are many strange ones among the old samurai. The times have made them that way.

Look carefully at the crumbled and broken walls whenever you pass the ruins of the old samurai homes. Observe all the mulberry fields with their lines of foundation stones still in place. You can read there the bitter histories of countless scattered families. Then go on up to Honmachi and Aramachi and see the affluence of the merchant houses there. You will, I am certain, be forced to contemplate the fearful effects of the passage of time. But if you go to other places you'll discover that the new men now making themselves prominent are for the most part sons and grandsons of samurai.

This old scholar now carrying his bow up the path on the grounds of the ruined castle was formerly a samurai in a certain feudal domain. The headmaster is said to have been a direct retainer of the Tokugawa. The retired captain of military police who now doubles as teacher of Chinese and school business manager once served the Komoro domain. The science teacher even went off to war when he was eighteen or so.

Here in the old castle grounds, I am enjoying a scene such as you probably cannot imagine: the wonder of looking out from the welcome shade of lush greenery upon distant snow-capped mountains. From here the snowy slopes of the Japan Alps[4] rise up like walls of whiteness, row upon row.

The rich perfume of the wisteria, magnolias, azaleas, and peonies in the Kaikoen, which have each bloomed abundantly in its season, has now been replaced by the scent of young leaves. You cannot see the Chikuma River unless you climb up to the old foundations of the long-vanished keep. This will perhaps give you an idea of how deep the valley is. From the dense shade of the pine trees, the vast slope of Mt. Asama looks like a broad sea wholly exposed to the June sky. Although the pastures at the foot of Mt. Eboshi and in Nezumura, which I've already told you about—that is where B—— lives—are not visible from here, you can pick out the direction in which they must lie beyond the dense forests. From the foundations of the old keep you can also look down on the zelkova and maple trees that shade our archery range.

There is a teahouse with a very pleasant view situated on the castle grounds. I pick up the archery equipment which I keep there and head on down the mossy stone stairway with the science teacher. Not all the people at this quiet archery range are connected with the school.

"Tomorrow it will be a full year since I took up the big bow."

"Even after a year's practice, if you stop for even a little while you can't hit a thing. I can't believe it!"

"This is awful! And the target is fifteen inches wide! Get yourself together!"

TWANG!

"That just won't do!"

This conversation takes place between the teacher of Chinese, who pulls the strongest bow, and the physical education instructor. The science teacher pulls the weakest bow of any of us but he works hard at it and is a good shot.

I have been talking about the castle ruins and I'm sure you've imagined a place that is completely uninhabited, even though I've already introduced you to the gatekeeper, who lives beside the main gate, and to the keeper of the teahouse. There is another person living here who keeps chickens. Being in poor health, he has too much time on his hands and he often comes over to watch our archery practice. He stands behind us and offers witticisms as we line up and draw our bows back until the feathers rub against our cheeks.

"Well now, how about it?" he will say. "If you gentlemen would just tell me that you're tired of archery and that I can go ahead and raise chickens on this range, then there would be something in it for me, but it looks like you're going to keep it up forever."

This chatter causes some of the archers to lose concentration. They ease their already-pulled bows, unable to shoot.

For the science teacher, who has hidden himself away in Komoro, this deep shade is like a still more remotely concealed home. As he sends his beloved hawk-feathered arrows off to the target, he seems to have forgotten everything.

A warm rain suddenly starts to fall. There is a rumbling of thunder and Mt. Asama is wrapped to its very foot in gray, smoky-looking vapor. Several low-flying clumps of cloud race over our heads directly toward the mountain. The shower ends quickly but another one begins almost immediately afterward.

"Looks like it's going to start in earnest," says the science teacher. He goes to take down his newly made seven-inch target. In the mulberry patch on the castle grounds some people are working on through the rain. As we watch the clouds, the early summer sun bursts forth again over the wet foliage. We archers have all stuck it out and now we begin shooting again but another heavy shower starts and we give up and go back to the teahouse.

Later, as the science teacher and I are passing down together along the ruined walls on the way home, we see a brilliant rainbow in the eastern skies. The science teacher walks very slowly.

Sketchbook III

A Mountain Villa

The little stream that flows down from Mt. Asama divides at the bamboo grove. One branch cuts across well behind my house and runs down toward the deep valley where the mill is located while the other flows along the street behind the stable compounds. The houses along this second stream make up the cluster to which my house belongs. I became a member of this group as soon as I moved in. There is no really level ground anywhere in this whole town of Komoro and with a bit of rain even the smallest streams begin to cut deeply into the ground. Whenever I go down to Honmachi to shop I must pass along the winding road alongside these houses.

The head of the neighborhood group is the hard-working owner of a tailor shop. One day the head clerk of a merchant family in Honmachi with which he has dealings came over to tell me that since business was slow they were relaxing at their summer home in Higashizawa and he invited the tailor and me to come out.

I've shown you around the castle grounds and its neighborhood a bit, but I haven't yet told you anything about the homes in the town. Let's talk about my visit to the merchant's summer home at the invitation of the tailor.

You have visited little provincial cities before. You've no doubt noticed that most of the people you meet there are men and women who have come from nearby to do their shopping. Very few will actually be from the town itself—that is the character of country folk, and Komoro is also this way. A great many people who seem familiar with the lay of the land are always coming and going through the back streets, along the pathways, or down the narrow passages between the paddies.

The tailor and I glance at the streets of Honmachi, lined on both sides with townsmen's houses, and then we cut into just such a passage between the paddy fields. When we turn to look down upon a part of the town of Komoro, we see a mixture of white plaster and mud-wattle walls built upon high stone foundations. Among them a tall, three-story building shaped like a castle tower glows in the dull light of the cloudy sky. The sharply contrasting color of its dark sun-shades when viewed from this angle reveals something of the state of the region's wealth.

It is time for the barley to ripen. The fields, which regularly take on their golden tints twice each year, lie on either side of us. Many of them have already been cut. About halfway to the villa we overtake a farmer carrying a straw bag of salt fish.

The tailor turns to the farmer, asking, "Is the rice transplanting all finished?"

"Yes. It finally ended about two or three days ago. Once it would already have been over ten days ago but nowadays it has gotten to be a lot later. There never was much grain in the heads as long as the fields were shaded, but nowadays they're all well filled."

"I wonder if that might be because it has gotten warmer."

"Well, there is that, too, but there's a lot more fields being planted than there used to be, and so the water in the paddies is muddier," the farmer said, looking around as he talked.

The people from the merchant's household are all gathered in the mountain villa in Higashizawa. The store has been left in the care of their wives and two or three boys and the rest have come up here. You are a native of downtown Tokyo: the needle wholesaler in Ten-machō, Nihonbashi, or the retreat in Saruyachō, Asakusa—those are names rich in nostalgic associations for both of us, and so I am sure you can readily imagine just what sort of people I am with at this moment.

The villa is a two-story house with a pond in front and it stands at the entrance to a peaceful wetland. The pine forest enfolding the shallow valley to the left is blanketed in mist and the sky is clouded over, but the summit of Mt. Fuji is said to be visible in fair weather. The wild iris blooming profusely at the edge of the pond lend a pleasant air to the place. The tailor points out the leaves of the Korean cryptomeria in the garden, saying that it was brought spe-cially from Tokyo. I do not find it particularly attractive.

We are conducted up to a second-floor room with a fine view. A man, short hair cut plainly, dressed in a striped homespun kimono and an indigo apron, proves to be the owner. Although he is not in complete control of the store he nevertheless gives the impression of being the respectable owner of a major business. With his grossly fat chief clerk sitting at his side, the owner offers us salt-broiled carp from the pond to go with our sake. Downstairs there are five or six shop boys, some of whom have been brought along to cook, others to run errands.

The austere style of a great merchant house is manifest in even the smallest details. The chief clerk notices that the cold tōfu served to the guests has shaved dried bonito on it while his and the master's have none, and he shouts down the stairway to the boys. "Hey, this is no good with just soy sauce! Shave some more bonito and bring it up!" Almost immediately a boy comes running up the stairs with two heaping plates of shaved bonito.

Presently the chief clerk brings the chess board upstairs and places it before the tailor.

"Shall I spot you the rooks?" he says by way of invitation.

The tailor has not played for twenty years but he laughs and says that since he has not sworn off for all time he might try a game. The owner seems to take a great interest. He watches each move and now and then cries out that the tailor is in a good position or that he has made a very fine play but in the end the guest is defeated. The chief clerk gulps down his sake and looks around as though to say, "I'll take on anyone!" The owner quickly asks for the board, saying, "I'll avenge you" as he begins a game with the chief clerk. He makes a very bad start. The clerk slaps himself on the head, clicks his tongue, and says, "Now I've got you!" The game soon ends in the defeat of the owner and they start a second game.

Downstairs in the garden a boy with a large bag hung from his waist is playing with a black dog of foreign breed, but he suddenly turns back toward the house and begins complaining loudly. The tailor notices and runs downstairs to comfort the child. I go out for a walk around the garden. The globeflowers are at the end of their blooming and as I pass under the wisteria trellis I see carp playing in the pond. Someone observes, "You just can't catch the carp when the water's that high."

As we continue to walk around the pond the chief clerk comes downstairs, his face a bright red.

"And how did the game come out, sir?" asks the tailor.

"Won both of them!" replies the clerk, impudently putting his fist to his nose and then bursting into a loud happy laugh.

It is with such people that I pass the time among these gloomy mountains. A downpour begins just as we leave. The clerk, who is slightly drunk, hands us an umbrella, saying, "I'll let you share an umbrella because it's much more romantic that way."

The tailor and I start to leave under one umbrella but the clerk bellows, "Bring another one!" and a boy comes running after us with the second umbrella.

The Medicine Peddlers

"Wouldn't you like to buy some medicine?"[5]

We suddenly become aware of the voices of women calling out these words in Echigo accents in front of each house in turn.

Dark and travel stained, their broad hats flashing in the sun, they move in flocks like swallows. They form these groups every year at some distant place and come to these deep mountains. Just as flocks of birds will break up so that a few can land on each roof, the women approach each gate in twos and threes. During the season I seldom fail to meet a group or two of medicine peddlers on my way to school each day. They even resemble each other in their rude, vigorous health.

Gin the Simpleton

"You'll always find a couple of simple ones wherever you go," someone has said.

As I pass along a certain poor street, I meet a candy seller with a black beard. He is standing below a high stone wall, playing his Chinese flute. We are on a back street near the station, at a place I often pass going to and from school. When I come out between the boulder-strewn mulberry fields, I see someone coming down the slope toward me, struggling to keep his heavy cart from running away with him. In the cart are the hams of freshly slaughtered pigs. I learn afterward that this is Gin the simpleton. Gin-baka is the sort of simpleton who slaves away in silence. It is said that his house has been taken over by someone else but that he works on unaware.

On the Eve of the Festival

Once the spring silkworm crop is finished, it is time for the Gion festival. You can count on your fingers the people in this town who do not raise silkworms. Even the priests in the temples gain the greater part of their income this way. People marvel that we do not raise silkworms in my home. This being the kind of country it is, I will never be able to communicate to you the joy which the Gion festival brings unless you first think of the dark frames on which the worms are raised, the awful stench, the worries about the pupation of the worms, the endless hauling of mulberry leaves, and the times when men and women labor desperately throughout the night.

People come in from Suwa and Matsumoto, hemp bags on their backs, scales thrust into their sashes. For a while all the inns will be full of these cocoon buyers. They add a bit of liveliness to the place as they come into town, take up residence in their favored lodgings, and a few days later pack out the year's harvest of cocoons.

The land has lain sodden under the rainy skies for twenty days but now, on the twelfth of July, the weather has cleared at last and the sunlight seems especially brilliant after the long rains. It bathes the distant mountains, so long hidden in mist, in a rich violet. This is the day for which all the people in the village, adults and children alike, have been waiting, new clothes all ready.

I have heard a little about the quarrels that smolder among the various cliques in the town but I don't propose to tell you about them here. All you need to know is that these resentments have been accumulating since long before the festival. For a time there were reports of arguments about whether or not to hold the festival at all but finally the archlike straw festoons that normally go up at the first of the month were hung overhead in every street. One consequence of all this is that some families have even gone so far as to move temporarily in order to avoid the nuisance of having the portable shrines carried in on them. This will no doubt give you some idea of the state of mind in which the townspeople await the festival day. Small though the profits from the silkworm harvest may have been this year, every last bit will all be spent at this time.

At nightfall there is a *yudate* or divining by hot water. This evening the more important people of the town gather at the shrine carrying paper lanterns. I go out to watch. The sky is brilliant with stars. At the shrine gate I meet a man selling candy. He is said to have had some reputation in nō drama circles at one time but it has already been a long while since he hid himself away here in the country.

The light of the red and white paper lanterns along the streets of Honmachi is reflected on the faces of the passersby. In their light I recognize I—— from the Hatoya and K—— from the paper shop, out together. They are two lively girls from the neighborhood.

The Festival on the Thirteenth

It is the thirteenth and school is out. Every year there is an argument about letting school out for the festival, with the principal taking the affirmative and the business manager opposing. But school is let out every year nevertheless.

The country girls come in early to gather in groups on the street corner. The small tradesmen set out wooden tubs, lay doors over them, and cover the doors with blankets on which they place the food and drink offered for sale. Rude benches improvised from fulling boards serve as seats. Even the couple from the greengrocers in Honmachi have put up a temporary stand at a corner in Ichimachi, where the pale-faced husband and plump wife are soon hard at work making sushi, each with a shoulder bared to the summer heat. The children of the poorer families, very much in the spirit of the festival day, stroll the streets in new, unlined kimono, manifesting the special air of those who have just received presents.

In the afternoon my wife and children go to the home of B—— and her sisters to watch the passage of the portable shrine. B—— comes to my house regularly to read Sei Shōnagon's *Pillow Book* with me, and my children often go over there to play.

The bell in the bell tower of the Kōgakuji reverberates ceaselessly across the skies over every quarter of the town. On this one day everyone is permitted to climb up the tower and ring the bell. Some time after three o'clock I set out with my family as usual to climb up the steep road bathed in summer sunlight. At the top we come out on the corner of Honmachi where the green sunshades hanging out before every house seem particularly fitting for this July festival.

The crowds of people out to see the festival pass before us like the unrolling of a picture scroll. There are men wrapped in broad purple muslin sashes, and there are women, their hair done up in buns with heavy-looking ornaments thrust into them. There are girls carrying foreign-style men's umbrellas and there are babies in little flannel aprons with their rear ends left bare. Other girls with fat, sunburnt feet thrust into white tabi, are all dressed up in kimono that are not quite long enough. They think nothing of walking four or five miles to attend. There is even a Western woman in the crowd. Probably over from Karuizawa, she is staring at everything around her with great interest. The children of the town are full of high spirits, darting about everywhere among the crowds.

At last the wooden mortar is rolled up from the bottom of the slope. The sightseers all flee to the edge of the road.

"Yoi-yo! Yoi-yo! Yoi-yo!"

Amid the shouts of the bearers the heavy shrine comes into view. From time to time the shrine is rested on top of the mortar in the middle of the narrow street. The lusty bearers temporarily take over the area. They run about in circles, throw their hands in the air, and shout. Then there is yet another round of vigorous cries as they take up the shrine and move on. A sort of rhythm is transmitted to the onlookers; on the way back I notice that everyone on the street, down to the very children, is walking to the same beat.

People are still a bit uneasy after the quarrels that preceded the festival. At about six o'clock, I decide to go back down to the corner of Honmachi for another look. Now even the shouts of "Yoi-yo!" from the bearers have taken on a threatening tone: "Gyoi-gyo! Gyoi-gyo!" The shrine is no sooner brought up to an intersection before it is rushed away again. The bearers are getting drunk. Some fifty or so onlookers are running about and shouting like madmen. Groups of police and festival officials are running back and forth. The sightseers have all left to go to dinner but the bearers only grow wilder. Each time the shrine is borne past the home of a wealthy merchant the onlookers wring their hands until the perspiration comes.

Suddenly the bearers turn into a sort of mob. Some are waving sticks menacingly in front of a house. Others are raising their hands to restrain them. The shrine tilts precariously under a rain of blows. People come out of their houses and try to push the shrine away. Some are trampled in the confusion and faces are bloodied. Police rush up bawling, "Put down the shrine!" After a heated argument, everyone but the bearers are moved away. A group of people in white hats and white garments gathers around the shrine to protect it. There are orders of "All right! Pick it up!" and the shrine is borne off quickly in the direction of Nakamachi. One of the participants, felled by blows, is left sprawled out in the street.

"You children there! Get going! Get out of the way!"

Everyone is yelling.

"That was a real workout for the police!"

"What a fine mess!"

The onlookers begin to chatter among themselves.

Paper lanterns are lighted all over town once it grows dark. Bamboo sunshades are rolled up, mats are spread in front of the stores, screens set up around them, and people in search of a bit of coolness take seats at the edges.

The shrine moves from Ichimachi to Shinmachi. On one steep street young girls pick up handfuls of the offertory coins that rain down around the shrine. Others come along afterwards, groping about, lanterns in hand like the descendants of Aoto.[6] Fifty-year-old women dart out from the shadows, clutching at pebbles and grasping at clods of earth. It makes one pause and reflect on the appalling greed of this world.

The Ichimachi bridge is near the home of the school's botany teacher. It is also close to the home of my close friend, Dr. T——. Along the railings of the bridge are the dark shadows of people enjoying the cool breeze. Some are singing in coarse voices while others are bestowing unwelcome attention on certain women.

Even after nine o'clock at night the lanterns in Baba'ura are still lighted as they were earlier in the evening. Our usual group is now gathered in front of the pawnshop and the tailor's shop, enjoying the cool air and talking about the festival. There are no stars tonight.

Fireflies wander up from the dark river out into the middle of the streets flashing their beautiful bluish lights.

After the Festival

It is the next day. A cool rain has been falling since early morning. Water drips from the green leaves of the persimmon and plum trees behind the house. The moist plum leaves look particularly cool.

Along Honmachi the previous day's crowding and confusion have vanished without a trace. Only the festival lanterns still hang deep beneath the eaves of the houses. The matchstick blinds hanging beneath the indigo shop curtains are so quiet that the sound of a pipe being tapped out on an ashtray somewhere behind them is startlingly loud. Only girls and children are out on the street, huddling under their umbrellas. The wooden mortar from the day before lies on its side in a corner, slowly getting wet in the July rain.

Today is the fourteenth and it is set aside for relaxing and for eating red beans and rice and vegetable stew. At four o'clock in the afternoon the sky still has not cleared. A man in a court hat, an old-fashioned sword at his side, looking as if he had just stepped out of the kabuki play *Shibaraku,* accompanied by a Shintō priest, festival officials, and a crowd of children, all dressed in pale yellow trouser robes, makes his way through the rainy town to cut down the sacred ropes.

Sketchbook IV

Nakadana

The window of the faculty room looks out over a shallow swale, the bottom of which has been plowed up and planted to mulberries.

There are many such swales in the vicinity of the old castle, all lying between steep banks covered with dense growths of pine. They grow deeper as they fall away toward the Chikuma River. We have dug up a grassy plot beside the castle gate to build a tennis court. Another swale begins just beside it. M—— painted watercolors of these swales while he was in Komoro. The physical education instructor says that in the distant past there was a great sloughing off of Mt. Asama and it must have been the waters rushing down from the mountain in the millennia since then that have created these formations.

I cut across this swale at the beginning of August on my way to Nakadana. My feet often carry me in that direction. Not only is there a mineral spring there but it is just the right distance for a walk from home.

There is quite a bit of good farmland around Nakadana. As I arrive at the edge of a cliff the snug little pavilion belonging to the headmaster comes into view on its site high on the slope. The flags at the hot spring are flying far below. Beyond them is an apple orchard and the Chikuma River glistens in the distance.

By a little after one in the afternoon I pass along the path between the paddy fields, just before it comes out on the bank of the Chikuma River. There, where rushes, scrub brush, and willows sprout among the boulders, I meet a student from the normal school in Nagano. He is part of a group that includes A——, A——, and W——, who have been coming to my house for extra lessons during the summer. There are also several other young men along the bank, treading down the hot sand to swim in the river. Among them are students from my school.

I often bring my students here to swim when it gets hot. If this makes you think of swimming in the Sumida River, then you must

remember that the current here is a very different thing. It has a diz-
zying speed even where the clear green water seems to flow as
smoothly as oil. When you look upriver, you see the water breaking
into white foam over the dark shapes of the rocks as it hurtles down
toward you and flows on downstream, swift as an arrow, to fetch up
against the red cliffs at Goribuchi with an awful force. It is impossible to walk straight across to the cliff on the other side. Moreover,
this seemingly clear water conceals huge boulders and you will be
swept away if they should cause you to lose your footing. This means
that you cannot possibly reach the rock you are trying for unless you
start well upstream.

Unlike placid lowland country streams such as the Tone, this river
pounds violently against its banks with the full force of its current.
We decide to spend a couple of hours here, sitting in the shade of a
boulder on the exposed river bottom, surrounded by rushes in
bloom. Some of the swimmers crawl out on the sand to dry in the
sun while others continue to leap into the water. Little girls also
come down to roll up their sleeves, tuck up their skirts, and dip their
feet into the water, without a care in the world.

Three straw hats appear among the boulders. They belong to the
group from the normal school.

"Catch anything?" I ask.

"Yeah. I got a lot."

"How about you?"

"I hooked five but every one got away."

"Oh well, you've had two hours to think up excuses."

They go on chattering among themselves as I join them to go back
toward Nakadana. The water at the mineral spring there is artificially heated but it is pleasant nevertheless to sit in the tub and enjoy
the scenery. The enjoyment continues after the bath when we have
tea and carry on the sort of talk that students are addicted to. Our
pleasure is enriched by the cool breeze that blows in from the apple
orchard and the grape arbors.

"Do you lose your taste for sweets when you grow older?" one
student asks, and the talk of food begins.

". . . because I sold my set of the *Chinese Dynastic Histories* to pay
my bill at the sweet shop."

"Sweets are fine but they sure cost a lot."

"I went without them for two years."

"That's really great. I couldn't possibly manage to do without sweets for two years. I have enough trouble limiting myself to three times a week."

"But I have to admit that when the third year started I couldn't stand it anymore."

"Now didn't one of the teachers recently say, 'I hear that you often go to the sweet shop. I've never set foot there myself but I'd like you to take me along next time'?"

"Well . . ."

"You boys are really fond of sweets. How much do you eat at one time? If your teacher asks you that, you will tell him 'ten sen worth' or 'twenty sen worth.' 'That's quite a bit—it's a wonder you don't ruin your stomachs,' he'll say. 'Some of you will come back to school unable to eat dinner, that's what happens!' "

"That's right. There are all kinds. Some fellows even spread stomach medicine on their candy before they eat it."

Everyone is in a gay mood. One of the three jumps up, clapping his hands and dancing as he laughs. I can't help bursting out at the sight.

After a while the three students head back to the inn where they are staying, whistling as they go.

Just up the hill, along the road that follows the stone wall, is the headmaster's mountain house. He has named it Suimeirō, the "pavilion of bright waters." It used to be his study, but he had it moved from an old samurai estate and reassembled here. It is an elegant little pavilion, sitting high up on the bank in a location affording an excellent view.

The headmaster was my English teacher at the Kyōritsu school in Kanda. He was in the prime of life at that time, teaching us about such things as Washington Irving's *Rip van Winkle.* Now he is hidden away here, an old man with white hair who finds pleasure in his flower garden and in pampering his aged body at the mineral spring. Sometimes the headmaster himself jokes about feeling like Rip van Winkle. But his vigor and passion do not seem to have diminished with age. He is an enthusiastic talker with everyone who drops by.

I enjoy looking over the headmaster's well-ordered study whenever I go to the Suimeirō. I can also lean against the railing of the study and enjoy the view of the Chikuma River to my heart's con-

tent. The smoke I see on the opposite bank comes from Ōkubo village. The rope bridge below is called the Modori bridge. The crowing of roosters that rings out across the river each morning and the
lights that glow in the village each evening bring all sorts of things to
mind.

In the Shade of Oak Trees

In the shade of oak trees.

We are in the grounds of the Kashima Shrine. I pass frequently
under these trees during the school vacation.

On this day I walk over the railroad crossing and along a path
through the green grass. A short-horned, soft-eyed calf is tied up
under a big old oak tree. I stop to watch it for a moment and as I do
so it begins to run, wrapping its long rope round and round the tree
trunk until it can no longer move.

Two horses, one brown, one white, are tied out to stakes in the
middle of the nearby grass.

Sketchbook V

A Mountain Hot Spring

One of those brief rains of the transition from summer to fall, neither a summer shower nor an autumn drizzle, is falling. It does not beat the plants down the way a summer shower does. Some old women from the neighborhood come around to sell the season's first mushrooms, both the reddish gold ones with leaves still stuck to them and the dark, tarnished-copper green ones which have been packed into boxes.

I went to the Tazawa hot spring just a month ago. I've forgotten to tell you about that. There are all sorts of hot springs, but there is something special about the ones in the mountains. The Bessho[7] hot spring near Ueda has all the conveniences, but the feeling of a real mountain hot spring is better realized at out of the way places such as Tazawa or Reisenji. It isn't that the inns themselves are poor or shabby, but they are more the kind of place where people from the countryside round about bring their own rice and miso and come up to forget their miseries. Most of the guests do their own cooking, renting only the rooms from the inns. A cooking stove is provided for each room and the guests can walk directly from the garden right up the stairs to their rooms, still in their wooden *geta*.[8] When I see such buildings, constructed so that outdoor footwear may be worn even in the halls and stairways, I know I am in a remote mountain hot spring. They say, however, that the Kazawa hot spring—the Mountain Baths—is the one with real backwoods flavor.

The train into Ueda runs on tracks wrapped in greenery on one side and clinging to the red bank cut into the mountainside on the other. Crossing the Ueda bridge—a red-painted steel bridge—one can look down on the immense flow of the Chikuma River. I walk through the farming villages in the level lands around Ueda. The roads in this area, with their long, tree-shaded stretches and their rude teahouses where one can sit and rest, have the feeling of real country roads.

What I see at the village of Aoki typifies the grinding labor of the farmers. They have thrust a few leafy branches into the backs of their clothes to make a bit of shade, and are hard at work weeding their fields.

The sun is blazing down with such force that I cannot walk without an umbrella. Once I pass beyond these fields I come to a road climbing up the bottom of a steep valley alongside a small, slightly milky stream. I can tell just by looking at the water that I am getting close to a hot spring. I reach the place where the signboard hangs:

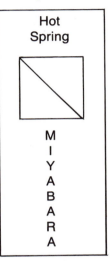

Hot
Spring

M
I
Y
A
B
A
R
A

As the slashed-square motif shows, it is the sign for the Masuya or "Measuring-box House," a hot spring that commands a splendid view. In this inn resonant with the sound of flowing hot waters I meet our headmaster's wife, who has fourteen or fifteen girls with her. Among the students are some whom I teach in my spare time. From the inn we can see a broad stretch of the mountains of the Asama region. The headmaster's wife confides that days when one cannot see Mt. Asama are depressing.

The light of the nineteenth day after the new moon shines into the valley. Most people have long since gone to sleep but the lights are still on in one of the rooms and a noisy argument is in progress there.

"I may be small enough all right, but I'm no savage!"—the kind of thing that argumentative people are always saying.

Next morning the sun comes pouring into the mist-filled valley. Even the nearby mountains seem distant and the smoke rising from

the houses seems still whiter than the mist. Mt. Asama is hidden
from view. Beyond the mountains, the early morning gray begins to
take on a bluish tint. The white clouds lift up to lie along the mountain ranges. Kuni-san, a lovable little boy who has come here with
his sister, is blowing on his toy flute up on the second floor.

The valley below lies between the Hōfukuji and the Jizō passes.
This evening the twenty-day-old moon rises late over the valley. The
sound of the stream keeps me awake and I get up to enjoy more of
the special quality of the moonlight here. As I lean against the high
railing, the voices of all kinds of insects blend in with the sound of
flowing water to fill the entire valley. There are other sounds down in
the bottom of the dark swamp: people locking up their doors, others
talking on into the night, dogs barking, and a happy-sounding farmer's song.

On the morning of the fourth day I get up in the dark and pack by
moonlight. By the time day breaks I am walking along the mountain
road to Bessho.

The School I

Summer vacation is over. I am once again seeing the science
teacher, B——, and the botany teacher every day. On the first day of
the fall term I stand by the window of the classroom which looks out
on the leaves of the cherry trees, still a lush green, giving the upper-
classmen a talk about Buddha.

I have chosen the *Shakafu*[9] as my text. In this work the life of the
Buddha is written up as a drama. From it I take stories such as those
of the Buddha's father and the young Prince Gauthama's friends.
The story of how the young prince, sunk in despair, went out in turn
from the north, south, east, and west gates of his palace seems to
catch the interest of the students. When he went out the first gate, he
met a sick man. From this he realized that all men must suffer illness. As he went out the next two gates he saw first an old man and
then a corpse. Then must all men age and die? The doubts he began
to harbor about life are shown very clearly and simply. The prince
made up his mind and, in order to free himself from this *life*,[10] he
began to free himself from everything.

Isn't that dramatic? Isn't it an effective story interesting to young minds? After I tell them this story, I go on to say, "Some of you may be planning to go into business while others may wish to join the army, but I hope that whatever you do, you will be able, as was this prince, to put all worldly considerations aside and lead a pure and priestly life."

I look around at the students. I'm not sure what they have made of all this but they are exchanging smiles. One makes a strange face and rests his head in his hands.

The School II

I was not previously aware that trees put out new growth three times a year. The new leaves for September are coming out now.

Quite a few trees have been planted around the school building. When the big cherries begin to ripen it brings back memories of my own youth,[11] and when I come back and look at this garden after the end of summer vacation, I find the slightly whitish leaves of the apples, the reddening leaves of the cherries, and the delicate coloring of the paulownia all blending in with the white birch to create a delightful shade. The cheery whistling of a student can be heard here and there. Now that the tennis court has been moved over by the castle gate, many engage in sumo wrestling in the shade of the cherry trees.

On the way back from school I drop in on the family of B——, who has been ill since early summer. The back way out of this house leads down over a stone wall to an apple orchard. The early autumn sun is shining there too.

A Country Pastor

The science teacher is fond of morning glories and he grows them every year. One day, on the way back from school, he tells me about a disciple.

Although I use the word "disciple" it is only in the matter of raising morning glories that this person is a disciple. Actually he is a pastor living in town who is affectionately known to some of the town children as the "Sunday school man."

Once a sudden violent shower came up while he was in the midst of a sermon. He had just entered into the discipline of growing morning glories and his thoughts turned to the garden plot he tended every day and the delicate leaves and lovely trumpets that were being beaten down in the rain. He broke off the sermon in mid-sentence and ran off to rescue his morning glories.

"Now isn't that just like a country pastor?" The science teacher laughs as he tells me about his new disciple. It seems that this pastor is every bit as fond of going to watch fires as he is of talking about morning glories.

September Rice Fields

I have come to where I can see, lined up across the slope, the houses of Akasaka, a neighborhood in Komoro.

At this time of day these streets at the foot of Mt. Asama are just waking up. Smoke from the morning cooking fires rises through the damp air and the crowing of cocks resounds from far and near.

Around the ripening rice fields are beans, their pods just beginning to take on weight, and the lower leaves of some of the rice plants are turning yellow. September is half gone. The heads are varied. Some have a bit of color while others are pure green, and others are still sporting red tassels. The rice fields that have turned dark brown are the ones planted to glutinous rice. Even I can tell that much.

The rays of the morning sun blazed into each valley.

The grass in the paths between the paddies scratches and dampens my feet. I hear the sound of a cricket as I walk along.

At this time of year Mt. Asama will sometimes spew out smoke as many as eight times in a single day.

"Oh-oh! Asama is firing up again!"

Such remarks issue almost automatically from people who live around here. When the men and women stop their work, rush out of doors, and look up into the sky, you can be sure that Mt. Asama is putting on a really spectacular show. It is only at these times that they remember they are living at the foot of a volcano. People accustomed to life here are apt to forget this during ordinary times.

Asama seems to have caved in after an immense explosion at some time in the past. The sawtooth formation known as Kippayama, or "fang mountain," is generally thought to be a remnant of the old crater. Travelers who come expecting to find something of particular interest in the shape of Mt. Asama are usually disappointed. This is not only true of Mt. Asama; if you look at the whole Tateshina range you'll find no mountains that are in any way unusual. The only peculiarity is due to that quality of mountain air which makes the mountains you looked at yesterday and those presented to your view today seem never to be quite the same.

Mountain Life

From the house where the science teacher lives you can see the windows of the huge soy shed belonging to the home of the daughter of K——, the vinegar dealer. If you turn off onto Aramachi street you'll find, tucked in among a tatami shop, sellers of dried bonito and tea, and a variety store, a rather large blacksmith shop. In a dark room beneath a high roof an old man with his hair tied up in the traditional style will be pounding away with his iron hammer. This old-fashioned blacksmith is the father of the physical education instructor at our school.

One day when the morning breezes are cool but the sun hot I enter this blacksmith shop in the company of two students. We pick up the physical education instructor and then go on out through the back door and begin to hike up the slopes of Mt. Asama. Even though I speak of our home as a "mountain home," the place we are heading for now is far deeper in the mountains, where the few residents live among dense alpine forests.

Our way passes along the hillside, through plantings of foxtail millet, beans, and barnyard millet for horse feed. Fields of white-flowered, red-stemmed buckwheat are also to be seen everywhere. Autumn is at its peak. The physical education instructor, being well versed in agricultural matters, points out the various types of crops. Over there, with the large, purplish red blossoms hanging from it, is *watari-awa* or "crossing millet," and these plants with the hanging, greenish black pods are called *kōrei* beans. I am always learning things from him. He can even distinguish the varieties of rice by merely glancing at the fields.

We observe a group of five or six trees standing on a steep slope. This is where Sasayaki Dōsōjin, the "whispering roadside gods," is located.[12]

We come next to a place called Terakubo or "temple hollow." Here five or six farmhouses are scattered about to make up a rustic mountain hamlet. I don't think I've told you yet about Mt. Kurofu, the "speckled mountain," but it's really just a part of Mt. Asama. Now if you were to stand on the highest platform of the old Komoro castle ruins and look out through the pines on the wall toward a slope that seems to be speckled black with pine forests, that would be the place where we are now walking. From that platform you can see a bit of wall looking like a white dot on the flanks of Mt. Kurofu. That wall is in this village.

A farmer walks by, bent under the weight of a sack of salt. The physical education instructor calls out to him.

"Time for making pickles already?"

"If we do it now it goes twenty percent farther."

It appears that these people, in their lifelong battle with a severe climate, are already thinking about preserving vegetables.

After the cool rains of the night before last and yesterday's bright sun there ought to be a good chance of finding mushrooms. The students and I enter a pine forest, still following after the physical education instructor, to whom this pine forest belongs. We find only a few yellow groundholders and ox foreheads[13] among the pine needles and so we push on through the bamboo grass to a place called *bubunboku no hayashi,* the "shared-yield forest."

Now quite deep in the pine forest, we come upon what appears to be the younger members of a family busily cutting green pine boughs and tieing them up in bundles. The woman is a young matron of around twenty with a filthy hand towel[14] tied around her head. She is wearing straw sandals and the skirts of her kimono are tucked up into her sash, showing her bare legs. Her tangled reddish hair and her coarse sunburned face make it difficult to be certain if she is a man or a woman; she is the kind of person you might see in one of Millet's paintings of peasants.

The faces of the three or four boys—they seem to be her younger brothers—are black with grime and their hair looks like so many tufts of weeds. Yet they are all singing childish songs in strong, guileless voices. Another person, apparently the mother, comes walking out of the forest and they all stop working and stare at us as though we were something strange and wonderful.

We leave these people at their work and go on up the mountainside to another pine grove on a stretch of level land. Here we meet a man carrying a big load of grass homeward along the narrow forest path. An occasional ray of sunshine penetrates through the dense cover to make the wet grass glisten. The heavy forest air somehow gives the man the appearance of a fish swimming through water. A cart loaded with brush comes rattling and pounding past, its sound reverberating through the lonely forest.

Still looking for mushrooms, we push our way through the brush and bamboo grass, but we are having little luck today. We find only an occasional inedible red mushroom or the decayed remains of the early mushroom here and there among the dead leaves. We have tired of our quest and our backs are beginning to ache as we carry our lightly filled bags of mushrooms past a field of melon plants in bloom. A small hut belonging to a mountain watchman comes into view.

A Mountain Watchman

The watchman's hut is in a place called Onoishi, directly below Mt. Kurofu. Before the main hut is a horse barn with its stock of hay, its sun-warmed earthen wall, and a paper amulet from Mitsumine Shrine pasted up on the wall to guard against robbers. It all seems quite remote from the normal haunts of man. An alert-looking red dog leaps out, barking furiously as though he has his doubts about us. He belongs to the watchman and seems to serve him in a number of capacities. When the owner of the hut comes out to greet us, the red dog quiets down and comes up to be petted. The watchman proves to be of the unshaven type that one so often finds watching over the forests. His wife, sleeves tied up, is hard at work cutting up the squash that they have grown in their mountain garden plot.

Four children then come into the garden. The oldest is a girl of around fourteen or fifteen. Although she is wearing a cheap narrow sash and rude straw sandals, she has a fine head of lovely dark hair. There is something awkward and uncertain in the expressions of the younger ones as they look toward me. A white rooster with a bright red comb and three hens had been close by but they have already hidden themselves away in the forest.

The hut has two rooms. One is a sitting room with tatami on the floor, although it would probably be more accurate to refer to its real use and call it a bedroom. The family eats, drinks tea, and entertains guests in the other room, which has a hearth[15] and thin rush mats spread on the wooden floor. All the implements of cultivation as well as of housekeeping are kept in this room. The bare, soot-stained walls are hung with calendars with lithographed prints or copies of woodblock prints, reminding one of the pleasure that even such crude things can bring to people living in remote places. I begin to understand why these prints are in such demand during the year-end sales in country villages.

We rest beside the hearth still in our straw sandals. The watchman's wife serves tea and pickled onions and the tea tastes good in our dusty throats. The watchman tells us that they never let the fire go out during the winter. The climate is quite different up here.

The students go around to the back of the house to have a look. They return to report that persimmons grown at this altitude never become sweet, the plums are bitter, and only the peaches seem to do well. It is time for lunch.

In the shade of the chestnut tree in the garden we roast the mushrooms that we have been given by the watchman. He spreads out three mats for us and our hostess provides chicken and eggplant soup and boiled squash. They are served in huge pots from which we all help ourselves. The students bring out bread and balls of rice and the physical education instructor has not forgotten to provide himself with his beloved sake.

They have tried to grow apples here but the insects from the wild pear trees, attracted by the nectar of the blossoms, keep them from bearing fruit. The wife tells us about this while we eat. After lunch the watchman leads us out to see the black soil in his fields. He tells us that he has a mulberry field of about a thousand *tsubo* beyond the pine grove while the fields here are about three times that in extent. The family has, however, grown smaller during his time and he has had to let some of the fields go wild because they don't have enough hands to work them.

The watchman seems to be greatly pleased by our visit. There is much in his conversation that does not seem to go with his shaggy, unkempt appearance. He has harvested about twenty bushels of buckwheat while the gingko, cryptomeria, and bamboo that he has planted have nearly all died. He has also planted twenty-five bushels of chestnuts but there have been fourteen forest fires during his time and although the remaining trees are now between thirty and forty feet high there are so few of them that the harvests are small.

We are also shown the nursery plot of larch that he has planted. The young shoots, soft as grass, are very pretty under the bright sun. There are also many wild pears around the edge of the fields. We catch sight of some fruit, ripened to a bright yellow, lying in the grass at our feet. But to tell the truth, there is nothing interesting about them.

We are told how terrible the forest fires are and about people who have been overtaken by wildfire and burned to death. We also talk about the charcoal burner's hut a couple of miles up the mountain where mountain beech[16] charcoal is being made.

It seems that Onoishi, where this watchman's hut is located, is part of a place called Takamine. It is less than half a mile from Onoishi to the Hishino hot spring and the watchman says they go over every day to bathe. Whenever I hear of Hishino I think of the girl who once came to our house to help care for the baby. She was a country girl from Hishino.

We are seeing some unusual places thanks to the physical education instructor's familiarity with the countryside. People like me seldom visit such remote spots. Once before, in the company of the history teacher, I stayed the night in another watchman's hut at a somewhat higher elevation. That place had just been brought under cultivation but the forest was not as heavy as it is here.

We make our farewells and leave Onoishi. After a bit I turn back for one last look in the direction of the hut. I see a steep narrow road leading to it through a grove of white birch and other trees, then the trees at the top of the hill, and beyond that the roof of the hut.

The trunks of the birch trees will catch one's eye in any forest, but here they are growing among wild cherries and their leaves are already beginning to turn a beautiful golden yellow.

Sketchbook VI

An Autumn School Excursion

It is the beginning of October and I am setting out in the company of the botany teacher and a group of students to explore the upper reaches of the Chikuma River. It promises to be a pleasant journey during a stretch of fine autumn weather. We will go from the slopes of Yatsugatake down into the old province of Kōshū, the present Yamanashi prefecture, as far as Kōfu. From there we will swing back through Suwa, where the science teacher, the art teacher, and some of the other teachers will be waiting to join us for the last leg of the journey back to Komoro. This grand circuit of the entire region will have us spending almost a full week in the long mountain ranges of Tateshina and Yatsugatake.

Among the places we will see is the region between the upper Chikuma River and the Nobeyamagahara plain, which I have visited once before. That time I went with my neighbor the tailor. I want to tell you about the present trip while those earlier memories are being refreshed.

The Kōshū Highway

When you go from Komoro to Iwamurada to pick up the Kōshū highway, you find yourself ascending a comparatively broad and level valley. Minami Saku county, gold with the colors of autumn, lies open to view and the Chikuma River flows through the center of its heavily cultivated valley.

There is scarcely ever a boat to be seen on the Chikuma River until after it has joined up with the Sai River. It is simply left to flow as it will. I'm sure you will be able to imagine the character of the river here and the scenery around it from that one fact.

Up to now I have only told you about the Chikuma River as seen

47

looking down from the high bluffs of Saku and Chiisagata. The country through which we are now walking is quite different. Once past Nozawa and Usuda the road lies quite near the stream.

We go along the banks upstream to a place called Managashi where the character of the stream changes once more. There is now a great litter of huge boulders that have washed down from the mountains, and the Chikuma River that flows through them could more properly be thought of as a mountain stream rather than as a great river. The teahouses facing this stream bear names such as Kōshūya, reminding you that you are getting close to that province. You also begin to meet peddlers who have come over the mountains from Kōshū.

The student T—— joins us near Managashi. His home is at Miya-ji, somewhat away from the main road on the quiet lonely shores of Lake Matsubara, and so he has waited for us here.

The river banks are thick with scrub willow, rushes, maple, lacquer trees, white birch, and oak. Along the banks we note villages such as Minami-Maki or "south pasture," Kita-Maki or "north pasture," and Aigi. There are small mills along the stream banks everywhere. The vast scars of old landslides on the flanks of the Yatsugatake range, the mountains of Kimbu, Kokushi, and Kobushi, with their towering major peaks, and a vast succession of unknown other peaks stretch off into the distance before our eyes. As the rays of the sun begin to slant, we become more and more aware of just how deep this valley actually is.

The students and I stop from time to time to watch the flow of the waters. From this angle the evening sun is reflected from one peak to another and the smoke from charcoal burners' fires rises through the heavy autumn air.

There is a village called Uminokuchi at the head of the valley. The river somehow seems to sound louder now and it is already dark when we enter the village.

A Night in a Mountain Village

I once wrote the following in a story about this mountain country.

At the end of the Sino-French war our army bought up the mounts that the French cavalry had been using and brought them to Japan. Thirteen of the stallions were brought to this province. This marked the introduction of the magnificently spirited Algerian bloodlines into Minami Saku county. They make up the greater part of the lineage of what we now refer to as the "mixed breeds" here. Later the famous American-born stallion Asama was also brought here. From that time on the quality of the horses slowly began to improve and the horse market at Nobeyamagahara has grown more lively with each passing year. Its reputation even reached the ear of a certain imperial prince. This prince was a colonel attached to the cavalry and a great lover of fine horses. It was due to his influence that the fine Arabian stallion Faralis was brought to Minami Saku on loan, creating a local sensation. As of this year there are thirty-four horses here that have been sired by Faralis. The prince must be greatly pleased. He has even deigned to come to Nobeyamagahara.

The last time I spent a night in a village at the foot of Yatsugatake I was in the company of the tailor. A peaceful night in a mountain village—houses set off by the edge of the plateau to escape floods; shake roofs weighted with heavy stones against the winter snows, just as they are in the Kiso valley; lights shining from the hills and valleys . . . Here on the second floor of our little inn I am once again seeing this countryside by the faint light of the stars.

This is a horse-raising district. There is not a single household that does not keep a horse or two, and this constitutes the main wealth of these people, who are so honorable and uncorrupted that a girl can ride her horse alone at night without the slightest fear.

The bathtub at the inn is built directly over the holding tank for night soil. How much this says about the hard life these people lead and their need to keep things as uncomplicated as possible! It gave me quite a shock when I first saw it.

Beyond here lie the so-called eight upstream villages. This district is said to be the most inaccessible and the poorest region in all of Shinano. Only the sick eat white rice there.

As soon as he learns of our arrival, a relative of the tailor comes
straight over to the inn, paper lantern in hand. A daughter of his
had come down to Komoro and worked in the headmaster's home
for a long time. I understand that this girl has not only had a husband adopted into the family for her but now even has a child. I find
the lives of these people who come out of such remote villages to go
into service somehow moving.

You have probably never eaten *harikoshi,*[17] and very likely have
never even heard of them. They are buckwheat dumplings baked in
hot ashes. One of the hearthside pleasures of this region is to sit
around the fire, still in one's straw sandals, talking and eating *harikoshi.*

In the Highlands

The next morning we go on up to Nobeyamagahara. The memories
come flooding back. It was over this very same road that the thirty-
four colts sired by Faralis and two hundred forty mares—more than
three hundred horses in all counting the stallions—passed that day.
Temporary buildings had been constructed at the horse market, purple and white curtains were hung, peddlers' stands were set up, and
more than four hundred people were on hand. The tailor and I
strolled through the fields but what has stayed in my mind most
clearly is the figure of the tall counselor with the white, supple hands
and the soft light step who came up from Nagano with the prefec-
tural governor. There was just a hint of quickness and shrewdness in
his actions. I was reading *Anna Karenina* at the time and so I tried to
think of him as a "Vronsky" type. The way he took up the binocu-
lars hanging from his neck to look at the distant pastures on the
slopes of the Yatsugatake range—this is no doubt presumptuous of
me—was exactly the way I imagined Vronsky might have done it.

The meadow that was so crowded that day is deserted now. Walking over the yellow and brown grass that is already showing the
effects of frost, and noting the play of morning sun on the trunks of
the sparse stands of white birch, we move on toward the village of
Itabashi. These highlands are nearly a dozen miles on a side. There

are fields of buckwheat and other crops here and there on the otherwise cold and deserted land, and the people who have planted them have gathered together in tiny, widely scattered villages. Itabashi is the very first of these villages.

In my earlier story I wrote about the region in this way:

How beautiful is the view over the highlands as the fog begins to lift! Only a small part of the base of Yatsugatake has been visible but the steep and mighty frame of the mountain now gradually emerges, and when the peak bathed in crimson light comes into view at last it casts its shadow on the other mountains. This mountain range, the boast of Kōshū, goes through an infinite number of changes of coloration: now purple touched with yellow; now a grayish yellow. The sun comes out suddenly to bathe the path along which husband and wife are walking. Clouds like torn wisps of cotton batting float overhead; the sky has turned blue. It is morning.

Otokoyama, Mt. Kimbu, Onnayama, Kobushi peak: every last one is aglow. Flowing among them in the distance is the beginning of the Chikuma River, and the village of Kawakami can just be made out. The Chikuma River glistens pale in the morning sun.

The "husband and wife" are characters I was trying to depict in that story. I used to like to write this kind of thing:

Farmers in narrow-sleeved jackets, short trousers, and straw sandals, with head cloths hiding everything but eyes, noses, and mouths, passed alongside the couple. Some men carried mattocks on their shoulders; others were bent down under the weight of night-soil buckets hanging from the ends of carrying poles. There was even a child following along behind with his father's tobacco pouch slung from his sash. Another autumn day's bitter struggle against weather, weeds, erosion, and the exhaustion of the soil was just beginning.

Some farmers were already at work. As they walked past a blackened, poor-looking field an unkempt, sweat-drenched man went on grubbing away without so much as a glance in their direction. His body so bent over he seemed on the verge of falling, he swung his huge mattock to turn up the clods. The aroma of the black soil was overpowering. As the couple left Itabashi village they met a group of travelers.

It was autumn in the highlands. In the scattered groves of trees every branch was bent toward the south, a reminder of the power of the winter winds here. The white birches, almost stripped of leaves, stood tall against the sky and the slender-leafed willows were bent so

low they seemed to be trying to hide. A brightness-burdened autumn
wind shrieked across the land, grasses bending before it in yellow
waves as oak leaves showed their pale undersides.

The sight of the autumn sun beating down on scattered, great boulders inspired thoughts of desolation.

Here the *arishiode* leaves hung down and the *kōbōna* were in bloom.
This is also where fallen *kashibami* fruits were to be found.

Again, the birds of the countryside were all hidden away. The lark,
which builds its nest in the shade of the bamboo grasses, lacked the
zest it had once displayed in the now waning springtime. An occasional quail rose to flee the passersby, spreading its awkward-looking
wings and flying up, only to drop abruptly back to earth a little farther
on where it could hide in the grass.

Among the withered trees there were occasional areas of green that
informed the traveler of the presence of a water course. Brush flour-
ished here, dangling branches into the water, roots thrust deeply into
the soil.

In this season, driven by the labors of autumn, few of the farmers of
the village could let their horses run free over the highlands. The
farmers from Yamanashi, to the south of the Yatsugatake range, find it
difficult to grow enough hay for the winters and they come all the way
up here to cut grass. . . .

These are scenes for the most part observed from the old highway,
which is the more interesting.

On my previous visit I took the new highway on my way back
across the open countryside. That day I met a farm couple leading
horses loaded with hay off toward Yamanashi. They were eating
their lunches as they trudged along. They told me that they had to
make a round trip of some thirty miles to come here to get hay. Even
though they had left Yamanashi in the morning while it was still
dark, they had no time to sit and rest while eating lunch. To be leading horses along the road and eating lunch at the same time—it
seemed to typify the hard-working life.

I tell such stories to my companion T—— as we walk along the old
highway. We see no more dwellings after leaving the tiny hamlet
called Sangen'ya or "three houses."

The plentiful grass makes the highlands suitable for pasture. We
don't see many horses at close hand but we do catch sight of a band
of horses running and playing in a distant swale.

The lower leaves of the white birch are all fallen now. The sound of the wind blowing fallen leaves and grass—particularly when the leaves are oak—is evocative of travel on this high land of hot sun and chill wind.

We see a *magusodaka* or "horse turd hawk" flying off in the direction of Yatsugatake. We pass on in view of scattered groves of brown-leafed oak. The way they stand out against the background of distant gray clouds somehow gives rise to thoughts of desolation.

Alongside the single narrow roadway across the highlands, purple flowers are in bloom. I ask T—— about them and he tells me they are called "pine-cricket flowers." This is the scene of an ancient battle; the place where, it is said, the lord of Uminokuchi castle fell in battle against warriors from Kōshū long, long ago.

Near the Kōshū border we come upon a wild pear bush as tall as a man. The leaves have all fallen but the tiny red fruit remains. We walk across the grass to pick some of the pears but most of them are still sour. Some, however, have already been touched by the frost and they melt in the mouth. Soon afterward we are able to observe the slope of Yatsugatake that faces Kōshū. We stand looking down on the great, nearly barren slopes and into the deep valleys.

"Fuji!"

The students cry out to each other before beginning the long steep descent into Kōshū.

Sketchbook VII

Fallen Leaves I

The first frost comes each year around the twentieth of October. I want to show this mountain frost to you, accustomed as you are to the groves and level fields of Musashino[18] and to the light frosts of the city which can seem so pleasant. Just look at the leaves in this mulberry field after the frost has struck three or four times. The leaves are so shriveled and scorched that the very soil around them seems inflamed—an awful sight. It's the frost that really shows the fierce and terrifying power of winter. It seems much more gentle once the snow comes; deeply fallen snow brings a feeling of peace to the land.

On a morning in late October, I step out the back door to find a beautiful persimmon leaf lying on the ground. It is richly colored by the abundant autumn rains, and being heavily fleshed, it isn't shriveled or damaged in any way. Nevertheless it fell, unable to bear its own weight any longer, as soon as the morning sun loosened the grip of the frost. I can only stare at it for a time, remembering that this morning's frost was particularly severe.

Fallen Leaves II

Once into November it suddenly becomes much colder. I get up on the morning of the third, the emperor's birthday, to find everything covered with frost. The mulberry field, the vegetable garden, the roofs of the houses—everything is white as far as the eye can see. Most of the leaves have fallen from the persimmon tree in the backyard, completely covering the path. There is not a breath of wind. Yet the remaining leaves are quietly dropping to the ground one or two at a time. The chattering of the sparrows on the roof seems even more boisterous than usual.

It is a day when the heavy skies take on an ashen color from the fog. I suddenly want to go back to warm my hands at the kitchen fire. The chill gnaws at my toes right through my tabi and I feel the dreaded approach of winter. In these mountains one must endure a winter that lasts from November through March, almost five months. It is essential to be prepared for such long winters.

Fallen Leaves III

The *kogarashi* or "tree strippers"—the chilling winds of early winter —have begun to blow.

I am startled into wakefulness this mid-November morning by a sound like the pounding of surf. It is the wind hurtling through the skies, seeming to slacken from time to time, then suddenly starting up again. The doors and the shōji rattle, particularly those on the south side since they are also being pounded by fallen leaves. In the rare intervals of calm the flow of the Chikuma River seems louder than ever.

Fallen leaves come flying into the room when I open the shōji. The sky is utterly clear except for a few white clouds but the willows along the creek in back seem to be waving their long hair in the fierce gale. Frost-blasted leaves blow back and forth across the mulberry field that has already been stripped bare.

As I cross the main street in front of the railway station on my way to and from school that day, I meet men with their heads wrapped in raw silk or flannel cloths and women with hand towels over their heads and their hands hidden in their sleeves. Everyone along the way is sniffling, red-eyed and weeping. Except for red cheeks, ears, and the tips of their noses, their faces are pale as they walk along with bodies hunched over and heads down. Those with the wind behind them seem fairly to fly along while those facing the wind seem to be pushing something heavy before them.

The soil, the stones, and the skin of human beings all seem to have turned an ashen gray. The sunlight itself is a yellowish gray. The sight of the day's tree-stripper raging over the fields and mountains is awesome, violent, even heroic. Every last bough is thrashing;

even the trunks are in motion and the willows and bamboos bend over like grass. The remaining persimmons on the trees are quickly blown down. The frosted leaves of the plum, damson, cherry, zelkova, and gingko trees will all come down today. Scattered heaps of dead leaves are caught up in the wind and the mountains grow suddenly desolate and bright.

Kotatsu *Tales*

Now that I've already told you about the frightfulness of the mountain winter, I must also say that the long, cold winter season is the most interesting and pleasurable time in Shinano.

Let me tell you how it affected my own health. When I first came to live in these mountains I was unaccustomed to the climate and I was constantly bothered by colds. I even wondered if I was going to be able to last it out. It's said, however, that the human organism will adapt to the stresses placed on it and that is exactly what has happened with me. I've gradually learned to resist the harsh climate and I sense that my skin is much tougher than it was when I was living in Tokyo. My lungs have become accustomed to the chill mountain air, and it doesn't stop there. As I listen to the wind in these forests of mountain beech where the dead leaves do not drop until just before spring, or gaze upon the onion fields white with frost or simply walk around outdoors, I feel the almost piercing sense of joy that comes only to people living in this kind of place.

The very plants that grow here differ from those of gentler climates. Even the somber greens of the many evergreen trees bring tidings from nature. I'm sure you would be startled by the difference in coloring if you were to look at the red pine that grows in this stony land with eyes attuned to the greens of Musashino.

It's a very foggy morning as I set out for school. On the streets one can see only a few hundred feet ahead. I meet a farmer setting out to work his fields, a guard at the railway crossing standing forlorn beside his watchman's hut, and a drayman, sopping wet from the fog, pushing his wagon. I realize—I can feel it directly—that these people are not flinching at all before the climate, even on this morning when their hands are red and swollen.

"Well now. I guess we'll need our coats, won't we?"

That is all they say as they go out, and it seems enough to make them warmer.

The fog gradually lifts after I join the people at school. Everything grows brighter. The lower slopes of Mt. Asama become visible and the clouds rush by. Occasional patches of blue sky begin to appear. Then it grows clear in the west and the sun suddenly bursts forth. All of Mt. Asama is revealed and I am struck once again by the coming of winter: snow covers the peak like a head of white hair.

This is the way winter comes, that most pleasant time of rest for those who must struggle against this harsh climate. Tea trays and plates of pickled vegetables, or even sake sets, are placed on the famed Shinshū *kotatsu*[19] and the *kotatsu* tales begin around them.

Little June

The weather keeps changing. This is not so noticeable on the warm Musashi plain but here one feels it keenly. Cold days will be followed by astonishingly warm ones, and then it will get even colder than before. High in the mountains though we are, we never sink straight down into winter. The days during the transition from fall to winter are one of the most refreshing and unforgettable times in this region. Their popular name, "Little June," makes clear how pleasant they are. I want to turn this story back on itself and return once again to early November to invite your imagination to picture the farmers working in the sun.

Hillsides in Little June

As you step outdoors into a windless, cloudless day, the sunlight is so dazzling that it is impossible to look about in the ordinary way, but it becomes cold the instant you step into the shade and you immediately crave the sun. It is this mixture of heat and cold that marks Little June.

In the afternoon of such a day I go out through the paddies of Akasaka behind Komoro. The paddies on this steep hillside are separated by the usual stone walls. I sit down on an embankment covered with dead grass and gaze out on the scene.

By this time the more successful farmers have already finished their harvest. Rice bundles are racked up like walls in the nearby paddies and the threshed-out straw is stacked alongside. Two women, their hair pulled up in rolls, are working alongside one man, who appears to be hired help. The man is dressed in a tight-sleeved robe and visored cap like a tenant farmer, and he keeps a watchful eye on the mood of the two women as he packs the threshed, unhulled grain into straw bags.

Aside from this one group, not a single person is working in the fields.

A man in an old derby hat walks along the lane between the paddy fields, carrying a pot of yellow chrysanthemums.

"Let's have a smoke!" comes the call. Visored Cap and Derby Hat lean up against a stone wall and begin puffing away. The two women continue to talk and work. The sound of their voices drifts up to me. "How are your eyes, Kin? —Oh, that's fine! —Yes, yes, that's exactly right." I listen without really intending to, thinking of the lives of people who spend most of their days out of doors. Looking back, I spot conical hats, wooden clogs, and packages that appear to contain lunches. Tobacco smoke, blue in the sunlight, rises above the men.

In a little while Derby Hat takes his leave.

"So long! Take it easy!"

Visored Cap takes up a mattock and begins to stir up the soil of the paddy field. Unlike the women so busily winnowing the grain to free it from clinging remnants of chaff, the hired man seems to be doing as little work as possible. He will start up only to stop almost immediately, lean on his mattock, and stand staring vacantly over in my direction.

The hillside is a sea of light. The black soil, the rough stone embankments, the withered mulberry branches and weeds between the paddies, the new straw spread out to dry on the ground, and the branches of the trees in the distant forests—the entire scene is filled to overflowing with the light of Little June.

Two hard-working men enter my field of vision. One begins to turn over the soil in a nearby paddy with powerful strokes of the mattock. The other is a tall, skinny young farmer. He appears again, half-hidden in the brown weeds beyond a stone wall, and starts to hull grain. Even when he is hidden from sight his mallet can still be seen, rising and falling. The blows of the mallet sound like a distant fulling block.[20]

I walk along the farm lanes behind Akasaka until around three o'clock in the afternoon. Flocks of sparrows are making an immense racket in the clumps of brush and among the persimmon trees. The barley sprouts in the harvested and replanted fields are already a couple of inches high.

Suddenly there is a sound of wooden clogs behind me. I stop abruptly at the sound of a small child's voice calling up toward the stone walls on the opposite side. Out beyond the brown mulberry fields I can see two people, parent and child, hurrying to finish the harvest. The younger child has come to let them know that tea is ready. I don't think that any people can be more fond of their tea than those in Shinshū, but even after the child calls out a second time the mother goes on threshing out the heads of rice as if begrudging every moment and her son continues hulling the grain without a pause. Although they are some distance off, I can see the mother, her head wrapped in a hand towel, bending down and rising up and the son's shirt as he continues to work, his back to me.

The child's shouts remind me that I am thirsty.

I start back down the lane, thinking of the cup of strong hot tea that awaits me at home. The slanting sun has taken on a yellowish cast, somehow making everything near and far look different. Up on the hillside several dozen sparrows come together in a flock only to scatter again instantly.

The Farmer's Life

Surely you've noticed how interested I am in the farmer's life. In the course of these sketches I've had a number of opportunities to visit farmhouses, talk with farmers, and observe them at work. I never tire of this; it only makes me want to know them still better. Their

life seems so *open*[21]—basic, simple, and exposed to the elements. But
the closer I get to them the more I think that they are in fact leading
hidden and complex lives, even though they might all wear the same
kind of clothes, carry the same kind of tools and implements, and till
the same soil. For example, their life appears to be extremely gray
and austere, but I have no idea of how many layers there are in that
gray. In my spare time from school I've tried wielding a mattock on
my own to grow vegetables but I haven't yet been able to penetrate
the farmer's state of mind. Yet I am so fond of farmers that I take
great pleasure in creating opportunities to draw nearer to them.

One day I find myself sitting, both feet thrust out before me, on a
heap of straw bale-ends beside a group of tenant farmers on an
embankment covered with reddish, frost-blasted miscanthus. One of
them is Tatsu the school janitor, the other is his father, and another
his younger brother. They have just started to work on a barley field
but now they have come over to rest and tell stories. Rain, wind,
sunlight, birds, insects, weeds, soil, climate—these are all things
that have to be and yet they are also enemies against which the farmers must do battle. The talk shifts to the weeds that give the farmers
around here the most trouble. *Mizuomodaka, ego, yobaizuru,* wild burdock, *tsurugusa,* artemisia, *hebi-ichigo,* akebi vines, *gakumonji (ten'ōsō),*
and still others—so many I can never remember them all—have to
be pulled out of the rice paddies.[22] Tatsu picks up a clod of earth
from the field and shows me the furlike green roots of a weed called
hyō-hyō gusa. The farmers can recognize all kinds of medicinal herbs.

"There are so many varieties of rice that most farmers can't tell
you what kind they are growing even if you ask them."

Tatsu's father loves to talk and he tells me about everything from
"male" and "female" grain heads to the fact that it is impossible to
grow good rice on the lower slopes of Mt. Asama, because there is so
much gravel. He tells me about the many birds that bother the barley fields and the insects that can devastate rice fields, and how the
farmer must take the character of each piece of land into consideration even when sowing barley. Since Komoro is subject to winds
from the east and west, making the furrows run from north to south
not only ensures the best exposure to the sun but also helps to pre-
vent mature grain from lodging in the wind. He says he is always
thinking of things like that.

"But if you tell that to the farmers from Jōshū, they'll be

astonished that you can grow barley on the basis of stuff like that!"
the old man says with a laugh.

"This old man knows a little bit about farmers, so why don't the
two of you just stay here and talk."

Tatsu picks up his tattered straw hat and goes back to the field.
His brother too rolls his drawers up to the knee and, barefoot beside
him, resumes turning the soil. From time to time the two take out
the sickles in their sashes to scrape off the soil that sticks to their mattocks. Then they bend over their labors once more.

"Mt. Asama is at it again," they all agree.

I smell the fresh-turned soil and listen to the feeble cries of the
insects and to the old man's stories. He says that he is sixty-three
and still hard at the tenant farmer's life. He has dabbled in moxibus-
tion and divination ever since he was fourteen. He pulled a rickshaw
for some ten years when he was in his thirties, the first rickshawman
in Komoro. He tells me about his marriage and how his father's
being run over by a train led to the gradual collapse of his own fortunes.

"Farming is for those who have no other talents . . . ," he says,
making fun of himself.

A tall, white-haired, sturdily-built old farmer, surrounded by a
group of contemporaries, greets us as he walks past. Each man is
carrying a mattock in his soil-ingrained hands. A young man carrying night-soil buckets on a pole over his shoulder hurries by in the
lane on the far side of the field.

Harvest

On another day I once more cut eastward across the back of the
Kōgakuji to the hillside above Komoro.

It is around four o'clock. I have come to a place with a rather good
view where I can look down on a part of the town of Komoro which
appears from here as though it were lying in the trough of a vast
wave. All around me are fields, some already harvested, others still
to be harvested. Only two families stay on in their fields hard at
work at the harvest.

The farmers all seem to be hurrying to finish their work before the first snowfall. Directly in front of me a man with partially gray hair and his thirteen- or fourteen-year-old son are swinging their long mallets to hull the rice, surrounded by a white cloud of dust. The sound of the blows seems to be transmitted through the ground. The mother, hand towel over her head and covers on the backs of her hands, is threshing out the rice heads, letting the grain fall into the flat winnowing basket in front of her. Beside her another woman, face deeply tanned by the sun, scoops up the hulls that are being removed by the man and his son. Still another woman, her sleeves tied up with scarlet cords and wearing indigo-dyed socks, is lifting a winnowing basket high above her head and shaking it gently to let the chaff and dust blow away.

The days are short now and everyone works steadily and silently, covered with dust. Another couple in conical hats is at work over on the other side of the hill beyond the rice paddies and the mulberry field. I can see that the woman lifts the winnowing basket especially high as she stands in the wind. The wind grows chill and sharp. The boy who has been working directly in front of me puts on the short sleeveless jacket that he left lying on a shock of rice. The mother also dusts off a jacket and puts it on. I find myself beginning to shiver. I gather the skirts of my kimono close around me and begin to rub my legs as I watch the work.

A man puts his mattock over his shoulder and starts to walk down the hillside toward his home. A woman carrying two sickles, baby on her back, greets the others by calling out, "You must be tired" as she comes past.

The rhythm of the mallets wielded by the father and son directly in front of me grows more hurried.

"Hun!" "Yo!" come their faint accompanying cries. Presently the father takes up a limp rice bag. A woman stretches up to full height to gaze through the cloud of dust. There is a mountain of rice hulls in the middle of the field.

Dusk is coming on rapidly now. Evening mists begin to rise in the streets of the town and in the valleys surrounded by mountains.

Farmers on their way home begin to appear in the lanes.

As I encourage myself to hang on just a little longer, the father ties a rope around the rice bag, loads it on his back, and sets out for home. The three women continue to work on their own. The hillside grows darker and fewer and fewer people remain working. I can barely make out the couple in the field beyond the mulberries.

The evening bell sounds from the Kōgakuji. Mt. Asama gradually grows dark and the lesser mountains that have been glowing in the sunset now take on a leaden hue. Only the white smoke rising from the very peak is visible in the deep purple sky. Suddenly the bell rings out again, seeming to make everything bright again for just an instant. A child passes beside me laden with wild green vegetables, and others—it's impossible to tell if they are men or women —hurry past me down the lane. A wild, unkempt-looking woman without a coat or undersash comes running past. Her outer sash appears to be completely undone.

A single bright star appears in the south, then another, some distance away. The two stars are brilliant in the purple evening sky. The tips of the mountains glow yellow in the skies off to the west, then quickly change to a scorched brown as they reflect the last sunlight onto the countryside. The head cloths and bent hips of the three women still at work catch this light for a moment. Even the tip of the boy's nose glistens. Now the rice paddies are wrapped in gray and the countryside in a deeper gray, while the branches of the zelkova trees in the Hachiman grove vanish into the darkening browns.

Lamplights begin to appear over beyond the town. Others gleam along the lower slopes of the mountains beyond the hillside.

The father comes back to pick up another bag of rice and then moves off again. The three women and the boy only work all the faster.

"It's getting so dark!" says the mother in a comforting voice.

"Find the broom! —the broom!" comes her voice again. The child begins to grope around the rice paddy.

The mother sweeps the grain together with a broom, picks up the mats, and gathers them together. In the darkness the faces of the women have become one with their head cloths so that it is impossible to make out their features even when they are looking my way. The couple in the field on the other side appears to be still at work but their moving figures can just barely be made out in the gray of the paddy. A train whistle emits its lonely sound. The wind suddenly becomes even more piercingly cold.

"Wait! Wait!"

It is the voice of the mother. The boy is still beside her, hulling grain with his sister. Homeward-bound people are dimly visible on the road across the way. Others rush past, but they do not forget to say, "You must be very tired!" It is no longer possible to see what the three women are actually doing. Only the faint whiteness of the hand towels on their heads can be made out. Even the mallets are lost in the dark as they rise up.

A voice comes out of the darkness saying, "Gather up the straw!"

The three women are still at work as I leave the hillside. I look back but I can see nothing but dark, moving shadows. It has become full night.[23]

Pilgrim's Song

A pilgrim with an unweaned child on her back stands before my gate.

The early winter clouds in the sky appear at first glance to be made of ice. They might be called markers of the freezing isotherm. Their white tips are like needles, clear and cold. Once such clouds appear it will begin to get colder with each passing day.

As I reflect on our condition up here in these mountains I am moved by the sight of this travel-worn beggar in her gray leggings and old socks. She shakes her bell and sings a Buddhist hymn in a pitiable voice. After the family has listened to her womanly song we give her a five *rin* (one-half *sen*) piece and ask her where her home is.

"I'm from Ise."

"You're a long way from home!"

"People like me always drift around like this."

"Where are you coming from?"

"I came over into Nagano from Echigo. I've been all sorts of places. It's getting cold now so I am going somewhere warmer."

I have someone go fetch a persimmon to give her. She puts it in her carrying cloth, thanks everyone, and sets out, shivering in the cold.

The sun has now receded far to the south of its midsummer

heights. As I step out of our gate to gaze at this setting sun of early winter, I think of the old line of Chinese verse, "Floating clouds like ancient hills." The bare branches of the nearby trees seem higher than the distant mountains of Tateshina. I watch the sun as it seems to settle between the roofs of the neighboring houses into the forests.

Sketchbook VIII

Penny Lunch

There is a household where I often stop to warm myself at a fire when I am out. It's the place across from the Kashima Shrine with a signboard saying it is the Agehaya and offering penny lunches and a place to rest.

I meet a great many familiar faces along the path from my house to this lunchroom. Near the road in Baba'ura, in a sunny, southward-facing spot that has been planted with rock iris and *ōmoto* shrubs to please the eye of the passerby, is the shop where the tailor is hard at work with his male and female apprentices. A little farther on is the shop of the couple who sell pastries, their storefront lined with bean-paste candy and sponge cake. There also is the long-haired fortune-teller, so often seen coming back from the Chikuma River, casting nets in hand. Coming out of Baba'ura onto the main road where only the old castle gate known as the "Third Gate"[24] remains is the dyer's shop, marked by the indigo curtains hanging from the eaves. Off to the right in the direction of the Kashima Shrine lives the shaven-headed blind woman who makes her way in the world as a masseuse. The good-natured bird seller peers out from a room where larks and mynahs are singing. The Agehaya is just this side of his place.

They also make tōfu at the Agehaya and the hard-working wife, who seems utterly indifferent to her appearance, regularly sets off with a load to sell in town, wiping the sweat off her face with the sleeve of her underrobe as she goes. I always recognize her voice whenever I hear it cutting through the morning or evening air, and we buy deep-fried tōfu or tōfu and vegetable cakes from her at our house. Their son, who has grown big enough to take his mother's place now and then, will also sell you anything you want in the way of tōfu products.

They have noodles at the Agehaya. Of course they are not fresh-made noodles, but simply boiled dried ones. People around here tend to be fond of noodles. I know a farm family that has noodles for their evening meal once a week as a special treat. And of course buckwheat noodles are a local specialty. Here it is good form to serve buckwheat noodles after drinking. And then there is what is called *onikake,* handmade wheat noodles boiled with vegetables, a standard dish. When I sit at the Agehaya, warming myself at the hearth with its hanging kettle while the roaring fire sends smoke into my eyes, I like to watch the people who are gathered around, still in their outdoor footwear, taking in the warmth of noodles boiled in stock. "How about some tōfu fresh off the fire?" the wife will say as she ladles tōfu soup into a huge serving bowl. Then the owner will come out, hand towel hanging at his hip, to speak proudly of how his son has been given the honor of presenting the bow at the children's sumō matches.

This is where the lowliest laborers, the teamsters, and the poor farmers round about come to have their sake warmed. I suppose I've come to take this dark place with its soot-stained walls and customers with unwashed faces pretty much for granted. Now I warm my chilled body here while listening to the whinnying of the horses tied on the street outside. I listen to the talk of unrefined people. They have gradually come to take me so much for granted that I've even been asked by the owner to do the calligraphy for his new sign.

In the Pine Forest

It is the day after the Ebisu festival[25] when my colleague W—— the history teacher calls to invite me for a walk in the mountains. W——, who graduated from school in Tokyo, is a young, lively person who still seems like a student himself; a good companion for such an outing.

At the gate of his lodgings in Yoramachi, just outside Komoro, we are told by the maid: "You can get it cooked for you up there, so you should take a whole *shō*[26] of rice with you. Why don't you take some persimmons along too?"

Ignoring the advice, we put just a little rice in a drawstring bag, accept some beef, sling blankets over our shoulders, and set out in our outlandish getups: drawers under tucked-up kimono, our European-style umbrellas taking the place of walking sticks.

We are starting an hour later than we had planned. It is four o'clock in the afternoon and we are already pressed by the waning day as we pass the Hachiman grove, setting out for Mt. Asama over the narrow path along the hillside. We go by another pine grove. The silvery evening moon comes out, evocative of the onset of night. The sun has already vanished beyond the mountains to the west and we repeatedly look back over our shoulders as we hurry along.

A single track through a quiet pine grove—as we continue to climb, the peaks of Mt. Asama grow purple above us. Our feet make no sound on ground spread deep with fallen pine needles. The remaining daylight filtering through the pine trees seems harsh to our eyes. There is only a bit of yellow remaining in the western sky and not a single bird calls out.

We go out of one pine grove directly into another. Moonlight shines in among the trees and the grove seems smoky from the evening mists that fill it, giving a grayish cast to the spaces between the slender trunks. The distance fades into darkness, the tree trunks are black. We are surrounded by a deep, lonely peacefulness.

Although it is completely clear, the light of the half moon is feeble and the path under our feet is dark in the shade of the pine trees. Still it is easy to distinguish the dark line of the path cutting through the pine needles. We are now far from human habitation and Komoro is lost to sight. We stop from time to time to listen to faint, distant, unidentifiable sounds, trying to see into the depths of the darkness around us. Groping through darkness so deep that I can't really make out W——'s face when he turns back to me, we move still deeper into the woods. All is wrapped in the somber shades of night. The mists make everything vague and shadowy in the feeble moonlight. Still we trudge on, only stopping from time to time to sit down on the grass, lower the packs from our backs, and stretch our legs out before us. I am already tired because my stomach has been acting up and I have been skipping meals. I collapse beside W—— whenever he stops to rest. Then, in a little while, I have to struggle to my feet once again with the help of my umbrella.

We pass through a number of pine groves and then out into a spacious clearing. Our two shadows appear on the ground as the moonlight now grows brighter, now dimmer. We soon catch sight of a huge black object. It is the formation known as the seventy-foot boulders.

"We've come quite a way already. I'm really tired out. My feet just don't want to move anymore."

"I've made night hikes before but I've never gotten this played out."

"Isn't this a good place to take a rest?"

"You're weakening!" comes the laughing reply.

We go on talking like this to keep each other's spirits up but in our fatigue we are dragging our feet and bruising our toes painfully on the rocks. Utterly limp, we collapse for yet another rest. We are now out on the middle slopes of Mt. Asama and around us stretches what appears to be a vast wasteland. From here the pine groves below that we have come through look like dark clouds and we can just make out the immense shadowy forms of the boulders wrapped in darkness. The moonlight dimly illuminates the mountainside. Far up in the skies among the ash-colored night clouds three stars shine crisp and bright.

Lamplight in the Mountains

It is impossible to describe how pleasing the light of a lamp glowing red against the shōji can be. We've at last managed to reach the mountain hut at Shimizu.

The caretaker at the hut seems to be out late, doing chores by moonlight. We enter the hut, wash our tired feet, and take our ease before the open hearth, still in our leggings. W—— wraps his blanket around him as he says, "The lady down at the main house asked me to tell Otake to come down tomorrow to wash daikon, no matter what. . . . And then the wedding gifts from K—— have come and she wants her to see them. They are really splendid."

Otake is the caretaker's wife and the lady at the main house is the person who tried to get us to take a little more rice along when we set out. W—— is on very good terms with these people and their conversation is relaxed and casual.

We take out the bag of rice, the beef wrapped in newspaper, and a woman's collar liner to offer as gifts.

The caretaker comes to the entrance of the hut, saying, "Will onions be all right with the beef?"

"Yes, onions will be just fine," replies W—— with a laugh.

"By the way, we've got potatoes too. —Right! We'll put some potatoes in," says the caretaker as he goes out. In a short while he returns with some of the onions and potatoes they have stored. We quickly gather around the open hearth, arranging the smoky wood fire with chopsticks and breaking up pieces of mountain beech to put into the hottest part. The blazing fire gives our faces a reddish cast.

It turns out that the caretaker is still quite young. He arrived here just this April and got married in May. His face glows with health in the firelight and his eyes, though small, bespeak his honest, hardworking character. He has a number of mannerisms: opening his mouth very wide when he speaks, shaking his head, and laughing so hard that his tongue shows. The laugh is just a bit on the crude side but its utter openness suits this cheerful young man. He seems ready to do any kindness. His wife, already known for her industriousness, is a plump, red-faced, black-haired, somehow girlish young woman. They seem to be a perfectly matched couple.

The room is lighted with a dim foreign-style lamp and only the fire seems bright. The outdoor cooking stove is set up in a corner of the front yard and now the smoke begins to rise from there, too. We listen to the sounds of the rice cooking and the wife chopping onions as she tells us about life on the mountain.

"I was brought up in a lonely place but I've never been as lonely as I was when I first came here."

The husband too seems delighted by our visit and he tells us about the quality of his onion crop this year as he helps his wife with preparations for the meal. The potatoes have been cooking over the outside fire in an immense cauldron that would be suitable for feeding a horse, but now they are being transferred indoors to a smaller pot over the hearth. After the wife puts the potatoes in, the husband replaces the lid. Right before my eyes I am witnessing the kind of life celebrated in the folk song "Even at the Cook Pot."

A kitten catches the scent of the meat and comes to press its nose against the newspaper packet, only to be scolded by the caretaker. It then comes around behind us and climbs right up into W——'s lap.

The caretaker shouts at it again and it shrinks up beside the hearth and narrows its eyes.

"I can't stand that cat but the main house insisted on giving it to us, so I had to take it," he explains, going on to tell us how the black field mice come into the hut and make trouble.

"It's getting a little smoky. Shall I open up?" says W——, getting up and opening the shōji a bit. He stands looking out.

"Ah, what a fine moon! It's perfectly clear out there!"

When my colleague comes back to his seat there is a white froth boiling up from the kettle and the steam is rising.

"Looks about right!"

"Put the meat in!"

"Is it time yet? Wait a minute! Let me check the potatoes!"

Our host scoops up a potato with a shell dipper, lays it on the pot lid, and cuts it into several pieces. Yes, it's done enough so that the meat can be put in. He unwraps the newspaper and the bamboo sheath inside. Then he puts the bright red meat slightly marbled with fat into the pot with chopsticks.

"Oh, that smells good! I wish we could get gifts like this every day!" he says to W——.

The wife takes serving trays, rice bowls, and lacquered chopsticks from the cupboard and begins serving up rice directly from the cook pot.

"How about it? Isn't this hearthside nice for a change?"

And so we begin our evening meal, gazing into the fire. Everyone is ravenous.

"The meat's done now too!" The wife begins to serve us with great solicitude.

"Keep a close count on me, Otake, because I'm going to eat a lot," W—— says, sounding completely at home. "Delicious! Those onions are delicious! But they're hot, hot, hot!" He trails off into puffing sounds.

"Meat really does it when it's cold out!" responds the husband.

I have a splendid appetite too and I finish three bowls of the soup. Both of us have to loosen our belts and undo the top buttons of our trousers.

"Come on! Have another! Nobody ever turns up his nose at food once he gets up here in the mountains!" As she speaks, the wife snatches up the rice bowl that W—— has just put down. W—— tries to grab it back but he is too late. The wife heaps it up with rice and hands it back.

W—— laughs as he put his hands to his face. "That's mean! Mean! You sneaked up on me!"

"Sneaked up, eh?" her husband says, joining in the laughter.

"Surely you can eat that much."

"How? I've eaten so much already. I really don't need it," W—— responds with a sigh but then adds, "Well, I'll give it a try. I'll have some fresh pickles with it!"

I finish my evening meal to the accompaniment of cheerful laughter. The wife now serves herself, her husband having urged her to go ahead and eat. Hungry-sounding cries begin to come from the kitten, which has been shut away in the cupboard. The caretaker, starved for news, spreads out the newspaper that the meat was wrapped in and begins to read. W——, stuffed beyond endurance, pulls a blanket over his head and stretches out on the floor.

The husband and wife take turns telling me about charcoal making and rabbit hunting. After a while the wife gathers up the dishes and puts a big kettle of bran mixed in water on the fire, explaining that it is for the horse. All the while she is describing how, one night on this mountain when her husband was away, the newly built shelter for hikers was blown over in the wind. She tells of how she was prepared to go to the rescue if the shelter should fall on the horse shed and of how frightened she was when it actually happened. She also explains that her husband, who almost never spends a night out, just happened to be staying over at the main house that night.

The restored shelter stands next to the horse shed. We are conducted there by our host and there we spend the night. Perhaps because it is still not completely finished, heavy paper is hung in place of a door and the moonlight seeps in around it. We wrap ourselves in our blankets, blow out the lamp, and go to sleep without another word.

A Mountain Breakfast

Around three o'clock the next morning, the laborers with whom we have shared the shelter begin getting ready to leave. We listened to their voices until very late the previous night and now, when we hear the cries of the pheasants, we too get up. It's still very early.

We find ourselves in a place where we can look out across layer after layer of mountain ranges. Dawn has not yet reached to the bottoms of the valleys. The distant peak of Yatsugatake is wrapped in dull gray and red strips of cloud stretch off from it. Gradually the tips of the mountains begin to glisten and when the red clouds have paled to pink we can see the deciduous forests through which we passed in utter darkness the night before.

The caretaker takes us around to inspect the vegetable plot, the onion field, and the chrysanthemum bed. Two ducks crawl out from under a box on which daikon are drying. They flap their wings with great gusto, pick up fallen scraps of food, and waddle around, pulling their necks in and clacking their yellow beaks.

The caretaker then takes us to the front of the horse shed where a bay horse puts its head out and nickers. It is a tall, gentle-eyed, big-boned horse, still wearing a long and shaggy winter coat. Its owner mixes boiled onions and potatoes with the bran, adds some hay, and puts it all into a large bucket which he hangs on the door latch. The horse watches all this with the greatest interest

"Turn around for me!" the caretaker says, and the horse understands perfectly, turning around inside the shed.

"Once more!" says the caretaker, pushing on the horse's nose, and then he lets the gentle creature plunge its nose into the bucket. It feeds noisily as its owner gives us the amazing information that it can drink as much as five or six gallons of water at a single draft.

The clouds on the mountaintop gradually turn white and the valleys fill with a light that gives a grayish cast to everything it touches.

The wife comes to tell us that breakfast is ready. We have our breakfast in this most unaccustomed place. When he finishes eating, the husband pours hot water into his rice bowl, empties it into his soup bowl, and drinks it down. Then he takes a dish towel from the box whose lid forms his serving tray and wipes down his bowls and his chopsticks for himself.

Once again we go out of the house with the caretaker to look up and down at the mountains gleaming in the morning light. The caretaker brings out a spyglass and points out Shibunosawa and, just this side of it, the marsh at Reisenji. Mt. Yatsugatake, the slopes of Tateshina, Mimakigahara—all can be taken in with a single sweep of the eyes.

Down in the succession of precipitous slopes below we can recognize the villages of Kikyō, Yamabe, Yokodori, Takeshi, and Yaebara. We can make out distant white walls and we can see the sunlight glinting off the Chikuma River.

In December the mountain pheasants come down to the cultivated lands, often flying up at one's very feet. Rabbits too come down to eat the barley lying in the snow. We find these details extraordinarily interesting.

Sketchbook IX

Christmas in the Snow Country

I will be spending Christmas night and the following day in Nagano at the invitation of a technician at the Nagano weather station. I leave Komoro, looking out from the train window upon Tanaka, Ueda, Sakaki, and the other stations as I proceed on to Nagano to meet people I do not yet know. The reason for this little trip is that I've been wanting to see the weather station there.

Christmas in the snow country; a weather station in the snow country. I'm sure this is enough to stimulate your imagination. But before I tell you about it, I think I should describe just how deeply this countryside is buried in snow.

The first snow falls around November 20 of each year. I awake one morning in our home in Komoro to find that an unexpectedly heavy snow has fallen. A fine, powdery snow that heaps up like salt is a specialty of this area. The scenery is so very white that it seems to have taken on a slight bluish cast. The movements of those who are trying to make their way to work, tormented by the snow that balls up between the cleats of their *geta*,[27] remind me of people groping their way through a dark night. The bands of grade school children, their heads wrapped in red blankets, straw snow boots on their feet; the chickens huddled under the eaves of the houses in the town; the loaded freight wagons in the railway station, each one heaped with snow—all tell of the massiveness of the snowfall. When the snow slides off the branches of the pine trees in the Kaikoen a great, whitish, smokelike cloud rises up from them. The bamboo groves at the bottom of the valley are all bent down like grass under the snow.

The stagecoach for Iwamurada sets out through the snow. The sound of the horn blown by the groom comes ringing back. The bodies of the horses are soaking wet under the thin straw mats tied over their backs. Meltwater drips from their disordered manes. The wheels of the stagecoach begin to crunch through the snow on the roadway. In the streets buried in whiteness the endless, winding paths beaten by pedestrians gradually take on a muddy, reddish

75

tinge. Only in this kind of country will you ever see anything like these crowds of people coming out of their houses to shovel snow.

A thin mist or fog comes up to envelop the snow-covered town. It is around sunset. Thinking that the snowfall is over, I step out of my gate but I immediately feel something cold settling on my collar. Impulsively touching my hair, I wonder if it has started up again. Only now do I realize that what looks like fog is in fact very fine snow. Roadways that have already been shoveled out at least twice are now turning white once more, and after dark we occasionally hear the sound of snow being knocked out of clogs outside our door. Each time we think someone is coming to visit us, only to realize that it's just a passerby.

On even the darkest night the light reflected from the snow makes it possible to follow a path, and rays of light from the paper hand lanterns carried by many passersby acquire a new brilliance. The effect is *picturesque*. [28]

Now that I've told you about what the first snowy day in this country is like, I want you to try to picture what happens when this snow does not all melt away. It stays in cool shady places, in gardens, and on the north slopes of roofs, and more snow soon piles up on top of it. This snow then stays frozen until spring. Just try to imagine that.

Nor does my story of what it's like to be in this snow country end here. On the next day after a snowfall there is a foot of snow on the roofs and slender icicles hanging from the eaves. An apple tree in the garden falls over. Even the crowing and cackling of the chickens sounds very distant; everything seems to be muffled. On the day after a snowfall bright light comes through the usually dark shōji on the north side of the house. Once the light from the gray skies begins to shine, the snow picks it up, glistening so brilliantly that it dazzles the eyes. The sound of meltwater dripping from the eaves all day long makes for a kind of monotony; while boring, it also gives rise to peaceful thoughts.

Out in the fields behind Komoro the tender young winter barley is buried in white and the rise and fall of the hills make it seem as though great waves of snow are rolling in at you. Of course bits of the larger stones of the low walls separating the fields and some of the dry remains of the grass that grew among them remain visible. The distant forests, the bare boughs, a row of houses—all have taken on a deep leaden hue. That leaden hue—with perhaps just a touch of purple—may be said to be the keynote for the color scheme that will dominate from now on. It is a dim, indistinct coloring that draws one's heart into an ineffably forbidding world.

On the second day after the snowfall I go out into the valley toward a place called Tsuruzawa. The sunlight beating down on me is intimidating, violent, and the reflection from the snow all around is almost unbearable. I cannot keep my eyes open enough to see clearly. Even after I pass through the most dazzling spots I can still feel the almost painful intensity and heat of the reflected sunlight. I am following a gentle slope that leads down into the valley. All appearance of contour is washed out; I cannot tell whether I am in a grain field or a mulberry field. The slope, carved into one terrace after another, is covered with dead leaves that are scorched brown in color and patches of reddish earth show through here and there. Above that great wave of red soil is a barren mulberry field where the snow lies in drifts under the brilliant sun. Once across the wave I can see over into the Tateshina range and even as far as the distant Japan Alps.[29] On this day I also hear the awesome roar of the Chikuma River.

Each new snowfall comes before the previous one has melted, and the exposed soil of the roadways is once again hidden away. Once into December the skies remain gray, the sunlight grows more weak and distant, and we are enclosed in a half-frozen world. The high mountains, hidden by blizzards, rarely show themselves completely. Water pours from the flume by the Komoro railway station, creating a thick column of ice. Sometimes, even on days when it has not snowed in Komoro, the roofs of the railway cars coming from Echigo will be buried in white and you realize it is snowing over there. As the solstice approaches, what appears to be thin streaks of water vapor that are not quite clouds will hang in the sky; I find their austerity particularly moving around sunset. The icicles at the eaves begin to grow, some reaching a length of more than a foot. The successive falls of snow in the garden pile up higher than the veranda. Rhododendron leaves peek out, shriveled in the cold; only the plump flower buds seem unaffected. On these cold evenings our bodies too draw in on themselves like the bodies of creatures hibernating through the winter deep in the soil.

It is late on Christmas day when I arrive in Nagano, having made my way through the frozen air in anticipation of the pleasure of meeting new people. I reach the home of the technician from the weather station to discover that he is still quite young. We have a most enjoyable conversation across the *kotatsu* about meteorology and his well-informed views on literature. Ruskin's study of clouds in his *Modern Painters* also comes up. When one considers Ruskin's division of clouds into three categories, we can see how much more advanced are the recent studies of cloud forms which recognize nine categories. Some women callers arrive in the middle of this conversation.

As my host introduces these young women I learn that one is the wife of a pastor and the other the wife of a close friend of her husband. They both have cheerful laughs. I also learn that among the Christmas songs that will be sung that evening are some that they have written. It is now time for the Christmas services and we leave the technician's house.

The churchlike building to which I am being guided stands on a sloping portion of the main street of the town. We pass through a number of dark snow-covered streets on the way. From time to time the technician and I pause on the frozen street, hearing the laughing voices of the women behind us. Their laughter is loud and filled with obvious pleasure; the sound on the cold winter air intensifies the feeling of a festival in the snow country. It is only afterward that I learn that the pastor's wife has slipped and fallen twice.

Reddish lamplight pours out of the windows of the church where I spend a countrified Christmas evening surrounded by children.

The Nagano Weather Station

The next morning the obliging technician guides me on the climb up the hill to the Nagano weather station.

Along the way he turns back to me to speak of his recollection that in one of my stories I describe fracto-stratus clouds as being red in the morning light around Mt. Haruna; he cannot see how that could be, since fracto-stratus clouds are low-moving. Trust a specialist to catch these things.

The weather station is small but it is located in a spot with a splendid view. It may be said that it does no more than relay daily reports to the meteorological observatory but to a first-time visitor like me its equipment is most impressive. The life led by these people who spend their days compiling charts of cloud forms and air temperatures is sympathetic.

I follow the technician up a narrow ladder to the observation platform. From here we look out over a portion of the early morning streets of Nagano. Wintry mists hang around the skirts of the mountains beyond, so that the more distant scenery can only be seen through the breaks.

Standing beside the wind gauge, the technician tells me of the difficulties imposed by the topography of the Nagano region on any attempt to make full observations of the clouds that precede a storm —in the way, for example, one might observe them in open places like the seashore. He explains that this is because the mountains are tall, causing the clouds along colliding fronts to break up.

"The heaviest clouds come in winter, but they're pretty monotonous. It's summer when you see the most changes. Summer is probably next after winter for the amount of cloud cover. But personally I find the clouds from late spring into summer most interesting."

The technician falls silent, gazing up into the many-layered clouds above our heads. Then, as though the thought has just occurred to him, he points at one, asking me, "What do you make of that cloud?"

I have been keeping a simple cloud diary during this trip but I find it difficult to answer this question from a specialist.

Railroad Weeds

Railroads have now reached into Nagano and on to the Japan Sea coast.[30] Some of their effects along the Chikuma River are startling. They are changing the quiet lives of the farmers.

The railways have even brought a revolution to the natural world. One example is the way the seeds of what is called "railroad weed" have been brought in with the railways. Now that noxious weed is growing everywhere, on cultivated and uncultivated land alike, ruining the soil and taking over the grasslands.

The Slaughterhouse I

I have heard of the slaughterhouse on the outskirts of Ueda but I've never had a chance to see it. Now the man who comes over from Ueda to sell beef has offered to serve as my guide.

It is New Year's day. It seems a bit odd to go off to see a slaughterhouse right at the beginning of the year, but this is an opportunity I can't pass up. I set out for Ueda from Komoro early in the morning.

There are few passengers waiting at Komoro station and the station workers are all sitting around playing cards. We pick up a few more passengers at Tanaka but that little country station is even quieter than usual. From the train window I can see some women playing at shuttlecock in the station.

It may be the beginning of a new year but it is a cold, yellowish morning sun that shines through the glass of the train windows. The stands of leafless trees outside are melancholy and there is not a soul out in the countryside. I see silent snow-covered valleys, mulberry fields enclosed by their stone fences, and the clinging brown leaves of the mountain beech. There is only a handful of passengers in the car. A solitary railway worker wearing an old hat and overcoat and with a blanket tucked around him dozes in a corner. He makes me think about people who spend their days on the railroad. (It's said that only people from Echigo can stand the monotony of the railroader's life in these mountains.)

We reach Ueda. Where Komoro is known for its stolidity, Ueda has a reputation for liveliness. It's the difference in the character of the land on which they stand that causes this difference in character. People who make a living through the heavy labor of building stone walls on a steep, sandy mountainside and farming between them grow strong and straightforward by necessity. The cold climate and poor soil have naturally created a hard-working people. Here the fields in Shinshū do not produce as rich a yield of vegetables as those in Jōshū. People in Komoro live on miso soup and tough, pickled

daikon morning and night. Whether the occasion is formal or informal, or just an everyday matter, well-to-do young men of Komoro
are not in the least ashamed of being seen in dress jackets of a type
that have been out of fashion everywhere else for ten years; in fact
they take pride in their rough-and-ready style of dress. Yet I find a
certain formalism in the Komoro austerity. I know of young men
who will change out of the luxurious clothing they have been wearing elsewhere to put on rough cotton just before reentering Komoro.

In general one may say that Komoro is poor on the surface but
rich underneath; cold and austere on the surface while in fact setting
great store by kindliness. I think this must be the source of the formalism in Komoro life. Putting aside for the moment the difference
in size and relative wealth of the two towns, there is none of the
Komoro gloom in Ueda. Komoro merchants may be brusque and
impatient but they tend to sell relatively high quality goods at attractive prices. The people in Ueda seem to feel that there is no room for
such a casual approach to business. It is the Ueda style to remain
ever on the alert, ever struggling to maintain the prosperity befitting
an old castle town. The stores vie with one another in their efforts to
make themselves attractive to customers. It is said that many of the
things handled by Ueda retailers, such as salt, dried bonito, and
lumber and building materials, are supplied from Komoro.

I see that in spite of myself I've begun a comparison of these two
mountain towns. Let's move on to the home of the butcher who is in
charge of the slaughterhouse; he has told me that today will see the
first activity of the new year there. I find waiting for me that very
same man who comes regularly to Komoro carrying a basket full of
meat for sale on his back. He introduces me to the owner of the
butcher shop, who proves to be a man of few words, careful and
thoughtful in his speech, and knowledgeable about cattle.

The apprentices are pulling an empty, rumbling cart over the road
just outside town. We all follow along behind, crossing a small
stream to come out at the base of Mt. Tarō. Five or six dull-eyed
dogs stand around the front of a new building which proves to be the
slaughterhouse.

Entering through a door painted black, we find about ten butchers inside. The head butcher is a man of some fifty-odd years of age
who speaks and handles himself with great assurance; a cheerful
smile stretches his plump cheeks as he gives his New Year's greetings

to the owner of the butcher shop. The inspection room and the waiting room are decorated with pine boughs and a red cow and two black ones are tied in the holding pen.

A big box containing a single pig sits in the central courtyard. The courtyard just outside the slaughtering room is surrounded by a board fence painted black.

The Slaughterhouse II

A veterinarian in billed cap and black overcoat comes in and everyone exchanges New Year's greetings. The butchers are all wearing white coveralls and their bare feet look cold in their straw sandals as they begin their preparations. Some of them are bent over in a corner of the courtyard, sharpening their already keen knives. The owner picks up a huge broad axe leaning against the fence and shows it to me. It looks as though it was made for splitting firewood except that a sharp steel tube some six or seven inches long is affixed to the side opposite the blade. The handle is encrusted with dried blood; it seems that it is used for killing. The owner explains in a very matter-of-fact voice that they previously used an axe equipped with a thick spike but that this tube has proved to be stronger and that the blow has to be very forceful.

A black bull of the Nanbu breed is now led into the central courtyard. The tip of his nose looks white. The other two animals still tied up in the holding pen suddenly begin to struggle. One of the butchers goes up beside the red cow, pushes down on its nose, and calms it, saying "Dō, dō!" The black mongrel bull tied beside it shakes its head from side to side and then runs around the post to which it is tied, struggling to escape. It looks as though they are putting up a final battle almost by instinct.

In contrast, the bull that has been led forward is relatively calm. A purplish film has settled over its eyes. Everyone watches as the veterinarian walks back and forth around the animal, pinching its skin, pressing on its neck, tapping its horns, and finally lifting its tail.

The inspection has finished. The butchers crowd around, urging each other on, shouting and scolding as they force the reluctant animal into the killing room. This space with its floorboards resembles nothing so much as an enlarged version of the washing area before the tubs of a Japanese bath. One of the butchers, watching his chances, passes a stout cord between the front and rear legs. When this is pulled tight the animal loses its balance and its heavy body falls over sideways onto the boards. Another man takes up the killing axe and delivers a smashing blow to the animal's forehead. It rolls its eyes, its legs quiver, its breath leaves in a jet of white vapor. It lets out a faint groan and stops breathing.

The butchers have already gathered around the body, one pulling on the tail, one retrieving the cord, and another cutting the throat. By this time a number of butchers have climbed up on the body, treading on its abdomen and chest. The dark blood pours out of the cut throat. A bar is thrust between the bones of the smashed forehead and vigorously stirred about. As long as any trace of consciousness remains the animal writhes and groans and kicks its feet but by the time the blood has run out it has lost all consciousness.

The fallen body of the black Nanbu bull lies sprawled out before my eyes, one foreleg and one hind leg tied up to the pillars of the killing room. One of the butchers makes a vertical cut in the brown skin of the abdomen and swiftly begins to peel the skin from a leg. Another butcher takes up the broad axe again. Two or three strokes to the head bring the sharp white horns falling to the floor. The body of the Nanbu bull, wrapped in fat, is rapidly being freed from its black hide.

The red cow is next to be led into the killing room.

The Slaughterhouse III

The black mongrel bull follows the red cow, falling in an instant. The bodies of the three animals now lie in the spacious killing room. Suddenly there is a loud cry from the pig beyond the fence. I go out into the courtyard to see the fat white short-legged pig raising its tragicomical voice and running desperately around the courtyard in search of a way out. A group of children have come and some of them chase the pig while others run from it. The owner quickly throws his cord while several others climb on top of the animal and tie up its legs. It is then dragged into the killing room.

"Cattle are no problem but pigs . . . There's nothing dangerous about them but they make such a fuss."

I follow the owner back into the killing room. Five men are holding the pig down but it is still moving its snout and making pitiful sounds. The broad axe that is used on cattle is of no use here. A butcher takes up a knife and plunges it into the living pig's throat. I become quite upset as it begins to cry out even louder right before my eyes. This is very different from the calmness of the cattle. The red blood flows out of the pig's neck. The sight is even more shocking because of the whiteness of the pig's skin. Two or three butchers climb on top of the animal and begin treading on it and it loses consciousness almost immediately.

The elderly head butcher walks here and there giving instructions. His hands and the knife he is holding are red with the blood of the cattle and the pig. The Nanbu bull that was killed first has now been almost completely skinned by the three men working on it. As I stand watching a short distance from the others I can see the steam rising from the still-warm hide. One man sweeps the blood off the floor with a bamboo broom while another sharpens knives. A cold sun shines in past the eaves that have been decorated with straw ropes for the season, lighting the heavy beams, the bodies of the fallen animals on the floor, the shoulders of the white-uniformed butchers.

Now one of the butchers puts his knife to the white belly of the Nanbu bull. The intestines come spilling out, wrapped in tissue the color of egg yolks. Another butcher begins cutting at the first joint of the legs to remove the hoofs, which he throws on the floor, while a third cuts into the flesh in the middle of the body. Grease runs out of the bull's body and its smell, mixed with that of blood, fills the killing room.

The Slaughterhouse IV

I watch the "quartering" of the red cow. They cut through the hipbones with a saw, run a wooden stake through the hock joints of the hind legs, and pull the body up with a block and tackle. It takes three men to raise it. "It's gonna get caught!"

"Better get that tail cut off!"

The head butcher quickly removes the tail.

"The cart! The cart!" some cry out while others shout with their exertions as the animal's body gradually rises up to hang suspended between two of the pillars. Now the backbone is cut into with a saw. It sounds exactly like sawing ice.

"I've gotta get this cut through!"

"Is it the saw that doesn't cut or is it you?" jeers the head butcher.

A policeman comes in. A crowd of children is watching. Even the dogs are looking on vaguely. The policeman gives New Year's congratulation to everyone he meets and then goes on to an outbuilding where there is a fire. The veterinarian moves around through the confusion keeping an eye on everything.

"Hey, it's New Year's day! All of you ought to get dressed up in your best clothes!"

One of the butchers dressed in old white coveralls turns to the veterinarian and says, "Yes, sir!"

"You all look as though you've been boiled in soy sauce."

The Nanbu bull has been reduced to four huge pieces of meat and each one is now hung up in the back of the killing room. The head butcher brings out a tin box and begins putting a big round black stamp on each quarter.

Incredibly, I find myself gradually becoming accustomed to the appalling sight of the slaughtered animals and beginning to see "beef" instead. The pig too has ceased to have the form in which it was crying out and struggling just a few minutes before and has become so much pink-tinged pork. The blood-stained head of the Nanbu bull has been tossed into a corner of the killing room where a butcher is washing it off with a sponge. The major bones, now stripped of their flesh, are being cut up like firewood with the broad axe. The head butcher washes off his blood-drenched hands, takes out the tobacco pouch at his hip, and begins to smoke as he watches the others at work.

"Get those guts out of here!"

The veterinarian shouts at the butchers, who then take away the stomach, which looks very much like a huge bundle wrapped in a carrying cloth, but the red cow's tail, hide, and two small horns remain behind at the foot of one of the pillars.

The apprentices from the butcher shop pull their cart into the courtyard. They line the bottom of the wagon box with matting and throw the beef bones in.

"Eighty-four pounds . . . sixty-nine pounds twelve ounces . . ." The sound of voices drifts out from the killing room where the butchers are manning the big scales two at a time to weigh out the meat of the black Nanbu bull and the red cow. The owner of the butcher shop takes out a notebook and begins to write the numbers down in it with a pencil.

The killing room is filled with the stench of meat and grease and fresh blood. Some of the butchers are dropping hooves into a bucket at the edge of the floor while others are washing away the beef blood. All of the cow has already been loaded into the cart and hauled out the gate.

"Thirty-one pounds . . ."

Next they weigh out half of the pork carcass. According to the owner of the butcher shop, almost nothing from a cow is wasted. The skull is sold for fertilizer. The internal organs and the horns are given to the butchers. This conversation continues as the owner of the butcher shop and I walk out through the front gate. Through the barren mulberry trees comes the happy and excited barking of dogs and the rumbling of the heavily loaded cart.

Sketchbook X

Along the Chikuma River

I'm sure that what I've told you up to now will give you some picture of this great, deep valley that lies between the Asama and the Tateshina ranges. I've taken you up onto the slopes of Mt. Asama and described the view of the Chikuma River; I've invited you along to the upper end of the stream and told you about the mountains and villages there. Indeed, I've always taken pleasure in exploring the Chikuma basin whenever time allows. I've started in Iwamurada, slipped over Kōsaka, and crossed the Uchiyama Pass to look down into Jōshū; I've followed the Yoda River, a tributary of the Chikuma, up to Wada Pass[31] and on over into Suwa; I've traveled from the Reisenji hot spring over the Umenoki Pass and around by the Bessho hot spring. I've also told you about the Tazawa hot spring. You and I have now seen the greater part of the upper reaches of the Chikuma River. This time I'm inviting you to join me as I go farther downstream toward the Echigo border.

The train crosses over the snowy highlands from Karuizawa and comes down into Komoro, and on the thirteenth of January I board it there. Try to imagine the huge icicles hanging in the tunnel of the Usui Pass, the place that might be called an internal customs barrier for this pass.[32] Try also to imagine how festooned with what seem to be flowers of hoarfrost are the larches around Karuizawa, telling us that this too is a part of the cold country.

As the train leaves Komoro the breath of the porters and workers on the platform rises in white puffs. The rice fields, vegetable plots, and mulberry plantations beyond the window glass are all covered with snow while far down in the bottom of the valley flow the dark blue waters of the Chikuma River. The roofs of the houses in each village we pass are also white and the walls dark. The farmers carrying their buckets of night soil look cold. As we pass Tanaka station, we see Mt. Asama, Mt. Kurofu, and Mt. Eboshi standing out against gray skies. Only the edges of the mountain ranges appear

87

vaguely white. *Unseen whiteness*[33]—only that English phrase can describe those deep skies. The furrows in the barley fields are filled with snow and among their parallel white undulations are a random scattering of bare-limbed trees and bushes.

How melancholy the snow country is! The train crosses the Sai River; with the addition of its waters the Chikuma appears even greater. The broad rice fields along the Sai River, the low-growing willows and the white earth of its banks, the villages with their numerous persimmon trees—everything is covered with snow. This low-keyed scene is not simply white; it carries purplish gray highlights. The forms of the more distant mountains are barely perceptible, almost hidden away beneath the dark heavy skies. The only things that relieve the monotony of the snow are the occasional dark groves of trees and the low-flying flocks of half-starved birds. Dark snow clouds are piling up ahead. I begin to feel as though I am gradually penetrating into the very depths of the snow country. Snow begins to fall just as we pull out of one station.

I am not making this trip alone; I have two companions from Komoro, I—— and K——, both girls who live near us. They have graduated from the Komoro grade school and are now going to enter the normal school in Iiyama. They are of an age where they relieve themselves of the boredom of the journey by looking back toward their parents' homes, eyes overflowing with tears; by poking at each other with their elbows; by laughing with a display of yellowish teeth; and by embracing one another from behind. Whenever I look at this *naive*[34] and charming pair I can't keep from laughing, too. They help to make this journey a pleasant one for me. I—— is the daughter of my landlord.

We get off the train in the broad stretch of fields at Toyono. The famous Obuse chestnut forest is nearby. Mt. Azuma and Mt. Shirane are almost completely hidden from view today. As I walk along the snow-covered road I recognize the bare branches of pear and persimmon trees. In one village I climb up a steep slope to a height from which I can look out over the Minochi plain. Once before I stood at the top of this slope in autumn and looked out over a golden ocean of ripening rice fields. I have also looked out from the other side at the glistening flow of the Chikuma River. We spot a fine grove of zelkova trees with branches like golden hair; the image of their dark sturdy trunks will always linger in my mind. We walk

as far as Kanisawa and there, for the first time, we see a boat on the
Chikuma River.

The Riverboat

It has been snowing off and on, and now it turns to sleet. We stand
waiting for the boat to Iiyama, listening to the sleet beat down. The
men wear quilted cotton hoods and straw snow boots and the women
carry indigo-dyed quilted jackets on their backs like tortoise shells
and keep a kerchief over their heads even in the house. These are the
most immediately striking aspects of the local customs. When we
leave the teahouse to walk out to the riverbank, we can only dimly
make out in the distance such places as the Kamitakai range, the
Sugadaira highlands, and Mt. Takayashiro. The rushes on the
opposite bank have withered and sunk below the surface of the
waters and the sandbar in the middle of the river is covered with
snow. Out of these deep, endless reaches of whiteness, the dark
waters of the Chikuma River come flowing like oil. I try to picture
them as the same waters that earlier broke white against the banks
near Komoro but they seem to have changed quality; they are now
part of a great river. Upstream there are many high rope bridges but
from here on there are also riverboats.

The passengers begin to gather. We walk along the snow-covered
banks and down to the landing. The riverboat cabin is low and our
knees touch each other across the aisle as we take our seats. The
sounds of the scull in the water and the voice of the captain as he
walks on the roof over our heads seem casual and relaxed. Beyond
the windows something that is not quite snow or sleet is falling into
the water. The waves are touched with golden highlights.

We leave Kanisawa. Two or three passengers are waiting on the
bank at Kami'imai. The captain leaps into the water and splashes
back and forth between shore and boat, carrying the passengers on
his back, men and women alike. There is the sound of the boat grat-
ing on the sand and then the creaking of the scull starts up again. It
resounds over the quiet waters of the Chikuma River like the lowing
of a cow. It almost seems as if the boat itself is crying out. It sounds

like anything one might want to make of it—if I think of the surname of my companion I——, it sounds like that, or if I think of the
surname of B——, then that is what it sounds like. The unsophisticated girls seem greatly amused by it. Here and there in the whiteness on both banks we can see houses belonging to villages, or stands
of brush, or forests, or people bundled up against the snow and cold
walking along the banks. The last time I walked along these banks
the beans and millet were just ripening in the fields and their vines
and heads were bent over the roadsides. And yes, now I recall I saw
a low stand of willows huddling below the bank, and how, when
viewed from beneath the frosted autumn leaves of a stand of brush,
they looked just like a herd of sheep. The riverboat is passing below
that spot right now. The bare limbs of the nearer willows rub against
the roof of the cabin and we can hear other limbs scraping the bottom of the boat as it passes over them.

It is fairly warm in the cabin of the boat. Although we are still in
the snow country, there is a readily sensible difference in climate
between here and the high country, even though the snow is deeper
here. In the low afternoon sun the mountains on the opposite bank
seem to cast purplish shadows on the water. I open the window to listen to the whisper of the waves and watch the water slide along the
sides of the boat, which is painted white with two red stripes.

The riverboat drifts clumsily past one end of a pontoon bridge. A
town comes into sight, lying along the broad floodplain of the Chikuma River with Mt. Kuroiwa in the background. The crowing of
roosters rings out over the snow and smoke rises thick from the
houses. This is the old castle town of Iiyama.

A Sea of Snow

It is said that from here on over into Echigo four feet of snow can fall
in a single night. Iiyama itself proves to be a town completely buried
in snow. It might be better to say that it is a town that has been
excavated from the snow. That impression is reinforced by the towering banks of snow that have been built up along the streets. The
snow that has been cleared from the roofs is gathered together and

stacked up higher than the eaves of the houses to form a white wall running down the middle of each street. Broad porchlike extensions have been built out from the eaves of the houses and people bustle back and forth through them. You can readily imagine how dark it must be inside the houses, but the heavy reed blinds that hang around them make them even darker. I leave the girls and strike out on my own. Lamplight is beginning to show here and there among the snowbanks. I look up toward the gray skies that are now touched with scarlet as though a distant conflagration were coloring the sky. It is sunset.

Smokelike wisps of snow come blowing by—something you will see only in a place like this. It is quite gloomy here; it feels as though something has been pulled over your head. The well-known devoutness of the local people seems to be no accident. There are more than twenty temples in this town alone. They almost make one think he is in the Kyoto-Osaka region for all that he is clearly in Shinano province. Even the speech is different from that of the highlands.

I decide to walk around until dark. Sleds are being used in place of carts and some are even pulled over the snow by horses. People walk past me in full snow gear: heavy hats woven of cattails, dark glasses, cattail leggings and footwear, bodies wrapped in blankets or shawls.

The sleet begins again. I go down to the boat landing on the banks of the Chikuma River. On the long pontoon bridge that undulates off to the far bank I see that the only touch of brown is the single line of footprints crossing it. From time to time I meet men wearing high straw snow boots, but there are few passersby. Takayashiro, Kazahara, Nakanosawa, and the other peaks that stand along the Shinano-Echigo line are only vaguely discernible and the distant villages are lost in the snow. The melancholy waters of the Chikuma River flow silently past.

Yet when I walk out onto the pontoon bridge, the snow crunching under my feet, I find that the waters are moving as swiftly as an arrow. Looking out from here over the floodplain, there is nothing to be seen but a sea of snow—that's it, a white sea! And this whiteness is no ordinary whiteness; it is a fathomless, melancholy whiteness. It is a whiteness that makes one shiver to look at it.

Tokens of Love

I hear that hand towels serve as tokens of love in Iiyama. When a relationship is broken off a hand towel is torn up. That is apparently the reason the girls around here take such care of their hand towels and particularly dislike to lose track of them.

This is rather close to the entire question of whether a relationship is a favored or an unfavored one. But it is a charming custom.

To the Top of the Mountain

"Minochi must have been one great swamp long ago—the fact that the town of Iiyama sits on sand and gravel is proof of that. You find that out as soon as you start to dig."

Having heard all kinds of stories about the land, I drop off the girls and leave Iiyama the next morning. I cross the pontoon bridge and walk over into the town to look up at the site of the old castle, and then I have myself drawn in a sled through the snow of the mulberry plantations along the riverbank. This sled consists of a rickshaw from which the wheels have been removed and replaced with runners made from a hard wood called *itaya*. There are shafts for the puller in front and a bar across the rear on which a second man can push. The sled is set so low that the passenger finds himself tilted back uncomfortably whenever the shafts are raised too high, but the very awkwardness of the sled seems to add to the zest of being on a trip. I listen to the heavy breathing of the men pulling and pushing me with the wide-eyed excitement of a child. As we hurtle over the frozen snow I feel that I am about to be pitched, sled and all, into a mulberry patch.

"Hooo! Yooo!" come the cries of the men, and with them the sound of the runners on the snow and the crunching of footsteps, all bringing joy to my ears. The snowy scenes along the bank that I previously observed from the riverboat now spin quietly past me once again.

I leave the sled near Nakano and walk the rest of the way. My feet remain warm as long as there is snow on the road but presently I find myself slogging through cold, deep yellowish mud and my toes begin to tingle. I have been given snow shoes by the thoughtful people at the inn in Iiyama and I have strapped them to the front of my straw snow boots.

It is January fourteenth and they are celebrating *monozukuri* in all the villages by hanging small lumps of rice flour moulded into the shape of cocoons on the reddish branches of a tree called *mizukusa*. They explain that this is all in preparation for the next season of raising silkworms.

On the way back I am dazzled by the sunlight and the reflection off the snow is painful. The waters of the Chikuma River have taken on a yellowish green coloring.

I get on the train again at Toyono and as we climb up into the mountains once more I can feel it growing colder and colder. All the same I have the feeling that I've climbed up out of a great mass of dark gloomy snow toward the bright sky and I breathe a sigh of relief.

Sketchbook XI

Dwellers in the Mountains I

Once on my way back from a previous trip to Iiyama—I was following the road on the opposite side of the river from the one on which I had my sled ride—I passed through the long succession of golden rice fields making up Shizumadaira before finding myself in a traveler's teahouse on the outskirts of a village. I found it very amusing that the lady there assumed I was heading for Zenkōji.[35] "Are you with a temple?" she asked. My companion, the painter B——, was wearing a suit of clothes he had bought while abroad and his sketchbook was in his pocket, but he went along with the joke, claiming to be a priest himself. The lady in charge of the teahouse was somewhat taken aback. The more we laughed the more convinced she became that we were priests. She went on in half-envious, half-teasing tones, saying that, even though we were dressed as ordinary people, she could see through that. What she had to say was revealing about one aspect of the life of priests in the countryside between Iiyama and Nagano.

In the course of talking about my recent trip to Iiyama, I mentioned how religious the people around there happen to be—there are more than twenty temples in that little mountain town and everything is still being done in the old style. Just how long will those old ways be maintained in this time of rapid change before they too are smashed down? At any rate it seems that there is something in the snowbound lives led during long winters that inclines most of these people toward religion. One is especially aware of that along the lower reaches of the Chikuma River.

In Nagano I've only had a look at the huge buildings of the Zenkōji while walking around the temple grounds to enjoy their splendid views. Seeing only a bit of the *dramatic*[36] ceremonials carried on within, I don't really know what kind of people live there. In Iiyama I did encounter an aged priest who seemed to have a lofty outlook. The elderly lady who accompanied him was also a most impressive individual. They were in charge of a huge old temple and they appeared not to have let up the least bit in their efforts in spite of their advanced ages. At their temple I caught sight of a man taking away a sacred painting, carefully packed in a box and wrapped with an impressively patterned carrying cloth, that was to be used in a service in one of the parishioners' homes. Even in this momentary impression I sensed how old-fashioned things are there.

Have you heard about the effort to retrace the life of the Buddha in India? One of the priests who is taking part in this is the son of this old priest. He was joined in the quest by a young college graduate married to the old priest's daughter. This young man had been pursuing advanced studies in England when, in spite of poor health, he joined the expedition to search for traces of King Asoka in the Indian hinterlands and in Ceylon before falling ill and dying there. A great many picture postcards sent by this young scholar are being preserved in the Iiyama temple.[37] I was particularly moved by their accounts of the hardships of travel in the tropics. I never met either of the young men, although I hear the son has been called up for military service. Such are the new people being produced out of the atmosphere of these mouldering old temples. Behind such people we can imagine that there are their parents and their parents-in-law; people like this aged priest and his wife who have devoted decades to the religious life.

It is, however, no accident that a scent of the old-fashioned and the religious should remain around Iiyama and that more than twenty temples are maintaining the old ways even in the midst of difficulties.[38] I learned from this priest that even among the lords of Iiyama castle there were those who broke early with the political world, robed themselves in priestly garments, and devoted their entire lives to the propagation of the Buddhist faith. Again, I've heard that there is a deep historical linkage between this area and such outstanding religious figures as Hakuin and Etan.[39]

There is not much of this sort of thing up in the highlands. It doesn't fit the local style in the first place, nor is there the same kind of historical background; neither will you find people like that aged priest continuing to hold the light of the law on high. I've met a number of priests around Komoro but on each occasion it has seemed little different from meeting with the laymen of the region. When it comes time to care for silkworms there will be silkworm platforms hanging alongside the main temple buildings. The priests too have to labor and build up their stores against the long winter.

Dwellers in the Mountains II

A broad distribution of learning is one of the boasts of this region. The big school buildings filled with students that you see in these mountains have few equals elsewhere. These buildings also double as meeting halls when the occasion calls for it. In Komoro too the greater part of the town's resources have been put into building a schoolhouse in no way inferior to those of the other towns. Its tall glass windows glitter in the town's forehead.

It's not surprising in such a place that so many youths should aspire to become good educators. Family conditions of one kind or another make it impossible for many of these studious youths to go very far away and so they think of ways to prepare themselves within the province. They make up a disproportionate number of the students who apply for admission to Nagano Normal School each year. Many of these students include a year or two of study in our school in their preparations.

There is a great respect for scholars here in these mountains. Even elementary school teachers get better salaries than in other places. Again, they also occupy an honored social position. In this respect their lot is nothing like that of educators in the cities. Here even newspaper reporters are addressed as *sensei*.[40] For that matter, it's not at all unusual for people here to invite reporters over from the Nagano region to deliver lectures.[41] Whenever they see anyone of any accomplishment, they want to acquire new knowledge from him. This has led to a truly remarkable number of outstanding people being welcomed to Komoro. It's almost as though we were maintaining one of the old internal customs barriers,[42] not letting such people get through without questioning them.

Thanks to these local values I've had the opportunity to listen to a great many masters since I came here. It is said that even the late Fukuzawa Yukichi[43] passed through here once, leaving the local people with a token of his wisdom. I learned this from the headmaster much later. We often see refugees from Korea. It is the kind of place where if a traveling painter is in trouble we will provide him with the needed travel expenses. There is a tendency to greet everyone in the same way: soldiers, newspaper editors, educators, artists, or whatever.

This tendency to receive anyone with the most passionate interest carries with it a matching tendency to create a very heavy and uncomfortable atmosphere—a provincial dullness, to put it bluntly. Even people of the most diverse personality types all prove unable to say anything but the same old things.

Moreover, in the Saku region one is particularly likely to encounter people who are blessed with a negativistic kind of courage. You'll find the most extremely casual people here as well as the most extremely argumentative people.

It's often asked why it is that Shinshū people are so fond of argument. I think it's because people's tempers are so violent here. Some local people will, at the slightest provocation, break out into violent trembling like oak leaves roaring in the north wind. I recall that when I first began to write fiction there was talk among the town leaders of establishing a youth group. When everyone had gathered in the hall of the Kōgakuji a lively argument broke out. I—— from our school and some others kept going at it with some of the youths until darkness fell. It left them all tired out, and although they did eventually manage to establish a set of rules, in the end the youth group went by the boards.

On the other hand, there are extremely quiet people like T——, who teaches botany in our school. He has a very scholarly, and therefore orderly, mind. I've never seen him looking the least bit put out. He comes from a village called Nishihara, just outside Komoro. I find the sight of his face more reassuring than anyone else's in the school.

Dwellers in the Mountains III

Many of the policemen and railway workers are from elsewhere; in fact, almost all the people in charge of maintaining the peace as heads of local police detachments are from other places. Yet even among these policemen there are those who have entered into service from around here and the sound of their footsteps is reassuring.

The railroad people have created a completely separate world for themselves around the station. It is said that no one but the long-suffering people of Echigo could bear up under the life that railway workers lead in these mountains. I learned something about the station master from the masseur who lives by the old main gate of the castle. It seems that he moved from Shinbashi in downtown Tokyo to Naoetsu on the Japan Sea coast and worked there for five years as a conductor and then for seven as an assistant station master before coming to Komoro. Even up here in the mountains there are people living lives completely different from those of the rest of us.

The masseur also told me about a previous station master.

"He had worked as a brewer and as a warehouse guard in Echigo and then rose very quickly to the post of station master. One day he pointed at the label on a wine bottle and asked a telegrapher if his English was good enough to read it. He promised him a *shō* of wine if he could. The telegrapher was fully aware of the station master's lack of learning and so he pretended not to be able to read it himself and asked the station master for help, offering in turn to give him a bottle either of sake or of grape wine if he could. 'Oh, is that right?' said the station master. 'I'm amazed that you got a job with the railroad when you can't read something like that.' Then he stalked out. The telegrapher, deciding he would use the wine as an excuse if he should be scolded, came before the station master with a slightly reddened face. 'Please forgive me. I'm afraid that what is written here is the simplest kind of English. Listen everyone, this is what is written on the label on this wine bottle.' And he read it straight off. 'Is that right? Is that what it says there? You really know a lot. I never dreamed you were so learned . . . ,' said the station master."

From that moment on, the station master and the telegrapher were at odds, but it was the station master who decided to leave Komoro soon afterward.

The switchmen who stand alongside the tracks are migrants who lead particularly lonely lives. They are on duty for two days and nights at a time and then they get one day off. It must be very difficult to work such long shifts. I often see switchmen standing beside the guard's station as I go over the grade crossing at the Kaikoen on my way to and from work.

Yanagita Mojūrō

The previous Yanagita Mojūrō was a Saku merchant who was always ready to start haggling. He was one of the most extreme manifestations of the Saku character.

Famous though he was as a merchant, at one point he had failed so badly that he was reduced to selling tōfu. He may very well have brought it on himself; when he first started a tōfu shop in Komoro he seemed so wretched that no one would buy from him. His family had originally been in the sake business but realizing that brewing sake tied up his capital and kept it from working as steadily as it might, he went into the tea trade. He was strict about his use of time. Whenever anyone quoted a high price to him for bargaining purposes he would go straight back home. He put several of his sons into the business and charged them rent as long as he was alive, but at his death he divided up his stores among them. People tell of the surprise a certain woman experienced when she received a memento after his death even though she had set foot in his house only once. The headmaster of our school often speaks of him when we are together, telling us how, when Mojūrō was invited out to a party, he would not drink excessively and would even move the sake bottle away.

"If you drink just as much sake as you want, that should be sufficient."

I hear that Mojūrō was that way in everything he did.

The Home of a Tenant Farmer

Since I've promised to visit the home of the school janitor, he has suggested that I come over on the day when he would deliver the year's rents.

There is a shallow valley at the bottom of the Shinmachi slope in Komoro. Tatsu's house stands there, just across from the mill. The courtyard is covered with matting on which unhulled rice is stacked mountain high, and Tatsu and his brother are hard at work.

His kindly father, now retired, escorts me straightaway into their dark tenant farmer's house. There my attention is caught by a cat shelter or something shaped like a foot warmer made of straw. The old man accepts the small gift I have brought, places it before the *kamidana* in the alcove, and rings the bell vigorously.⁴⁴ He then escorts me to the *kotatsu,* where he begins to tell all kinds of stories. A thin, extremely taciturn woman of about fifty is also at the *kotatsu* and Tatsu's little daughter sits beside her, completely taken up in her play. The taciturn woman and a younger woman, whose kimono is held closed by the narrowest of sashes as she kneels before the cook stove, both seem to be living here. I try to ignore them as I listen to the old man's stories.

The sociable and interesting old man begins with a comparison of Jōshū and Shinshū farmers and then goes on to talk about various kinds of agricultural tools and about the relations between tenants and landowners. I learn from him that the tenant farmers in the Shinmachi neighborhood occasionally engage in what would have to be called minor strikes. He explains that the main reason there is tension between the tenant farmers and the landlords is that hereabouts a hundred *tsubo* is said to require one *shō* of unhulled rice for planting and one *tsuka* is calculated as three hundred *tsubo* while one *shō* of unhulled rice is counted as two hundred eighty *momme.*⁴⁵ Even though each unit of land is called one *tsuka,* it is in fact not three hundred *tsubo.* A proportional allowance is made for the difference and that difference is split between tenant and landlord, but that is grossly unfair. That is where the dissatisfaction of the tenants begins. The helpless and unsophisticated tenants take revenge on the landlords in various ways. For example, they may make life difficult for the landlords by putting stones inside the rice bales to increase the weight, by letting dampness into the bales, or by ignoring the rice heads and taking scrupulous care of the straw. This is why they run out of food around the third or fourth month.⁴⁶ Yet, to be sure, the barley harvest will be coming along about then.

"In my time, I would always make sure to buy a *shō* of sake and offer some pickled vegetables with them whenever the landowner came. But now I have turned things over to my son this year and I have no idea what he will do . . . That's the way I always did it," the old man says, laughing.

Soon we hear Tatsu's voice outside saying, "I wish the landowner would get here; I wish he would get here right now."

The sunlight suddenly begins to shine in through the doorway and the southern window brightens too. Tatsu's voice comes again.

"Ah, the sun's shining. That's good! It was looking like snow a little while ago."

The woman with the narrow sash prepares tea and brings it over to us. The taciturn woman with us at the *kotatsu* abruptly gets up and goes off to the kitchen.

The old man lowers his voice.

"I'm all alone and usually I have no visitors. It's because I'm old . . . So I asked them to stay with me. My son doesn't like it. 'What do you mean bringing in such people without telling anyone?' he says."

"Do they prepare your meals?" I ask.

"That's right. That's what everyone thinks. But I don't have them cook for me. If I did they would eat me out of house and home . . . I'm pretty tricky about such things. But people don't appreciate that. They say it would be tough without them."

The old man goes on, tapping on the tasseled cover of an old, foreign-style umbrella that has been pressed into service as a *kotatsu* cover while he speaks. His pleasures in his old age consist of such things as predicting the agricultural fortunes of his neighbors by means of the "aspects from three worlds" system[47] and curing them of their illnesses by means of the "six-three" system of divination.[48] He is respected throughout the neighborhood as a knowledgeable old man, but even so I was startled when he began to question me about an entry in *Genkai*, a scholarly dictionary of the Japanese language.

"I don't want to be telling you about my old disgraces but when I was a young man I pulled a rickshaw for a while. There were times when I was making eight *ryō* per day.[49] Eight *ryō*! And I spent it like water. I was young and foolish then. So I've done just about everything a man might do. The only thing I've missed out on is gambling and jail—yes, that's just about all."

As the old man laughs, another man comes in. He is about fifty, dressed in a cotton hat and a somber jacket.

Tatsu simply calls out, "The landlord's here!"

The landlord comes into the room and begins to warm himself at the *kotatsu*. As I step out into the garden a young woman comes over the bridge from the mill to toss a measuring box out on the heap of unhulled rice. Tatsu begins preparations for paying the rents. His five-year-old daughter comes over to cling to his sleeve. Tatsu gives comfort in a voice filled with fatherly solicitude but the girl's head and shoulders begin to quiver and she bursts into tears. It is impossible to tell just what she is saying.

"Don't cry. Mama will be here right away."

"My hands are cold . . ."

"What? Your hands are cold? Well then, let's run in and warm up at the *kotatsu!*"

Tatsu grasps his daughter's icy hand and leads her into the house.

There is a bare-branched persimmon tree in the tiny garden overlooking the valley. The mill opposite us is now also surrounded with straw. The spray from the sluice has formed a column of ice while the little stream itself looks frozen over. The cold yellowish sunlight passes through the branches of the persimmon tree to shine on the courtyard heaped with unhulled rice. The self-important landlord comes out of the house, his gray hair hidden by a cotton hat drawn far down over his ears. As he leans on the beam running along the south window, his desperate efforts to keep himself warm make him appear to be enfolding himself in a tight embrace as he watches Tatsu and his brother making the preparations.

"How does the rice look to you?" asks Tatsu.

The landlord puts out his hand to pick some up. He puts a grain in his mouth.

"You've got a lot of blank heads!"

"The sparrows have been after them. There aren't any blanks. Shall I put up a bale for you?"

The landlord discards the rice he is holding and goes back to wrapping his arms around himself.

The younger brother has Tatsu gather up some rice in a winnowing basket so that he can put it into a round one-*to* measure. The landlord seems doubtful. He carefully checks the top of the measure.

"Sound off! It just doesn't seem like paying the rent if you don't say anything!" Tatsu says to his brother.

"Well then, I'll go to it!" says the brother and he begins to chant, "One load! Two loads!"

Six woven straw containers for unhulled rice are laid out in a row and six *to* three *shō* are measured into each one. Tatsu takes up straw caps and attaches them to the tops of the bales but he soon begins to

protest to the landlord, who now is leaning on the bales. The landlord listens to him, narrows his eyes, and looks thoughtful. In less
time than it takes to tell of it, Tatsu's quick-witted brother has run
across the bridge and come back with a jug of sake wrapped in a carrying cloth. He is smiling, his cheeks red.

"The year's rent, is it? Congratulations!" The owner of the mill
has joined them.

I've drawn back to the shed where straw articles are made in an
effort to be out of the way as much as possible. I sit down on a rice
bale cover and watch the proceedings. Tatsu puts his foot on a rice
bale and wraps it three ways with a straw rope. His brother is help-
ing him but the dry rope breaks from time to time.

"It looks like the ropes around the bales are breaking! You're in
for a bad time!" laughs the miller.

"Just pick up one of these bales. They're really full. A good hundred and fifty-five pounds . . ."

"That's really something!"

"A hundred fifty-five pounds would mean that it's really good
rice."

"Of course there's also the weight of the bag."

"That's true, but we've already allowed for that."

"At our place we already count a hundred fifty pounds as good."

"Well, that's because you always have to give the landlord the
best of the crop."

The chatter grows more lively. The miller turns to the landlord
and begins talking about the price of rice. Then he goes away, walking right over the unhulled rice with his wooden clogs.

The men grow playful.

"How about it? You look like you ought to be able to handle two
bales easily!" the landlord says and the younger brother grasps one
bale in each hand and lifts them up, his face turning bright red.

"Please have some tea."

Tatsu includes me in his invitation to the landlord and as the landlord enters the house, stripping off his cotton cap, I follow in search
of warmth.

"Shall I make the deduction two *to* five *shō* from the six bags?"
asks Tatsu.

The retired old man sits at the *kotatsu* listening with disapproval to
Tatsu's proposal. As he unwraps the jug of sake before the landlord

he says, "How could we deduct just two *to* five *shō*? It'll have to be four *to* five *shō*."

"Four *to* . . ." the landlord's voice trails off.

The retired old man speaks up again. "It can't be four *to* five *shō* either. Four *to* seven *shō*. That's it . . ."

"Four *to* seven *shō*?" The landlord stares at the old man.

"Four *to* seven *shō*, is it?" says Tatsu over his shoulder as he goes out into the courtyard.

We all remain around the *kotatsu*. The old man brings out a battered wooden cover to fit over the *kotatsu* frame, sets it on top of the quilt and begins to serve up huge bowls of a stew of *konnyaku*[50] and fried tōfu. He also sets out a bag of red pepper on a small plate to go with it. Next he takes the cover off the teakettle with a rag, puts the sake jug into the boiling water, and begins to urge us to drink.

"It's still cold. It's not warm yet. . . . But the landlord is here."

The old man speaks without constraint. The landlord wedges his old-fashioned pipe in between the boards of the *kotatsu* cover and begins to drink the cold sake thirstily. He looks up at the old man and says, "It would be nice if your wife could be with us now."

A faint smile shows on the landlord's face for the first time. The old man, playing the conscientious host, says, "This year will make twenty-five years since the old woman left."

"She ought to have stuck it out with you."

"No, listen here! She had seven children and every last one of them died. . . . Tatsu here is adopted. . . . And then what? She waited until I was away one day and took everything in the house with her. That's the way it is with men and women, so I can overlook most of it. . . . I can overlook it but . . . It's the stealing that was bad. And now people are saying that even though I pretend to be all pious and proper the reason I've got this old woman here now is that I've got an eye on her savings. I hate that. Even if my wife did come back we'd just start quarreling over what she stole. There's not a thing to be done about it. I know! I kept making spells and I found out who stole it. It's a terrible thing."

The old man goes on to tell of interesting things that only a tenant farmer could know about. He and the landlord also discuss the two women in the kitchen who are living with him.

"You say that's her daughter?"

"Well, she's got a kid. I felt sorry for her so I let her stay here. But people have funny ideas about it. . . . After all, I'm sixty-seven years old. . . . It's awful to have people saying that I've taken in that kind of woman at my age. That's what I can't stand."

"It's always the same no matter how old you get."

Thanks to these people I'm able to pass the time under this roof where I've never been before and listen to the farmers' talk. I eat my fill of *konnyaku* and fried tōfu and leave the old man's house soon afterward.

Sketchbook XII

Roadside Plants

Walking to and from school each day through a landscape buried by snow has caused me to take pleasure in those plants that appear to anticipate the coming of spring from shelters such as the cracks in sun-warmed stone embankments. It has been a long winter and my feeling of closeness to these plants is a source of comfort.

In mulberry fields with a southern or western exposure, I am often greeted by the metalwort,[51] the very edge of its leaves outlined in purple. It is also called "wheel-weed," and wherever that wheel-shaped weed is growing on bare banks and the like, the green chickweed will also be flourishing. The janitor at the school tells me that the farmers feed it to the baby chicks.[52] Among the stones of the walls dangle the purplish green leaves of the "devil's shin-pieces" and the *kishiya-gusa* with its thick flat leaves that appear to be bundled in heavy winter clothing. Among the dead twigs of artemisia and other herbs killed by the cold, some of the short slender blades of grass stay green while others have turned yellow and some have gone dead. There isn't much moisture around our school and the old samurai quarter, and so a number of tiny streams have been directed toward them. One flows directly in front of the gate of the school. It keeps the grass green so that there is more life here than in other places.

I want to tell you about the kind of world it is in which these plants show their faces and in which some of them are preparing to send forth their tiny buds. The cold is at its worst from around the twenty-seventh to the thirty-first of January until around the sixth of February. Even though I've become accustomed to living in the mountains there are days when I'm overwhelmed by the violence of the climate, days when my fingers freeze and I come down with a cold and fever. The snow piles up on the north slope of the roof or in the garden and it shows no sign of thawing as the days go by. . . . I've seen it become impossible to close the sliding panels in certain rooms of our old house because of the frost heaving up out of the tortured earth. The icicles along the northern eaves will grow to two or three feet in length. Whenever I wrap up and go outside I soon find my coat collar turning white from my frozen breath. The only creatures that seem unaffected by it all are the dogs and the swallows that fly over the rooftops.

Speaking of plants, we have potted up an Amur adonis and put it in the alcove. It turned quite cold just as the yellowish buds were forming but the plant rises up on the warmer days only to collapse again with each attack of renewed cold. The nandina was really surprising. Even though the water in the vase was frozen the fruits on the branch we brought in retained their bright red and the leaves stayed fresh and green to the end.

I doubt that you've ever seen frozen milk. It loses its fragrance and takes on a faintly greenish color. Even eggs freeze here. When they are broken open the yolk and white have a granular texture. The water that runs out below the open kitchen sink all freezes. Onions and used tea leaves freeze too. The sight of someone using a heavy kitchen knife to chop the ice out from under the sink by the feeble light coming in through the windows is something you'll never see in a warm country. Water left overnight in a washbasin will be half frozen by morning. You have to set it out in the sun for a while before you can knock the ice out and replace it with fresh well water. Pickled vegetables freeze so hard that they crunch when you bite on them. Sometimes you have to pour hot water on them. The maid's hands turn black, the skin cracks, and blood oozes out. She has to put on gloves and wrap a cloth about her head when she goes out to get water. Mornings when the moisture left behind by the cleaning cloth immediately freezes white on the floor behind each stroke are not at all rare. Sometimes when I am reading late at night to the accompaniment of the sharp cracking sound made by the pillars of the house as they freeze, it seems as though the cold has penetrated to my very bones . . .

It actually turns warmer when it snows. The feeling when it starts snowing after dark is different from the gloom of rainy nights; there is a different kind of stillness. On some snowy nights it feels so warm that I start thinking about plum blossoms.[53] But then once the snow has fallen it gets almost unbearably cold again. The frozen fields are like arctic scenes. In such times even the Chikuma River freezes over.

From under the ice comes the sound of the waters, still flowing with the same power.

The Death of a Student

O——, a student at our school, has died. I set out for O——'s house in the company of my colleagues, thinking of how, during my year as a teacher in Sendai—I was still only twenty-five years old then— another of my students died. All kinds of people who have died come to mind.

O——'s house is in the district of Komoro known as Akasaka. As I walk there with the old science teacher, we pass in front of the house where the watercolor artist M—— once lived. It is in an old neighborhood of samurai residences and the house which M—— rented for that year is a quiet and peaceful place with a fine gate. M—— was diligent during the time he was in Komoro and he produced a great many pictures on subjects such as "Morning" and "Pine Forests." I would often invite myself over and spend many hours there, either watching him make sketches or talking with him about the paintings of Millet.

We walk alongside a small stream to the bottom of the slope, where we have arranged to meet our colleagues T—— and W——. It's said that O—— went off at dusk to help his older brother the tailor replace the paper on his shōji and from there went to the bath in spite of being terribly chilled.[54] He quickly took to his bed but the fever moved from his lungs to his heart. There were three doctors in attendance on him and it's said that they drew off more than a pint of fluid from around his heart. He was just eighteen years old when he died, after an illness of some forty days. The science teacher and my other colleagues talk about his life. O—— began taking care of his invalid mother when he was around ten years of age, cooking breakfast in the mornings and putting up her hair before going off to school. It's said that even during his illness he had his bedding placed where he could keep an eye on his mother.

The funeral ceremonies at O——'s house are simple. His relatives, the people of the neighborhood, his teachers, and his classmates are gathered there to mourn him. It is ten o'clock on this morning of January thirty-first. Since O—— was a Christian, a black cloth has been draped over the coffin with a green cross placed on top of it. A bouquet of artificial peonies has also been laid on the coffin and a group of fellow believers sing a hymn before it. Next there is a prayer, then a recounting of the life of the deceased, and finally a reading from the Bible, the first verse of the fifth chapter of II Corinthians. The headmaster of our school gives the elegy. While O——'s mother weeps over her Bible, he speaks of how we must always mourn the departed as a brother.

The students and I accompany O—— to the samurai graveyard. His body is buried on a small peaceful pine-surrounded hill. Another hymn is sung. There, under the pine trees, beside the stone monument, O——'s classmates gaze out over the scene.

Warm Rains

It is February and the warm rains have come.

On this day when the sun is obscured by low-hanging gray clouds, rain starts in the afternoon and a life-restoring warmth quickly spreads over everything. It will, however, take many, many rains like this before we can overcome the springtime shortage of food.[55]

People go about under umbrellas beneath skies that seem as much smoky as cloudy, and the horses passing by are soaked to the skin. The sound of the rain dripping from the eaves is pleasant.

I feel an indescribable pleasure as my body, chilled and drawn in on itself for so long, seems to loosen and expand. When I go out into the garden I can hear the rain soaking into the dirty snow. The falling rain melts the remaining snow everywhere, revealing the dark soil beneath. As the sandy face of the earth makes its appearance, it's as though the fields are beginning to awaken from their winter's sleep. The yellowed bamboo groves, the trunks of the still-bare persimmons, the plums, and the other trees are all wet with rain and there is not a one of them that does not present an unkempt and sleepy-eyed face to the world.

The sound of flowing streams and the voices of the sparrows all

seem cheerful. It is a rain that soaks into the very roots of the mulberry trees in the fields. Amid the mud, the melting snow, and the
shattered wreckage of winter the first signs of growth in the willow
branches are most encouraging. In the evening I look through those
branches at the yellowish gray southern skies.

As night falls, the dreary sound of the falling rain somehow brings
thoughts of the approach of spring.

The Wolves of the Northern Mountains and Other Things

I hear all kinds of stories about the countryside as I walk about with
the students. One student tells me about the wolves of the northern
mountains. Their tracks are larger than those of domestic dogs and
there is hair and bone in their droppings—which, after they have
weathered a bit, are used by the farmers as medicine for fever. They
say this is because the wolves eat rabbits and birds. I have the feeling
that the world of folk tales is being revealed to me in these little
stories.

I hear some brutal, savage tales. There are people around here
who live by stealing chickens. Some of them go to where chickens
are running free and throw out a line with a baited fishhook. When
the birds are firmly hooked in the throat they take them away. Others steal dogs. They use brown sugar to lure other people's dogs out;
then they kill and eat them, stretch the hides, and dry them to use
for rugs.

These local tales remind me of something else. You often see
huge, blank-eyed Daruma[56] on the household Shintō altars around
here. In Ueda there is a hall called Yōkadō, or "hall of the eighth
day," and on its festival days a Daruma market is held there. It is as
lively as the Rooster Market[57] in Tokyo. When a wish is realized, the
eyes of the Daruma are painted in. When I spent the night in the
desolate hot spring lodging at Uminokuchi village I noticed that one
of these Daruma was being displayed even in that remote place.

This is a silk-producing district and there is a silkworm festival
here. They observe the day by molding rice flour into the shape of
cocoons and laying them out on bamboo leaves.

The festival of the roadside gods, held each year on the eighth of February, is specially for children. In the local dialect they are not called Dōsōjin, but Dōrokujin. The custom of putting rice cakes on straw horses and leading them out to the tiny roadside shrines of these gods so beloved by children is an ancient and innocent custom. The little ones always enjoy this day.

The Bow

The headmaster of our school chose to make a speech he gave in the auditorium of the Komoro Elementary School the occasion for an attack on the fecklessness of physicians. I did not hear the speech myself but I learned later from the science teacher about the unpleasant problems it caused. Now the headmaster is one who already had a long career behind him when he came up here to teach the youth of this remote district. He has been an influential person here in many ways. Even the development of the peach orchards around Moriyama is credited to him. He is an active and virile person who always has to be doing something and, being as he is, it is not all that surprising that he got carried away on the lectern and gave offense to the physicians. This worried the timid science teacher and he came over to consult with me.

One evening a messenger from the restaurant Okagen comes with a letter from the chief of police. I open it to find that it is a summons. I have heard hints that the chief of police has undertaken to mediate the dispute. It turns out that all the members of the Komoro Medical Association are assembled there on the second floor of the Okagen. I have been called out to offer them an apology in place of the headmaster. Since I really know nothing about the headmaster's speech it is difficult for me to know whether or not there is anything in it that calls for an apology. I decide that if any apologizing has to be done the headmaster should come and do it and that I should do nothing at any rate until I hear what he has to say about it. As soon as the chief of police realizes that I am going to take that position, he leaps to his feet and, for the sake of peace in the town, turns toward the assembled group and makes a deep bow. There is an immediate change of mood among the physicians. Since I still don't know what it is all about I am no more inclined to yield the point than before, but after the chief of police's display of good faith there is nothing for me to do but bow also. I make my bow and leave the second floor of the restaurant, reflecting on what distasteful duties may fall to the lot of a country school teacher.

The next day I call on the headmaster at Nakadana. I laugh as I tell him how I was made to bow in his place. The headmaster responds angrily that there was nothing that called for a bow. It turns out to be a losing proposition all the way around.[58]

Forerunners of Spring

From late February into early March, each passing rain brings an increase in warmth. The cherry and plum buds gradually swell, the snow on the north slopes melts at last, and the gray soil begins to turn yellow. After a pleasant spring rain the wet boughs of the plum take on a new reddish tint. The green moss on the thatched roofs, so long buried under the snow, quickly returns to life. A replenishing breeze blows and the color of the blue sky gradually intensifies. The yellow-tinted white clouds, looking like flocks of sheep, are carried along on a gentle breeze like forerunners of spring.

I have often noted those clouds in the southwest sky that are filled with spring light. They seem to appear suddenly, gradually grow larger, longer, brighter, and then, as they move to the south, fade away. Then another cloud appears in the same place to develop in the same way. It is particularly beautiful when a distant white cloud slightly shaded with gray floats in the soft milky sky.[59]

Stars

On an evening when the moon is due to rise at about midnight I gaze at the southern skies where a bluish star is shining. There is a reddish star in the eastern sky. Those are the only two stars in the sky. The stars up here in the mountains are one of the sights I want to show you.

The First Flowers

"Heat and cold last until the equinox," the local saying has it, and we breathe a sigh of relief when the equinox comes. We have at last made it through another long, long winter—more than five months of it. Until the equinox there was nothing that did not serve to remind us of the season we have just passed through: the oak trees, still retaining their dead leaves; the hard fat buds of the rhododendrons that have held out under the snow.

The cherry trees outside the faculty room at school have taken on a reddish luster on trunk and branch. Once back home, I never tire of looking out at the garden and the shadows cast on the embankment by the apple and persimmon trees. The flying insects that have emerged from pupation in the warmth are swarming at the eaves now. I've already told you about the plants, but the weasel-grass that grows out of the stone walls in March, the vetch, the artemisia, the snake-grass, the jinseng, the bride-grass, the lesser plectrum weed, and countless other varieties are now lifting their heads. Again, on the twenty-sixth of March I find plectrum weed[60] and another plant with tiny purple-spotted flowers whose name I do not know. These are the first flowers I've found in the mountains this spring.

Spring in the Mountains

Now the preserved vegetables are all gone, there are only a few onions and potatoes left, and it is still some time before we can get fresh vegetables. There is nothing for it but to make do with dried seaweed in our miso soup, morning after morning. As I gaze at the blue smoke that creeps along the wall under the eaves on mornings after a spring shower, I'm struck by what fine weather we're having but the poverty and monotony of our diet are still a discouragement. I shudder each time I'm confronted by yet another serving of the oily-smelling, frozen, dried tōfu that hangs on the kitchen wall. It is a pleasure to hear the voices of the women sellers of *kusa mochi*—rice cakes with the earliest spring greens mixed into them—crying out their wares while walking along streets muddy from a short-lived snowfall.

There is nothing that leaves a stronger impression of the difference in climate between this place and the city where you live than to make a visit there in late March or early April and then come back up here. When the cherries are in bloom in Tokyo I will see plums in bloom in Jōshū,[61] but once we cross over the Usui Pass and arrive in Karuizawa, it still looks like winter. When I look out from the train window on the familiar scenery of Musashino with eyes accustomed to the late spring in these mountains, I cannot help commenting to myself on how soft and gentle the rains are. Of course Komoro is not as cold as Karuizawa, and as the train draws closer to Komoro the fields that once looked so dead are replaced by those in which the barley is beginning to sprout vigorously. The old yellow leaves of the barley mixed with the bright green new growth are a fine sight from a little distance.

From around the fifteenth of April we will begin to enjoy a world overflowing with flowers. The plums, which seem to be holding out until then, will open all at once. The cherries come immediately after the plums, and after the cherries come the damsons, the apricots, and the oleasters, their white flowers blooming in profusion all around us. Opening the kitchen window or stepping out into the garden—there's no place that isn't overflowing with the scent of blossoms. Even when I go with the students over to the castle grounds at the Kaikoen, the short but intense spring brings intoxication to our hearts . . .

Notes

1. Yoshimura Shigeru was the son of Yoshimura Tadamichi, in whose Tokyo home Tōson had grown up. The second character of Tōson's given name, Haruki, was chosen by them to write Shigeru's name.

2. The *Tōsonshu,* or "Tōson Collection," of 1909.

3. Since most weights and measures in the highly regular Japanese system are incommensurable with the highly irregular English system, it is less confusing to leave the Japanese units untranslated:

Capacity

1 *shaku* = .0318 pints
10 *shaku* = 1 *gō* = .318 pints
10 *gō* = 1 *shō* = 3.18 pints
10 *shō* = 1 *to* = 3.97 gallons
4 *to* = 1 *hyō* = 1.99 bushels
10 *to* = 1 *koku* = 4.96 bushels

Area

1 square *ken* = 1 *tsubo* or 1 *bu* = 3.95 square yards
30 *bu* = 1 *se* = 119 square yards
10 *se* = 1 *tan* = .0245 acres
10 *tan* = 1 *chō* = 2.45 acres

Weight

1 *mō* = 0.058 Troy grains
10 *mō* = 1 *rin* = .58 Troy grains
10 *rin* = 1 *fun* = 5.8 Troy grains
10 *fun* = 1 *momme* or *me* = 58 Troy grs
160 *momme* = 1 *kin* = 1.3 lb Av.
1000 *momme* = 1 *kan* = 8.27 lb.

Linear Measure

1 *rin* = 0.012 inches
10 *rin* = 1 *bu* = 0.12 inches
10 *bu* = 1 *sun* = 1.2 inches
10 *sun* = 1 *shaku* = 0.994 feet
6 *shaku* = 1 *ken* = 1.90 yards
6 *shaku* = 1 *hiro* = 0.994 fathoms
10 *shaku* = 1 *jō* = 3.31 yards
60 *ken* = 1 *chō* = 114 yards
36 *chō* = 1 *ri* = 2.44 miles

4. Since the late nineteenth century, the central range of mountains in Nagano prefecture, lying to the west and west-northwest of Komoro, has been known as the "Japan Alps" (Nihon Arupusu).

5. The medicine in question is *dokkeshi,* a standard remedy (of various formulations but usually including creosote and bear gall) for gastrointestinal upsets that was the mainstay of any home medicine chest. The Takase family of Fukushima, into which Sono, Tōson's eldest sister, married, had made such a medicine for generations and after the Meiji Restoration it became their primary source of income.

6. Aoto Fujina, entrusted by Hōjō Tokiyori with ten *bu* of offering money, accidentally dropped it into the Nameri River in Kamakura and then spent fifty *bu* to recover it.

7. Bessho, literally "separate site," was originally a settlement of self-ordained priests *(hijiri)* of the Ji sect who traced their lineage from a visit to this region by the founder, Ippen Shōnin (1239–1285). *Hijiri* of all allegiances, being outside the officially recognized ecclesiastical structure, would live apart from official temples and established villages in these "separate sites" in various parts of the country, leaving the name to modern hot springs and villages where the priests have often been forgotten.

8. *Geta* are footware consisting of a flat piece of wood with two parallel cleats

an inch or so high across the bottom which are held on by cloth straps running between the toes. Satisfactory in a surprisingly wide range of footings, they are almost impossible in wet, sticky snow.

9. Hayashi Isamu, one of the students who heard this lecture, reports that he and the other students were too young to understand what it was about. He describes the *Shakafu* as a volume with large pages, bound in traditional style, and apparently quite old. See Hayashi Isamu, *Shimazaki Tōson,* p. 82. A note in *Shimazaki Tōson Zenshū,* vol. 1 (Tokyo: Chikuma Shobō, 1981), p. 353, suggests that Tōson was probably using a popular abridgment of a life of Buddha originally written during the Liao dynasty.

10. English word used in the original text.

11. A foreshadowing of *When the Cherries Ripen (Sakura no Mi no Juku-suru Toki),* Tōson's autobiographical novel of his school days at Meiji Gakuin, which first appeared as a magazine serial in 1913–1915, then was expanded and thoroughly rewritten before its publication as a book in 1919.

12. For a study of these arresting roadside devotional objects, see Michael Czaja, *Gods of Myth and Stone* (New York and Tokyo: Weatherhill, 1974).

13. *Kishimeji* and *ushibitai,* the first of which, a close relative of the pine mushroom *(matsutake),* is highly regarded.

14. Hand towels, consisting of a piece of light cotton fabric measuring about twelve by eighteen inches, played a wide range of roles in traditional Japanese life. Many people carried them dangling from the hip, one corner tucked into the sash. Not only were they used both as washcloth and towel in the bath but they also came in handy for a variety of additional uses: worn over the head as a kerchief, folded into a narrow width and tied around the forehead as a *hachimaki* or sweatband, etc. Still frequently given as favors by businesses, places of entertainment, and the like, they are usually printed in indigo with trademarks or with sophisticated and elegant designs. For another use, see Sketchbook X, "Tokens of Love."

15. The *irori,* or open hearth of the traditional Japanese house, consists of a square opening in the floor which is enclosed by a flush timber framing and filled with sand to within an inch or so of floor level. There is no chimney; the smoke from the wood fire irritates the eyes and nose before it eventually finds its way upward, through a grill in the ceiling if the room has one, into the attic and then out through a sheltered opening in the roof. An adjustable wooden potholder, often of interesting design, which has either a cook pot or a perpetually boiling teakettle suspended from it whenever there is a fire in the hearth, is fitted into the lower end of a heavy bamboo pole suspended from the ceiling or the roof beams.

16. *Kunugi,* a variety of beech that grows in the high mountains.

17. Literally "beam crossers," because they were tossed over the beams in the high-ceilinged hearthroom in the course of preparation.

18. Musashino is that part of the extensive plain to the north of Tokyo Bay that borders the city. One suburb still carries the name of what was once a region renowned for its natural beauty but is now almost entirely built over.

19. The *kotatsu* consists of a square depression in the floor some eighteen

inches deep and usually of a size that can be covered in summer with a removable half mat of tatami. On the bottom is a wooden grill beneath which is placed a small charcoal brazier. A quilt-covered framework is set over the top of the *kotatsu* to make a winter retreat from the chill and drafts of the traditional Japanese house. Too long a time sitting in the *kotatsu,* however, is likely to result in a headache or worse from the charcoal fumes. A second variety consists of a somewhat taller framework that can support a table top and quilt over a brazier set on top of the tatami. A modern version that looks like a short-legged, folding card table has an electric heating element under the top.

20. Throughout East Asia, the now-vanished, rhythmic sound of a woman beating cloth on the fulling block carries deep resonances of a homely, rustic peace and tranquility.

21. English word used in the original text.

22. Most of these are local plants that are no more likely to create a picture in the mind of a boy from Tokyo than in that of the typical reader in New York or London; they are listed for the express purpose of demonstrating how different the vegetation is around Komoro. Those plant names that have been translated are more common throughout the country.

23. Tōson's many conversations with the painter Miyake Katsumi, both in Komoro and in his home in nearby Chiisagata, about European art in general and Millet and Corot in particular and the deep interest that photoreproductions of the works of these two painters aroused in him are reflected in all his descriptions of country life.

24. All sources, including Tōson himself in other contexts, agree, and a brief walk through Komoro will confirm, that this is in fact the *ōte mon,* or main gate. The outer walls had been taken down but the old main gate, from which Ōtemachi—the "town before the main gate"—takes its name, still stands, some distance away on the opposite side of the railroad tracks. The Third Gate, which serves as an entrance to the Kaikoen, was part of an inner range of fortifications. See Komoro-shi Kyōiku I'inkai, *Bungaku Tanpō Komoro Tōson Kinenkan* [Literary Explorations: The Komoro Tōson Memorial Hall], 2nd printing (Tokyo: Sōkyūshorin, 1984), p. 17.

25. The Ebisu rites, which seem to date from the early eighteenth century, were carried out at different times in different parts of the country. In merchant families the rites consisted of a miming of buying and selling before the statue of Ebisu, one of the seven gods of good fortune. Mandarin oranges and small coins were sometimes distributed in the streets before mercantile establishments while dry goods stores held clearance sales.

26. See note 3 above.

27. See note 8 above.

28. English word used in the original text.

29. See note 4 above.

30. The rail line from Tokyo over the Usui Pass and past Komoro and Nagano to the Japan Sea coast was completed only in 1893.

31. Wada Pass was the scene of the fierce 1864 battle described in *Before the Dawn,* bk. 1, chaps. 9–10.

32. The internal customs barriers were a fixture of travel in Japan from the eighth century until the Meiji Restoration of 1868. The Usui Pass was the location of one of the most important of these barriers.

33. English phrase used in the original text.

34. English word used in the original text.

35. The great temple in Nagano that for centuries has been one of the major goals for pilgrims in this part of Japan.

36. English word used in the original text.

37. These postcards, chronicling the son-in-law's growing weakness and his death in a hospital in Ceylon, were the source for the story "In the Shade of Palm Trees" *(Yashi no hakage)*, published in 1902. *Zenshū* 2:455–467.

38. There was a persecution of Buddhism during the early years of Meiji under the aegis of zealots from the National Learning movement. Many temples and their furnishings were destroyed, priests and nuns were often forced to return to lay life, and many surviving temples fell derelict, having lost most or all of their parishioners. Tōson is describing a town in which Buddhism is faring better than in other parts of Japan but not at all well by any absolute standard. Conditions in Komoro seem to have been closer to the national norm.

39. Hakuin Ekaku (1685–1768), who was responsible for the revival of Rinzai Zen, spent a crucial seven months in 1708 with Dōkyō Etan (1642–1721) at the latter's Shōjuan, a hermitage in the village of Taruzawa near Iiyama. Their meeting and association are described in Heinrich Dumoulin, *Zen Buddhism: A History, Japan* (New York: Macmillan, 1990), pp. 371–373.

40. Literally "[one who was] born before [me]," *sensei* is a title of respect with many subtleties of usage.

41. In the cities journalists were at this time generally held in low esteem.

42. See note 32 above.

43. Fukuzawa Yukichi (1835–1901), one of the most active figures of the "Japanese Enlightenment," published key popular works on subjects such as world history, medicine, ballistics, and mass education. His fascinating autobiography is a major source on the period. See Fukuzawa Yukichi, *The Autobiography of Fukuzawa Yukichi,* trans. Eiichi Kiyooka, 3rd and revised edition (Tokyo: Hokuseidō, 1947).

44. The *kamidana* or "god shelf" is a small Shintō shrine usually mounted on a high shelf in a main room. It was customary to place offerings before this shrine and small gifts from visitors were particularly welcome. The bell is rung to attract the attention of the gods.

45. See note 3 above. The *tsuka* is a measure of tax or rental rice equivalent to 10 *kin* or 13 pounds avoirdupois.

46. Like most members of the older generation at the turn of the century, the old man speaks in terms of the old calendar, in which the new year starts from four to six weeks later than under the Gregorian calendar. The expression used here is *kui-jimai*, "the end of the eating." See note 55 below.

47. The *sanzesō* is a system of divining that draws on a mixture of the three Buddhist "worlds" of past, present, and future, on the yin-yang school, and on the mutual production and precedence of the five elements of fire, earth, water,

metal, and wood to predict good or bad fortune depending on the birth dates of the person whose fortune is being told.

48. In this system nine parts of the body are defined according to the stars, after which nine is subtracted from the patient's age and the remainder is used to determine the location of the disease.

49. Since the *ryō* was replaced by the *yen* in 1871 it is most likely that the old man is following the common country practice of calling the new currency by the old name.

50. *Konnyaku* is a tough, almost chewy gelatin made from the tuber of a plant related to taro. Commonly served as a heavy noodle, it has little nutritional value and almost no flavor of its own but takes on the flavor of food cooked with it.

51. The *kanamugura,* a small vinelike annual related to the mulberry.

52. The association that gives the plant its English name carries over even though it is not literally present in the Japanese name.

53. The Japanese plum blooms in February in the lowlands and it is not unusual to see a tree in full bloom standing in snow.

54. It was customary to repaper the shōji in preparation for the new year. This was a common cause of colds and worse since the old paper was removed by soaking the shōji in cold water, either by standing them up against the side of the house and dousing them with buckets or by laying them in a stream.

55. There are frequent references in folk literature to the *kui-dome* or *kui-jimai,* the "end of the eating"—that harsh time when the foodstuffs put by for the winter begin to give out and it is still too early for harvesting the crops from the new season. See "Spring in the Mountains," pp. 113–114.

56. "Daruma" are dolls representing Bodhidharma, the putative founder of Zen Buddhism. They usually consist of a larger sphere for the body with a smaller sphere for the head filleted onto the top (the classic snowman is called "yuki-Daruma" or "snow-Daruma" in Japan). The bottoms are weighted so that the dolls will always return to an upright position. They are painted in strong reds and blacks and the faces have fiercely staring eyes, the pupils of which are often left blank, to be filled in when a wish is fulfilled. Even today one frequently sees politicians celebrating an election victory by painting in the eyes of a Daruma before the television cameras.

57. The Tori no Ichi, or Tori no Machi, is held on those days falling under the zodiacal sign of the Rooster during the month of November, two in some years and three in others. See the description in Paul Waley, *Tokyo Now and Then* (New York and Tokyo: Weatherhill, 1984), pp. 209–210.

58. Once the chief of police bowed, Tōson's refusal to bow with him would have been received, not as a reflection of his perfectly reasonable position on the matter of the speech, but as a humiliating and gratuitous personal affront to the chief of police on the part of the school that he was, willy-nilly, representing. That could have incurred the enmity of the chief of police and those associated with him, creating a new and even more ugly feud in the town.

59. A self-conscious echo of the famous opening lines of Sei Shōnagon's *Pillow Book.*

60. *Nazuna,* which is also known as *penpengusa* because the leaves of the plant are shaped like tiny samisen plectra. *Penpen,* an echoic for the percussive sound of the samisen, is a baby-talk name for the instrument. In English the plant is called "shepherd's purse."

61. See note 53 above.

Afterword to the
Chikuma River Sketchbooks

I held these sketches back from publication for a long time. They are only some of the many I made while in the mountains of Shinano but none of the others were fit to be shown to anyone. I selected only those that seemed likely to be suitable for young people, touched up the writing a bit, and published them in monthly installments in the magazine *Chūgaku Sekai*. That was during the years in late Meiji and early Taishō when it was coming out from Hakubunkan under the editorship of Nishimura Shozan and it was then that I made up the title *Chikuma River Sketchbooks*. They were subsequently published by Sakura Shobō in 1913 and that was their first appearance in book form.

> In truth, from the time on that first morning in Komoro when I gazed out upon the mountains like a famished traveler—those distant, snow-capped peaks—Mt. Asama, and the range shaped like fangs, the deep-shadowed valleys, the ruins of the old castle, the clouds clustered like wisps of smoke over the mountain peaks—from the time I first caught sight of them bathed in morning light, I felt that I was no longer the same person as before. It was as though something some-how different had begun in me.

I wrote that later but that was exactly the kind of desperate hunger I felt then. After I published my fourth volume of poetry I was beset by a determination to see things more correctly, a determination so intense that I dropped into silence for some three years. Then I found myself writing these sketches. Entering them into my note-book became a daily exercise. It was just then that the watercolor artist Miyake Katsumi built his new house in Fukuromachi. He lived there for about a year, coming over in his spare time to teach in the Komoro Gijuku. His art developed greatly while he was in Komoro and I particularly remember his painting called "Morn-ing," shown at the exhibition of the Hakubakai, as well as the one of the pine groves around the Kaikoen. At his suggestion I even acquired an easel which I would occasionally take out into the countryside in an effort to enrich my mind through what nature had to teach me. These sketches, then, were born from the plateau at the foot of Mt. Asama; from the lava, the sand, and the fierce winds.

I want to write here about those days now gone by. My work as a member of the group producing the magazine *Bungakkai*[1] was already completed when I returned to Tokyo from Sendai, but those five years of work have now received unexpected recognition and I even hear voices calling me a "young romantic." When I look back over those times I wonder about the aptness of that title. At any rate I had just set out on my career and I was inexperienced. It makes me break out in a cold sweat just to think of how I was in those days.

Our greatest weakness was in our lack of historical spirit. If we had not been lacking in such a spirit we might have investigated the classics of our own country, we might have studied the European Renaissance, we might have found ourselves able to advance still further. As Hirata Tokuboku[2] has put it, Ueda Bin[3] is the only scholar that *Bungakkai* produced. He had a genuinely literary outlook and it is regrettable that he failed to leave to this country the study of Greek literature that only he could have produced. Ueda would have been uniquely qualified for such a work because the way to the European Renaissance lies through Greek literature. He did not, however, go far in that direction, being distracted by his undertaking to introduce and translate modern symbolist poetry.

While I was writing these sketches I received a complimentary subscription to the *haikai* magazine *Hanmen* from Okano Chijū[4] in Tokyo. There was an article by Saitō Ryokū[5] in the first issue and he mentioned me in that article: "He has taken up residence in Kita Saku county but he's just a bit too pale to become a true mountain monkey."

That is how Ryokū was. It is impossible to say whether this kind of thing constitutes cleverness or excess but no one could beat him at it. Yet for me, isolated as I was from my Tokyo acquaintances, this must have been the last thing I ever heard from Ryokū. I learned virtually nothing about literature from him but I have been enlightened to no small degree by his knowledge of the ways of the world. It was he who gave me news about Ōgai,[6] Shiken,[7] Rohan,[8] Kōyō,[9] and other writers. After his death, Baba Kochō[10] wrote about his association with him, and, recalling him now that he is dead, I have to agree that there was something about him that set him apart from the ordinary run of men.

I will never forget hearing of Kōyō's death while I was in Komoro. I was only able to come up to Tokyo and see my friends once a year, and I seldom heard any news of my elders in the field, but I could be certain that Ōgai, being the kind of person who simply does not know about rest, would be in his study, quietly observing the comings and goings in the world of literature. He would be paying close attention to the new works of Ryūrō,[11] Tengai,[12] Fūyō,[13] and the others and watching over the development of the writers who came after him. It was surely between 1897 and 1907, the thirties of the Meiji era, when Meiji literature underwent a major change of direction and that was when preparations were being made for the next age.

It is pointless to destroy old things. If it is possible to create something really new, then the old things have already been destroyed. That has been my belief ever since Sendai. Moreover, preparation for the coming age meant nothing to me but self-renewal. Yet a broader world had gradually opened before me. It was not easy for me to obtain good books while I was an impoverished country schoolteacher, but I was nevertheless able to realize some long-held desires and I was learning something new from my books almost every day. I was moved by the flourishing spirit of inquiry into the natural world in Darwin's *On the Origin of Species* and *The Expressions of the Emotions in Man and Animals* as well as by the psychologist Sully's studies of children.[14] It was then that my bookshelves took on a different aspect, being no longer filled exclusively with books of modern poetry. English translations of continental European fiction and drama now appeared there one after another. Tolstoy's *Cossacks*[15] and *Anna Karenina*, Dostoevsky's *Crime and Punishment,* and *Memoirs from the Dead House,* Flaubert's *Madame Bovary* and Ibsen's *John Gabriel Borkmann* became my favorites. *Cossacks* was not, in fact, the first work by Tolstoy that I had encountered. The year after I graduated from Meiji Gakuin I found an English translation of a small pamphlet called "Labor," and that memory alone makes him seem like an old acquaintance; what was more, I admired the accuracy of his depictions. Whenever I set out for the highlands along the upper reaches of the Chikuma River, I would be thinking about Tolstoy's characters, my thoughts running even to that as-yet-unseen land of the Caucasus. I was getting my foreign books from Kelly in Yokohama at the time, and of the novels by Balzac that they sent me, it was the English translation of *Tsuchi*[16] that stayed in my mind the longest. I was amazed to find that this growing familiarity with recent literature taught me to reread those things that had been present in my own country since ancient times. I discovered how much there was to be learned from the high-spirited personal attacks in *The Pillow Book*.

To look back upon the time between 1887 and 1897, the twenties of the Meiji era, is to look back upon my own youth, but it was early in the twenties when Ōgai came onto the literary stage with his "Dancer,"[17] and I believe it was in 1891 that his story "The Courier" appeared in *A Hundred Varieties of New Writing*.[18] Looking back on it now, we find that the events and the atmosphere of those times have not been all that clearly transmitted and most people recall them only vaguely. Yet it may still be said that it was during the twenties that the true Meiji literature began. The mere fact that the greater part of what we perceive today as Meiji literature was the work of people who were active in that decade is sufficient to demonstrate that the twenties constituted an age of youth, when writers could move forward. There seem to have been a number of reasons for this. One was that most people were preoccupied with the idea of a "New Japan" and the demand from society for a new literature was also strong. It was because it was able to satisfy that demand that Hasegawa Futabatei's *Drifting Clouds*[19] aroused such a sensation of novelty in our breasts; novels dealing with contemporary problems were then rare. On the other hand, our introduction, through Ōgai's fine translations, to such works as Lessing's *The Prisoners* and Andersen's *Improvisations* not only raised the standards of our literary culture but exerted a great influence on many writers. *Sea Foam*[20] seemed perhaps a bit too old in spirit to be considered a volume about youth, but the early spring of the twenties is to be found on every page of that book. If only the literature of the twenties had been able to continue on in that way it would surely have achieved something remarkable, but there is no shortage of reasons why it lost its early purity and freshness.

There can, at the very least, be no quarrel with the proposition that the foundation for the ongoing unification of the spoken and written languages was not yet adequate. Even a writer of the stature of Ozaki Kōyō kept drifting back and forth between a mixture of literary and colloquial on the one hand and a unified style on the other. In those days there was still a heavy remnant of the rhetorical conventions handed down from antiquity and the resulting diction inhibited the clear and natural exposition of feelings and the rendering of fine shadings of meaning. All progress came to a halt. Then the demand for change and for freedom gradually arose as even the established writers seemed to find the prevailing modes of expression to be inadequate. I know that intelligent writers like Saitō Ryoku suffered constantly. Is it not because he worked too hard for rhetorical effect that he was unable to exploit fully the great gift that he showed in such works as "The Hell of Oil" and "Hide and Seek"?[21]

Later Ōgai wrote one of his rare original works for that period, publishing the essay "Cloth of Many Colors"[22] in the magazine *Shinshōsetsu*. When I read it I realized that even this man had changed his course. As the very informality of the title itself suggested, Ōgai was no longer determined to force his way through with the elevated style of "The Courier" or "Sea Foam." By that time the short careers of Kitamura Tōkoku and Higuchi Ichiyō were already over and a new peak of literary creativity had appeared. Kōda Rohan had written a "New Hagoromo," shortly before Hirotsu Ryūrō wrote his work of the same title, and Kōyō had already written *The Gold Demon*. Looking back from the perspective of Ōgai's "Cloth of Many Colors," the beginning of the Meiji twenties seems like another world; for the writers of Meiji a decade was not a short time.

Surely the years from the end of the twenties to the beginning of the thirties (early to mid-1890s) were the most productive period for Meiji writers. This was when Ryoku was still close to Ōgai and Rohan, and I believe it was around then that established writers began to issue symposia on new writers.

As I look back at their labor of introducing European literature, I am struck by how very good most of the pioneers of Meiji literature were at what they did. The special qualities of their own country had something to do with it. They could draw not only on the heritage left them by the writers of the Tokugawa period but also on a long nurturing by Chinese literature. At any rate, it was Mori Ōgai's great asset that he came back to Japan with direct knowledge of nineteenth-century German literature while most of the other writers of the time were taking eighteenth-century English literature as their standard. When one recalls that even this man hesitated at first to experiment along the lines suggested by the movement to unify the written and spoken languages that was just beginning to take root in this country, one realizes just how far ahead of their time Yamada Bimyō[23] and Hasegawa Futabatei really were.

I am unable to think of the new literature of Meiji apart from the unification of the written and spoken languages because no matter how many and varied the ways taken by those who came before us, that was the most direct route. It was not without effort that our writing was liberated from the old rhetorical conventions and stock phrases to achieve its present unification of the written and spoken languages. We must not forget that it began in literary experiments and that many years passed before its adoption throughout society for everything from newspaper editorials and scientific writing to private correspondence and children's composition lessons.

What a brilliant light the *haikai* poets and *jōruri* playwrights of the Tokugawa period cast on the world of language with their espousal of plain, ordinary speech at all levels of their work! Next came the National Scholars who, with their studies of the *Manyōshū* and the *Kojiki,* brought to light the ancient world of language that had hitherto been obscured. I believe it was these two great accomplishments, together with the efforts of those who labored so hard for the unification of the spoken and written languages in Meiji, that created the foundation upon which our literature stands. Nor was it any passing fantasy that led me to pursue the study of the unification of the written and spoken languages at the same time that I was writing these sketches.

In the end, I spent seven years in the mountains.[24] I will never forget receiving Osanai Kaoru,[25] Arishima Ikuma,[26] Aoki Shigeru,[27] Tayama Katai, and Yanagita Kunio in the house in Baba'ura during those years. I frequently set out in the company of the bachelor of science Samejima Shin and the watercolor artist Maruyama Banka to cover the whole length of the Chikuma River with the students. These sketches are, in any number of senses, a memento of my life in Komoro.

Notes

Tōson Zenshū 5:587–592.

1. One of the most influential literary magazines of mid-Meiji, the first series of *Bungakkai* [Literary World] was published between 1893 and 1898 under the editorship of Hoshino Tenchi.

2. Hirata Tokuboku (1873–1943), born in Tokyo, was baptized at the Nihon-bashi Church in 1887 where he became acquainted with Hoshino Tenchi, who brought him into the *Bungakkai* circle. After graduating from the Department of English of the Tokyo Normal School in 1898, Hirata spent 1903–1906 as a student at Oxford University. His early writings in *Bungakkai* were strongly influenced by Christianity but his attention soon shifted to the Renaissance. In his later years Tokuboku turned to informal essays *(zuihitsu)* and translations, most notable among which are *Vanity Fair* (1914–1915) and *David Copperfield* (1925–1928).

3. Ueda Bin (1874–1916), literary scholar, critic, translator, poet, and novelist, was born in Tsukiji, Tokyo, where his forebears had been associated with the Shōheikō, the Confucian academy that in Tokugawa times fulfilled many of the functions of a national university. Hirata Tokuboku brought him into the *Bungakkai* group around 1892. In his short life Ueda left a heritage of seminal translations and essays, notably *Kaichōon* [Sound of the Tide] (1905), the most important volume of translations from European poetry to appear up to that time. It contains works from Italian, English, German, Provençal, and French, including the first introduction to Japanese readers of poets such as Baudelaire, Verlaine, and Mallarmé.

4. Okano Chijū (1860–1932), *haikai* poet who founded the *haikai* journal *Hanmen* in 1901. He advocated novelty and freshness in *haikai* while at the same time pursuing historical studies in the field.

5. Saitō Ryokū (1867–1904), a novelist and critic who enjoyed a highly ambiguous reputation among his contemporaries.

6. Mori Ōgai (1862–1922), whom Tōson always calls Ōgai Gyoshi, was, along with Natsume Sōseki and Tōson, one of the three dominant figures of late Meiji letters. See Translator's Introduction, note 7.

7. Morita Shiken (1860–1897), an important early journalist who originally trained in Chinese studies but became a pioneer translator of European writers such as Verne, Hugo, Dickens, Hawthorne, and Irving.

8. Kōda Rohan (1867–1947), novelist, essayist, thinker, and independent spirit, drew heavily on his erudition in Chinese literature for a highly creative traditional stance completely free from the Europeanizing that was so much in vogue throughout his life.

9. Ozaki Kōyō (1867–1903), the leading figure in the highly influential Ken'yūsha group, and one of the first to profit from the rediscovery of Saikaku in the late 1880s, was a representative practitioner of the elaborate and highly literary style of fiction which Tōson's *Broken Commandment* played a major role in rendering obsolete.

10. Baba Kochō (1869–1940), the younger brother of the popular rights leader

Baba Tatsui, was born in Kōchi prefecture. In 1891 he graduated from Meiji Gakuin, where he had become friends with Tōson and Togawa Shūkotsu. Between 1906 and 1930 Kochō taught European literature at Keiō University, publishing translations of Daudet, Gorky, Hawthorne, and Tolstoy and editing anthologies of poetry. He was active in a broad range of other activities, serving as literary advisor to the influential literary magazine *Myōjō* [Morning Star], and as editor of *Geien* [Literary Meadow]. Kochō left behind extensive collections of essays and an important memoir, *Meiji Bundan no Hitobito* [People of the Meiji Literary Establishment].

11. Hirotsu Ryūrō (1861–1928), a member of the Ken'yūsha, specialized in stories of tragic implication.

12. Kosugi Tengai (1865–1952) began as a writer of light fiction, but upon discovering Zola he became an early pioneer of the Japanese version of naturalism.

13. Oguri Fūyō (1875–1926), a member of the Ken'yūsha remembered as another of the early naturalist writers.

14. James Sully (1842–1923), a British psychologist prominent in the development of child psychology.

15. Katai himself was painfully aware that his 1893 Japanese translation from an English version was inadequate, but this seems to be what Tōson first read. See Tayama Katai, *Literary Life in Tokyo,* trans. Kenneth G. Henshall (Leiden: E. J. Brill, 1987), pp. 79–81.

16. *Land.* Most likely a reference to "Qui terre à guerre à," the first section of *Les Paysans.*

17. "Maihime" (1890) is called "The Girl Who Danced" in Rimer, *Mori Ōgai.* It has been translated under that title by Leon Zolbrod in *The Language of Love* (New York: Bantam Books, 1964) and by Richard Bowring under the title "Maihime (The Dancing Girl)" in *Monumenta Nipponica* 30, no. 2 (1975): 151–166.

18. "Fumitsukai," which appeared in *Shinchohyakushu,* a serial anthology of original works and translations, one work by each author, primarily by members of the Ken'yūsha group, in eighteen volumes published by Yoshioka Shoten which appeared between April 1899 and August 1901. See Karen Brazell's translation, "The Courier," in *Monumenta Nipponica* 26, no. 2 (1971): 101–114.

19. See Translator's Introduction, note 21.

20. *Minawashū,* an anthology of Mori Ōgai's translations of stories, plays, and poetry along with some of his most important early original stories, including "The Girl Who Danced" and "The Courier," was published in 1894. The first comprehensive representation of Ōgai's program for the modernization of Japanese literature, it was immensely influential in the years immediately following its appearance, going through a number of editions and revisions.

21. "Abura Jigoku" and "Kakurenbō" (both 1891).

22. See Translator's Introduction, note 23.

23. Yamada Bimyō (1868–1910) was the first of the Ken'yūsha group to gain wide recognition, although he was later expelled. At first basing his style on Bakin, he later wrote groundbreaking works in the colloquial style that were greatly admired in their time but are almost forgotten now.

24. Tōson spent six years almost to the day in Komoro, but since he arrived at the end of March, 1899, and left at the beginning of April, 1905, the time span touched on seven calendar years. *Ashikake shichinen* (straddling seven years) would be the Japanese expression and this way of counting would seem natural to his Japanese readers.

25. Osanai Kaoru (1881–1928), actor, playwright, and novelist, was one of the key figures in the creation of a modern Japanese theater.

26. Arishima Ikuma (1882–1975), a highly respected painter and an important advocate in Japan of Cézanne. A brother of the writers Arishima Takeo and Satomi Ton, he became perhaps Tōson's most intimate friend. He accompanied Tōson on his trip to Buenos Aires in 1936 as Japanese representative to the International P.E.N. Club conference and on his subsequent travels in South and North America and in Europe.

27. Aoki Shigeru (1882–1911), an artist in the Western style, was born in Kurume in Kyushu. He was inspired by Tōson's *Fresh Greens* to go to Tokyo, where he graduated from the Tokyo School of Arts in 1884. Best known for his painting "Umi no Sachi" [The Wealth of the Sea], he became one of Tōson's circle of friends during his Komoro days.

At the Foot
of Mt. Asama I

I was on my way back to Tokyo from my sister's house in Kiso-
Fukushima when I recalled that Kimura-sensei was living in
Komoro, which was on the way. Kimura-sensei had been my teacher
at the Kyōritsu school in Kanda, Tokyo. Later, while I was attending Meiji Gakuin, he lived nearby in Takanawa. I used to visit him
regularly then, but I hadn't seen him since he had gone off to
Shinshū. Now I felt I wanted to see him again and so I called at his
house in the Mimitori section of Komoro. That was the first time I
ever set foot in Komoro.[1]

Life is extraordinary. If I had not called on Kimura-sensei just
then, I might never have known that Komoro Gijuku existed and he
might never have invited me to join him there as a teacher. I told
him I would think it over carefully and went on back to Tokyo. Nevertheless I was quite impressed that a person like Sensei should have
withdrawn to such a place as Komoro to found a school where he
could devote himself to working with provincial youth.

Even though I kept working after I returned to Tokyo from Sendai
I found myself unable to muster the strength to maintain the tranquility I had known when breathing deeply of the ocean air on Shō-
buta beach, or walking in the pear orchards and vineyards near the
Doi district on the outskirts of Sendai, or going out to see the Abu-
kuma River. Nor was that all. There were few models along the path
I was trying to open for myself, and with nothing but darkness surrounding me, I needed considerable courage if I was ever to ensure
the survival of that to which I was beginning to give birth.

I wanted to renew myself. That was what was on my mind when
the subject of Komoro Gijuku came up in a letter from Kimura-
sensei inviting me to become a country teacher.[2]

A man by the name of Seki came all the way down from Komoro
to bring me words of encouragement from Kimura-sensei and various people of the town. Seki was a graduate of Meiji Gakuin and an

old friend of mine. I had an offer to teach in Kyoto[3] but since I had already made up my mind to retire to the country to improve myself, I chose the Komoro school instead, even though the salary would be low and the work hard. In April of the following year I went to Komoro to begin my life as a country teacher.

The new way—the new way—everything I saw and heard reflected the new way. To begin with, the very school where I was to teach was only then getting settled into its new building. Yet, once I had gone to the second-floor windows to gaze out at the distant Tateshina range or the highlands of Minami Saku, I felt that I was once again in the countryside and would be able to pursue my studies in tranquility. Those windows also offered a near view of the thatched roofs of the old samurai quarter of Komoro, where the branches of the willow trees were touched with green. My arrival in Komoro had coincided with the belated arrival of spring at the foot of Mt. Asama. The school was small, but I was looking forward with pleasure to working with the other teachers.

On the far side of Honmachi in Komoro there is a place called Baba'ura. That is where I rented a house, a thatch-roofed former samurai residence. My time in Komoro consisted of seven years under that thatched roof.

Ever since that morning following my arrival in Komoro when my eyes first caught sight of the distant peaks still covered with snow —Mt. Asama, and the range shaped like fangs, the deep-shadowed valleys, the high-reaching scars caused by landslides, the clouds clustered like wisps of smoke over the mountain peaks—I felt that something altogether new was beginning in me.

Notes

From *Chikaramochi* (1940), chap. 7; *Tōson Zenshū* 16:424–426.

1. Tōson had, in fact, visited Komoro and borrowed money from Kimura in November 1896 on his way back to Sendai after interring his mother's ashes in Magome.

2. In those days the title of "country teacher" *(inaka kyōshi)* had a very special resonance, that of the man of intellectual interests who had lost his way to the Tokyo where everything worthwhile was happening. As such (women were not to achieve full status as teachers for many years) he was doomed to a life of iso-

lation, frustration, and economic deprivation. These associations were later strengthened and focused by reader response to Tayama Katai's novel *Country Teacher* (1909), which has been translated by Kenneth Henshall (Honolulu: University of Hawaii Press, 1984).

3. All other sources, including Tōson's own writings, say the offer was from Nara.

At the Foot
of Mt. Asama II

How quickly the time has passed! It is already the fifth year since I came down from the mountains.

When I collected the practice pieces that I had written while in Shinshū I wrote the following in the preface:

> I stayed in Shinshū until April of 1905. What I was able to teach the young people of the Komoro district was nothing more than the first steps in learning but what I learned from their elders was the meaning of country life. I went out as a teacher; I came back as a student. In Komoro I lived in a place called Baba'ura—that alone brings up all sorts of memories. Let me mention just a few. My house was located between two small streams that flow down from Mt. Asama behind Honmachi, the main district which itself lies along the Hokkoku highway. Across the mulberry fields and vegetable gardens, it faced the pawnshop, the tailor's shop, and the water mill. There, under that thatched roof, listening on winter nights to the frequent loud crackings of the beams and pillars of the house as they froze around me, I wrote most of the things you will read in this book.[1]

I spent eight years[2] in Komoro—a place I will never forget as long as I live. There, on that cold and desolate Saku plateau where men and women work so very hard, I learned about the harshness of what we call nature. Even now, when we are back in Tokyo, I find myself recalling that place at the foot of Mt. Asama in every season. Each year, when the time approaches for the Gion festival in Komoro, the main street in Honmachi seems to appear before my eyes and I can see the blinds hanging before all the eaves. My children used to play in Baba'ura, but now the gentleman next door has died and his wife and family have moved away. Both of the daughters of the owner of the Shiokawa gun shop have married and left. Baba'ura itself must have changed. Does the old man at the Hatoya still go out with Iso and the others to gather hemp bags full of mulberry leaves? Are the hard-working tailor and his apprentices still toiling away? How about the dyer before the old main gate? And the

couple who sold sponge cake and sweet bean paste at the Kansendō?
Is the lady of the Agehaya, the penny lunch room whose signboard I
once drew, still selling her tōfu, and is she still so totally indifferent
to her own appearance?

Strange rumors begin to circulate once you move away. I understand that in Komoro they have been saying that I have lost my
mind. I think the rumor got started when I lost all three of my children, but the wife of the tailor once spoke of it when she came up to
Tokyo, expressing her relief in finding that I was all right. That is
how far I am from Komoro now.

I went down to Inage on the east shore of Tokyo Bay at the end of
last year. When I caught sight of grasses hanging down at random
from an embankment in a clearing in a pine forest, my mind immediately took me back to the Kaikoen in Komoro. In May of this year
I went to call on my nephew in Suwachō, in Asakusa here in Tokyo,
and as I passed by Onmayabashi I saw a shop selling potted flowers
alongside the road. There were poppies among them. Again I
thought of Komoro and a recollection of the way those colorful flowers had bloomed in the back garden of a house near the registry
office rose unbidden to my mind. That was a place I used to pass by
each day on my way to and from the Komoro Gijuku. Dressed in
baggy cotton trousers, I would leave Baba'ura, turn at the bathhouse on the main street in Ōtemachi, and then come out in front of
the Kaikoen, or else I would go down the street in Aioichō, pass
behind Tomioka's house, and follow the stone embankment to the
railroad crossing. There I would usually meet Samejima and the students coming from Akasaka and we would all go on together to the
Komoro Gijuku.

For eight years I experienced the hardship of carrying on an educational enterprise in the provinces. Yet, only a year after I came
down from the mountains, I found myself mourning the Komoro
Gijuku. It is truly lamentable that the determination of the founder
and headmaster, Kimura Kumaji, and of those who worked with
him should have come to this. Ide died while I was still in Komoro.[3]
Now the rest are all scattered, each going his own way. Kimura is in
Nagano, Samejima in Takazaki, Watanabe in America, and Maruyama and I are in Tokyo. Out of all of us who were there in those
days, only Tsuchiya is still in Komoro.

It is reassuring to know that you are still there at the foot of Mt.

Asama, Tsuchiya. People like you, able to continue with your studies whatever the adversities that might overtake you, are surely rare. It is your tranquil heart, even more than your knowledge of botany, that I envy most of all.

Whenever I think of Tsuchiya's complete lack of greed, his humility, and his studiousness, I am reminded of Father Jacquet of Sendai.[4] Father Jacquet is a Frenchman who came to Japan as a Catholic missionary, but I became aware of his qualities during the short time I was his language student. He is the kind of person whom one might meet among the Zen priesthood, dressed in plain black robes and living a tranquil religious life. He has been in Sendai for more than thirty years now. When I went to Sendai I found the Protestants very hostile to him, and I was repeatedly told that, fellow Christian though he might be, he was no ally of ours. Yet now, long after most of those people have gone back into trade, Father Jacquet continues to go his own quiet way. Thinking of Tsuchiya still back there at the foot of Mt. Asama gives me the same sort of pleasure I get from thinking of Father Jacquet in Sendai. Different in age, in race, and in belief, they are like each other in the tranquility of their hearts.

I have received a letter from Watanabe, who went to America after leaving the Komoro Gijuku.[5] He informs me that he is now tending more than two thousand chickens in Berkeley. I have not met Kimura since then, but his handsome beard must surely have become even more silvery by now.

This district in Asakusa where I now live is very much like Baba'ura in Komoro. It is a place where one hears samisen music and songs from the pleasure quarters, but it is still an old Edo-style district. The descendants of Hanabusa Itchō[6] and those of the family of Zeshin[7] live around here. So do the heads and senior teachers of various schools of traditional Edo music. I am managing to continue the same kind of country life that I carried on in Komoro here in this urban setting. It is now the season when people come round selling string beans in the city and we have just been sent some fine miso from a friend in Shinano, so it will be miso soup with green beans at our house today.

Notes

From *Shinkatamachi yori* [From Shinkatamachi] (1912); *Tōson Zenshū* 6:5–8.

1. This passage does not appear in any of the prefaces and afterwords to various editions of the *Chikuma River Sketchbooks* reprinted in *Zenshū* 5:585–592.

2. Elsewhere Tōson calculates the time he spent in Komoro as seven years, although it was closer to six. See "Afterword to the *Chikuma River Sketchbooks*," note 24.

3. Ide Shizuka, the business manager of the school, was a retired soldier and the model for Captain Masaki in "Among the Boulders" and "An Impoverished Bachelor of Science."

4. The Révérend Pére Jacquet went to Sendai around 1882 and served as priest of the Motodera Kōji Catholic Church from 1893 until his death in 1927.

5. Watanabe Hisashi, teacher of history and the model for W——in Sketchbook VIII, "In the Pine Forest."

6. Hanabusa Itchō (1652–1724), a disciple of Bashō in *haikai* and an important painter, lived in Edo his entire life except for a twelve-year exile to Miyakejima in the distant south, for reasons that are unclear. He did not take this name until after his return to Edo in 1706 and the greater part of his production seems to have occurred during those final years.

7. Zeshin (1795–1872), a poet-priest born in Iwaki, was for nine years the priest in charge of the Saikyōji in Edo.

Among the Boulders

Headmaster Sakurai and Captain Masaki met near the gate of the Kaikoen, alongside the stone wall at the edge of the mulberry fields. There they exchanged greetings as colleagues will who see each other every day at the school.

"Where is Oto-san?" asked the captain, referring to the school janitor.

"Over at Nakadana, I suppose," replied Headmaster Sakurai.

A mineral spring had just been discovered in Nakadana, at the bottom of a deep swale just a few hundred yards away.

In the vicinity of the old castle site at the foot of Mt. Asama the slope was carved up into a number of deep swales that almost seemed artificial. In the area around the old samurai quarter of this castle town, the shallower upper portions of these swales were all under cultivation. Headmaster Sakurai's home stood just in front of these mulberry fields and bamboo groves, but at the moment the sturdily built headmaster was walking down a path leading into one of the pine-forested swales, gesturing vigorously as he talked with the captain.

The two strode along the path through a swale enfolded in greenery, going along the foot of a high bank before coming out on a small patch of cultivated high ground. Here the uneven undulations of the land were abruptly replaced by a red clay cliff that extended the slope down toward the riverbed. Halfway down the cliff they came upon Otokichi the janitor and his younger brother, who were widening the road and clearing away stones. Otokichi was a farmer by origin and he still did some tenant farming in addition to his duties at the school. His brother was also a hard-working young farmer.

When they got to where the brothers were working, the headmaster and his companion found some people from the town already there. Everyone was talking about the quality of the mineral spring and the plans for the new bathhouse. Some children had also come by to have a look on their way down to swim in the Chikuma River. Among them were some students from the school, all of whom turned to the headmaster and bowed. Then the playful students returned to rolling boulders down the hill and watching them smash into other stones, sending up puffs of dust as they bounced down toward the bottom of the cliff.

The headmaster and the captain stepped around the boulders that had been dug out of the excavation, taking turns looking into the dark pit. The mineral deposits from the spring clung like dark moss to the submerged stones in the quietly moving waters.

The new bathhouse was to be built on the level ground at the foot of the cliff. In his inspection of the site the headmaster led the captain through the stands of mountain beech and other trees growing in this wild valley. He told the captain about his plans to move his present study to a spot near the mineral spring.

The villages and the rustic rope bridges visible across the river, the level ground alongside the streambed, the distant mountain ranges, the nearby peaks—all of this delighted the headmaster. He was also pleased by the excellent exposure to the sun. The fertile swale was cultivated all the way up to its head and the fields of growing crops presented an expanse of green to the eye. The headmaster liked to stroll down here along the tree-shaded path from his home in the old samurai quarter.

The headmaster had begun walking down to oversee the work almost every day. He could usually find a little spare time as soon as he'd finished his teaching, and so it was a rare day when he was not seen there, even if the man who was to run the new bathhouse did not happen to put in an appearance. The placement of clay pipes here; moving stones for the embankment over there—nothing escaped his eyes. As the crops started to ripen in the green fields along the river's edge, the headmaster's little villa up on the hillside also began to take shape. Work both above and below the cliff was pushed forward as quickly as possible in order to beat the frost.

The deep snows came to bury the swales and valleys for three months. When they at last began to melt, the headmaster once again dressed himself as though going for a hike in the mountains, even wrapping leggings around his powerful calves before descending the path. He would keep his arthritic left hand tucked into the breast of his clothing. The mineral waters had soaked everything right out to the path. The half-finished construction and the brown leaves of the mountain beech that had clung to the branches throughout the winter lay among the remaining patches of snow. The headmaster went all the way down to the bottom to inspect a stretch of riprap that had nearly been brought down by the frost.

By the time the partially finished bathhouse below the cliff opened for business the villa was approaching livability and a gate of unpainted wood was already in place before it. In the meantime an elderly couple had built another little shed on the face of the cliff itself, hoping to make enough profit from the sulfur waters to support themselves in their old age.

In April, just before the beginning of the new school year, a sign was posted in front of the school announcing that it was now a town-supported institution. A new teacher by the name of Takase was welcomed to the faculty at the same time. Takase, who had come up from Tokyo, was being shown around by the headmaster during the final days of the vacation preceding the start of the school year. As they stood at the top of the hill, they could see the banner marking the Nakadana Mineral Spring flying from a pole at the bottom of the hill beside the faint smoke rising from the bathhouse chimney.

The headmaster led Takase down the new path running along the face of the cliff. In his prime the headmaster had been a teacher of English in a private school in Tokyo and Takase had been one of his students there. Later, when the headmaster became the pastor of a church in Takanawa while teaching in a women's school on the side, he had been searching for someone to be his heir—he had no children eligible to inherit from him at the time—and he had even hinted at adopting Takase. Now Takase had come to work under him as a teacher in his school. The headmaster looked upon Takase as one of his own children.

They walked along the winding path that led beside a stone-faced embankment to the bathhouse, still fragrant with the scent of freshly worked wood. Once inside they found that a grape arbor and the newly opened field beyond were visible through its glass windows. A thin haze rose from the transparent, dark blue waters brought down from the mineral spring. The headmaster lowered himself into the luxurious bath with a deep sigh. As he scrubbed the perspiration from his face with a dingy, countrified washcloth, he repeatedly glanced over at Takase, taking obvious pleasure in their being reunited after such a long time. He told of his satisfaction in taking up a mattock in his own hands to dig out this mineral spring, even though the waters were cold and would have to be artificially heated.

"Masaki came too, shovel on his shoulder, dressed just like a farmer . . ."

Masaki's name came up constantly in the headmaster's conversation. He explained that the captain was a locally born former soldier who had retired on pension and returned to the vicinity of the beloved old castle grounds in order to spend the rest of his life in reading and in tilling the soil.

"Masaki and I hold the stock in this mineral spring," the headmaster said as he went over to the smaller tub of water to wet down his graying hair.

Takase, just arrived from Tokyo, was filing away fresh new impressions from everything he saw and heard.

The two left the bathhouse and climbed the path back up the face of the cliff. The headmaster called out when they reached the hut about halfway up. An old man with a forthright farmer's face peered out and then handed over the key that the headmaster had left with him.

"I want to show you my villa," said the headmaster, conducting Takase toward the small pavilion set against the face of the cliff. He pointed out the source of the mineral waters as they passed by, opening the black-painted door that had been installed among the boulders so that Takase could see the waters rising up from the depths of the earth to form a pool.

"Well, let's go in and have a look. Not all the tatami are in yet, though."

The headmaster took up the key he had received from the old farmer, rattled the lock, and then led Takase into the dark, deserted interior of the house. Once he had opened the heavy rain shutters they found themselves peering out over the green, new tatami of the room all the way down to the turbulent flow of the Chikuma River far below.

Takase went over to the railing to listen to the faint cackling of chickens coming from the farms across the river. The headmaster stood beside him, sharing the view.

"You may remember this house . . . ," the headmaster said, and Takase did in fact remember it. He had visited the headmaster at his home once before and although the villa looked different now, it was still recognizable as the headmaster's former study.

"At any rate, now that I've got this building all fixed up I can loan it to everyone. Please use it as often as you like while you are here," he said as he showed Takase the newly added rooms. Then he took Takase downstairs to see what appeared to be an area that could be used for cooking or for storage. The dark stone wall that had been laid up on the embankment when the site was first cut out of the face of the cliff was still clearly visible.

The two returned to the sitting room overlooking the river. The headmaster opened the cupboard and began rummaging around for a smoking set.

"You've really gotten gray!" Takase suddenly said.

The headmaster had let his long luxuriant beard grow out since coming to Komoro.

Takase left the villa following the headmaster, who set a vigorous pace for one his age, and the two climbed back up toward the town along the same path they had descended earlier. It was that season when each passing rain brought a little more warmth to the mountains and the sun shone down on the moist earth.

"Sakurai-sensei![1] What ever became of the house you had in Takanawa?"

"The Takanawa house? That's a sad story . . . I really let myself get taken in on that one . . ."

Takase knew all about the headmaster's life in Takanawa. He remembered the fine house, well sited on spacious grounds that had been planted with fruit trees, a house that the headmaster had built with the intention of living there for the rest of his life. Takase had also been acquainted with the headmaster's second wife, who had lived there with him. The headmaster himself had still been young then and he would frequently have his wife dress in light, comfortable European clothing when the two of them set out for a walk up toward Sarumachi. Takase was fully aware that the headmaster had once known that kind of life.

The two continued to talk as they climbed up the steeply sloping portion of the path bringing them to the edge of the old samurai quarter. Many of its former residences stood abandoned. In some the garden walls had been broken down and the pillars were rotting; in others nothing remained but the outline of foundation stones among the mulberries. Part of the town of Komoro could be seen from these ruined samurai residences.

"Asama's smoking again!" said the headmaster, pointing out the plume of smoke stretching across the sky toward Jōshū. To Takase the not unfamiliar mountains of the Asama range now seemed more clearly defined than when he had observed them with a traveler's eye.

Next to the headmaster's home stood the gate of a former samurai residence. Students from the school were passing in and out of it. They were residential students, all of them from farm families in the outlying districts. Takase, having temporarily taken a room in this building, unpacked only the things he needed immediately. He would be taking his meals with the headmaster and his family. The headmaster opened the door at one end of the garden wall and invited Takase into the garden of his own residence.[2]

Here the headmaster had adopted a manner of living almost like that of the local people. There was a rustic storehouse in the backyard, and a holding tank for night soil. A vegetable garden had been put in and a large chicken coop stood near the veranda with chickens running loose around it. The child of the headmaster's present wife, who was treated like a little gentleman, had been burned to a dark hue by the sun, in contrast to the paleness of children who lived in the city.

The house itself seemed dark and gloomy to Takase's eyes, accustomed as he was to the bright and airy residences of Tokyo. He could scarcely believe that such a fastidious person as the headmaster could sit nonchalantly smoking beside such a hearth.

Students who had learned of Takase's arrival came around to meet him. Their greetings were straightforward as they asked him why he had come to such an out-of-the-way place. The headmaster's present wife was a mission school graduate, much younger than the headmaster, but she took good care of everyone. She invariably used the familiar forms "Sensei" or "Sakurai" whenever she spoke of her husband to guests.

"I think it would be nice if we offered Takase some coffee."

"I was just thinking that myself . . ."

After this exchange with his wife, the headmaster took Takase along the veranda, where the children were playing, to his own room. It was a peaceful spot looking out on the flowerbeds in the garden and it alone was neat and clean in conformity with its owner's taste. A small, old-fashioned writing desk[3] held volumes of Chinese poetry and the like, while to one side stood a folding screen dating from the youth of the headmaster's first wife. He took out some poems in Chinese that he had written to show to Takase. They were recent compositions and the scenes they portrayed—the little, hidden paths, the villages across the river were all related to the Nakadana mineral spring. The conditions of life such as they had presented themselves to the headmaster were revealed in the wording of these Chinese poems, a life in which he had reached an advanced age without establishing a permanent home anywhere.

That evening Takase went back to his room in the neighboring building to write a letter to a friend in Tokyo. He could hear the muffled voices of some resident students several doors away; it appeared that other people were also renting rooms here. Fragments of dispirited and desultory conversation came drifting in through the broken sliding panels. Takase laid out his bedding alongside his wicker trunk but the strangeness of the place and the sounds of the mice kept him from sleeping soundly. His mind was still half in Tokyo and the faces of people who had concerned themselves about him appeared in his thoughts until late in the night.

Takase went out early the next morning to look at the mountains. Mists were still scattered over the more distant mountains but they had already dissipated around Mt. Asama. The fanglike range of peaks, the dark, deep valleys, and the scars created by great landslides all stood out clearly. Thin smokelike clouds floated over the peaks, bathed in the morning light. To Takase, fatigued by city life, these mountains offered vigor and stimulation. He drew the clean, sharp mountain air deep into his starved lungs.[4]

On the day when lessons were to begin for the new school year, Takase, thinking of the new people he would be meeting, walked along the garden fence to ask the headmaster to join him. But the early-rising and impatient headmaster had already left the house. Only his wife was in the backyard, casting a housewife's eye over the garden.

"We're really out in the country, Takase. Everything all the way back to those mulberry fields goes with this place," she told him.

Takase walked past the flowerbeds, where weeds were already sprouting, and went out the back gate onto the path between the mulberry fields. The high ground on the other side of a small, shallow swale marked the beginning of the schoolyard, and bits of window and white wall could be glimpsed through the trees. Takase walked around the swale and caught up with the headmaster just as he started to pass alongside a gently sloping field.

"I'm trying oats here. The school janitor is looking after it," said the headmaster as he gestured toward the stony field.

In the schoolyard there were young flowering cherry trees around the classroom building and on the surrounding earthen embankment. The red-tinged branches with swelling buds hung within easy reach. Along the fence at the front gate, acacias had been planted. Otokichi the janitor was bent over industriously sweeping the grounds. The day students, who walked in from as far as four or five miles away, were all wearing straw sandals on their feet.

It was still early and Takase had time to see the headmaster's office. A foreign-style *desk*[5] and bookcase stood in a corner on the second floor above the classrooms. The headmaster seemed to be recalling the pleasant times he had known in America as he sat down in front of the bookcase, inviting Takase to be seated also.

"What a fine study!" said Takase, walking over to the window. The view took in the Tateshina range and the distant highlands beyond Minami Saku. In the samurai quarter nearby thatched roofs were visible and the boughs of the willows were faintly touched with green. The late spring was coming at last to these mountains.

"I'm giving this to you, Takase," said the headmaster, taking out a small leather-bound foreign book. He placed a pair of pince-nez spectacles on his high-bridged nose and thumbed through the old volume redolent of his past life before handing it to Takase.

Captain Masaki made his appearance outside the faculty room. The headmaster and Takase joined him and they entered the room together. By the time the captain reached his seat behind a large Japanese-style desk in the corner, Takase had already made his acquaintance.

"Captain Masaki has quite a collection of Chinese books and some fine models of calligraphy," the headmaster told Takase. "I'm sure he'll be willing to loan you whatever you need."

"Yes, I've been getting a few together. There are just no books around suitable for children, so I thought I would try to supply them with a few . . ."

The captain thrust both hands into his wide, black Japanese-style trousers and laughed. Takase met the bachelor of science Hirooka for the first time that day. Old enough to be Takase's father, Hirooka commuted by train from Ueda.

"Takase has joined our faculty with a commitment to stay three years," the headmaster told Hirooka.

When Takase returned to the faculty room after completing his first day of teaching, the day's second outward-bound train from Tokyo was just arriving. The sound of escaping steam reverberated from directly outside the schoolhouse and the younger children all ran out the door to cling to the fence along the tracks and watch.

"The train makes a terrible racket. It's so bad the windows rattle. If it comes when class is in session we can't do a thing," said the captain, coming over beside Takase. The two looked out the window toward the station and caught sight of Bachelor of Science Hirooka running out the door in a great hurry, doing his best not to miss the train for Ueda. He had everything with him, from a walking stick to his bundle wrapped in a carrying cloth.

The inward-bound train from Echigo came in just afterward. As it pulled out for Tokyo Takase walked across the schoolyard on his way home. The quiet that soon gathered around him was like that of a seaport after a ship had just sailed. The branches of the cherry trees cast sharp shadows in the schoolyard. Walking alone along the valley and through the mulberry fields, Takase reflected on how he had fled from the city. He thought of his escape from the life that had begun to threaten him—a life of futile resistance and fatigue—and how he had fled all kinds of other things. Wasn't there some way to make himself more fresh and simple? It had been with that thought in mind that he had turned down another teaching position to come to this lonely countryside. He even thought he might try tilling the soil a bit.

"Just how old are you, Takase?"

It was Mrs. Sakurai who asked this question as he came over from the neighboring house. She had come out to the veranda to show her little boy the chickens.

"Twenty-seven," replied Takase, who was standing in the garden.

"You're still young!"

"But how old are you? I can never guess a woman's age!"

"Me? I'm two years older than you," she replied, with a look that suggested the question had been uncalled for. She gave a sharp laugh and again turned to her child and the chickens. A mother hen was covering her pale yellow chicks with her wings.

The headmaster came through the garden to conduct Takase out the back way to show him a house for rent that he had found in town.

Once past the stone memorial tablet in front of the castle gate they crossed the railroad tracks and began to walk along a sandy, deep-set roadway. Ahead of them was a cultivated rise lined with stone walls and dominated by the old main gate of the castle.[6] The headmaster pointed out its soaring tile roof to Takase. He told him of how he had taken temporary lodgings behind its heavily grated windows when he first came to Komoro—it sounded like a fairy tale.

At the top of the slope they came to the site of the old fortifications that had once stood before the gate. A tiny stream flowed from there down toward the old samurai quarter. They talked about the bachelor of science Hirooka as they moved on. The headmaster spoke with sympathy.

"Hirooka has a school of mathematics in Ueda but it hasn't been going at all well. We've tried to help out by having him give us a hand here. And besides we wouldn't get very far in our plans to be accredited as a middle school if we didn't have someone with formal qualifications."

Takase laughed.

They walked along a little stream in a neighborhood behind Honmachi. There the headmaster brought Takase to a thatch-roofed house surrounded by a hedge of larch. Until recently it had been rented by someone who sold sweet bean soup. What immediately stood out upon inspection were the holes in the sliding panels between the rooms, the walls black with soot, and the filthy shōji. The tatami had been scorched around the opening for the *kotatsu*[7] and crudely patched with paper.

"Well, that's it," said the headmaster. "It hardly looks like a place you'd want to rent right now. But you just wait and see! Paper the walls, put in new tatami, and it will be quite livable!"

Even though the house maintained the style of a samurai residence it seemed to have been built much later than the others. It belonged to a merchant who sold the papers with silkworm eggs attached that served as seed for the local silkworm growers. Takase decided to rent the place, along with a little of the adjoining farmland.

Takase moved from the house next door to the headmaster's residence as soon as Otokichi the janitor had installed a new, three-foot-square hearth.

In back of the house there was another small stream, tumbling down among the stones. Its cold, rough water came straight down from the mountains and, though unsuitable for drinking, it was splendid for washing. Takase found a pure excitement in this. He made preparations to bring his fiancé to this humble, but still relatively new, dwelling and they were married at the end of the month.

After living in Tokyo for so long, Takase found much to be impressed by just in the neighborhood of the school itself: the cherry trees in the schoolyard that came bursting into bloom; the double blossoms that formed dense masses like huge bouquets directly outside the classroom windows; the way the rich colors of the flowers tinted the faces of the teachers as they walked in the schoolyard during recess; even the white walls of the school buildings. The children played among the trees like little birds while hiding behind tree trunks or grabbing at branches.

Takase commented to Headmaster Sakurai and Captain Masaki on the fact that Hirooka paid no attention to his appearance.

"It's not that he doesn't pay attention; it's that he is incapable of paying attention," said the captain, laughing.

The captain himself made do with kimono of the skimpiest cut, determined as he was to give his all to the school.[8]

To Takase the school had come to seem almost like a family. Returning home one day, he found that the mattock he had recently ordered had been delivered. Koyama, the physical education instructor, had brought it over. His family did the town's blacksmith work and the mattock had been forged by his father, who still wore his hair in an old-fashioned topknot.

Takase took up the heavy mattock by its massive handle and walked out to the farmland he had rented behind the house. With a cloth tied close around his face and the skirts of his kimono tucked up into his sash, he made a strange-looking farmer. He owned no work drawers such as farmers would wear and he was barefoot. Passersby snickered at him from the street but he worked on, ignoring them. Almost immediately he turned up a sad little plum seedling with its not-yet-unfolded leaf still attached to the seed. An ineffable joy flowed directly from the soil into him. He would occasionally take up the soil of the garden and rub it against the pale tender skin of his legs. The school janitor became his teacher, coming over to teach him everything, beginning with how to hold the mattock.

As soon as he completed each day's duties at school, Takase would rush home to his vegetable garden. On the day Otokichi brought over a basket of seed potatoes, he found that Takase had at last finished tilling the garden. His wife, Oshima, showing her red underrobe as she pulled weeds and hauled rocks, presented an image of totally displaced urbanity. Her hair had been wrapped but it still retained the shape of her wedding coiffure.

"You're really hard at it, madam!" Otokichi called out with a laugh as he inspected the land that Takase had cultivated. The furrows were too shallow. Otokichi took the mattock from Takase and showed him how to dig more deeply.

"There's nothing here but sand and volcanic ash. The vegetables just don't do much around here. It's not like Jōshū," he explained.

He showed them how to plant the seed potatoes he had brought over and then went on to explain the planting of onion sets.

From this plot where Takase was trying to grow at least a few of his own vegetables he could see the white walls of the merchant household next door and the roof of a water mill off to one side of the valley. It was the kind of place along the back streets where one would occasionally hear the sound of pots and pans being washed in the stream. Takase reflected on the fact that he and his wife were actually living here on the lower slopes of this volcano where men and women had to work so very hard.

Another addition to the classroom buildings was under construction. But there were still not enough teachers and so the bachelor of science Hirooka moved his family over from Ueda before the beginning of the next school year.

On his next visit to Tokyo Takase brought back another new teacher by the name of Koyasu. He had never met the man before; they had been introduced by a third party. Koyasu's arrival at the school was awaited with considerable curiosity. He turned out to be a gratifyingly well mannered and energetic scholar.

The faculty room grew more lively. Headmaster Sakurai would converse with them while sitting before the large brazier, his eyes alight with youthful vigor. Captain Masaki rolled his strong-smelling cigarettes and was fond of saying "when I was in the army." Sometimes Otokichi would go on talking beside the brazier even after someone rang for him.

"Just give these glasses a try, Masaki."

"I don't need reading glasses yet. —Say! This is amazing! You can see even better at a little distance than you can close up. How about it, Hirooka?"

"Yes, I really can see better!"

"You're in bad shape!"

And so the time passed in pleasant banter.

The nearby bathhouse in Nakadana was another place where everyone gathered. Once Koyasu had settled in, Takase invited him to go down to Nakadana directly from the classroom. Barely a month had passed since Koyasu's arrival from Tokyo. The swale, hung with wisteria blossoms, lay in deep shade beneath the fresh new foliage on the trees.

As they came out onto the hilltop they found a warm breeze blowing across the yellowing barley fields. They could actually hear the sound of the barley heads rubbing together, and the overwhelming scent of growing grass reduced the two to silence. They tried exchanging a word or two but then walked on without saying anything more until they started down the path along the cliff. There they both burst out laughing. Near the hut of the retired couple they were greeted by Captain Masaki's wife, fresh from the bath, leading her children up the steep hillside.

Hirooka and the headmaster were at the bathhouse. The headmaster was just drying himself off and the bachelor of science was relaxing alone in the mineral waters. Young grapevines were growing in profusion outside the glass door and beyond them was a new apple orchard.

"You've got a fine build, Koyasu," said the bachelor of science. Koyasu's firm calves seemed to bespeak past rigors as he rubbed them down.

"What do you think of that finger?" said the bachelor of science, spreading the fingers of his left hand to display a half-missing third finger.

Koyasu gasped in surprise and stared round-eyed.

"You hadn't noticed, had you? That has a history behind it—it's a baseball souvenir."

Recalling his brilliant college days as he spoke, he even went so far as to demonstrate how he had been struck on the tip of his finger by a hard-driven ball.

The three left the bath together and began to climb up the hill toward Sakurai's villa. The headmaster was sprinkling water on the stones in the garden as he waited for them. He showed Takase the acacia cuttings that he was trying to root above the stone wall. Planted inside the gate were the flowers he was so fond of.

A plaque bearing the name of the villa now hung in the entry. When they entered the sitting room overlooking the Chikuma River, they found it flooded with a brilliant light. The greenish cast it took on from the vegetation outside suffused even the bath-fresh faces of all present. The view beyond the railing would turn to yellow twice each year, but now it was like a painter's study in green. As the headmaster served tea he spoke about the intensity of the insect songs in this time of green fields and about the evening lamplight in the villages across the river.

Shortly thereafter the three left the headmaster in his hideaway to return to town. Hirooka was such a slow walker that the other two would frequently have to stop and wait for him before striding ahead once more.

"Even the women really work hard here," Koyasu said to Takase as they were about to part.

Takase came to a halt.

"But it's probably because they do work so hard that the women here seem so strong."

"I'm sure it is. They really do work. But they are so plain! I'm telling you, Takase, charming qualities are absolutely lacking in the girls around here."[9]

Koyasu laughed at the intensity of his own speech before adding, "They're all like a bunch of solid stones."

"But you'll be amazed when you see just how fine those stones will start to look!" Takase teased him.

Koyasu went his way and Takase waited for the slow-moving Hirooka beside the tall stone wall just beyond the railroad crossing.

"I'm here to become Komoro soil, Takase," he said in a voice uncharacteristically humbled as they walked down the stairs along-side the stone wall into the poorer district at the back of the town.

"I'm growing morning glories now. I grew a lot of them in Ueda, but I don't know how they're going to do this year. Would you like to come and see them?"

It suddenly began to rain in big drops. The bachelor of science, apparently worried about his morning glories, took a hurried leave of Takase.

The rain was beating on Takase's face as he reached the coarse gravel strip at the edge of the overpass. Under the eaves of an impoverished-looking house stood a girl with brownish-colored—grayish would be more accurate—unkempt hair, staring listlessly out at the passersby. Takase walked on, unhurried, actually taking pleasure in the rain on his face. It pleased him that he had at last acquired some resistance, after a winter in these mountains when he had come down with one cold after another. He reached the house, drenched in perspiration, to find that this year's potato crop was in bloom. The scent of the rain on the dry soil reached even into the study lined with new books.

In July Hirooka received Takase in his house behind Aramachi. It was not far from where Takase lived; a short walk up a narrow path brought him to the blacksmith shop operated by the family of the physical education instructor. The bachelor of science's residence was set against the base of a high stone wall, upon which stood a white-walled storehouse. Being so close to the rice fields made it damp.

"Good morning!" called Takase as he walked around the main house toward the back garden.

There in the heavy dew Hirooka was pacing among the morning glory benches lined with rows of potted plants. His wife had been working with their eldest daughter at the kitchen door but now she came down into the garden, speaking in impatient but well-bred tones.

"He's just crazy about morning glories. No sooner had we arrived in Komoro than he had the whole backyard full of pots. Oto-san came and put up the benching. Such fine benching—"

She spoke as if she had no time to indulge in morning glories, but she obviously shared her husband's pleasure in them and she knew the name of every variety he had planted.

"This is the one I particularly wanted you to see," said Hirooka as he took a *tenaga* from one of the unglazed pots. He brought it to the edge of the veranda facing the garden and had Takase sit down before he placed the pot between them.

His wife, her attention partly on the children, said, "Shigeru! There's a teacher from the school here! Won't you come out and bow to him? Isamu! Why are you standing there? Really, Takase-san, the older I get the more impatient I become."

Her scolding reached even to the eldest daughter, whose childish cheeks flushed as she brought out tea for the guest and her father.

In spite of the distractions from the children, Hirooka seemed able to forget all his troubles when he gazed on the potted morning glory.

"The only ones that are blooming now are the plain ones and the peony shapes," he explained to Takase. "The lions and the *tenaga* come later. I'd like you to come over again then. I've been thinking of having everyone over for a drink, but—"

When Takase reached the railroad tracks on his way to school the next morning, some of the students from the school were, as always at this hour, just crossing over. Each morning he would meet Koyasu here just as though it had been prearranged. Takase waited up for Koyasu, who came in from Yoramachi, and the two of them went on to school together. They caught sight of the bachelor of science walking by the fence that ran alongside the tracks.

"There goes Hirooka," said Takase.

"Why did a person like Hirooka ever come to a place like this?"

"Nobody knows . . ."

They overtook the bachelor of science at the gate. He immediately began to talk about his morning glories.

"A few more bloomed again this morning, Takase."

"I'm afraid your morning glories are still more than I can understand," replied Takase with a laugh.

"Townspeople are starting to come over to see them. Some really seem to like them. But I'm not quite settled in yet."

Hirooka seemed almost to be talking to himself.

Captain Masaki came striding around the end of the wall by the mulberry fields, a big smile on his face. They all walked into the faculty room together to find Headmaster Sakurai hard at work. He reported that he had already been down to Nakadana that morning.

The trees in the schoolyard cast a dense shade. On a stone

beneath the refreshing acacia trees a student sat reading a book. A sumō ring had been set up under the luxuriantly growing cherry trees and matches were being called in naïve, childish voices. The hills and valleys visible from the window had grown familiar to Takase, who had now experienced two summers in these mountains. Whenever he had the time he took pleasure in going to sit on the grass at the edge of the fields, in smelling the earth, in watching the farmers at work—even in listening to the sound of a child nursing in the fields. The white summer clouds that had been absent from the window for so long were back. Takase could now distinguish every kind of cloud, from the heat-bearing, deeply shaded masses to the distant puffs of steam that seemed to flow through the blue skies.

Memories from his early childhood rose up as he looked out the window during each recess. He remembered himself as a country child, with his hair still long and his feet shod in homemade straw sandals. He remembered going to the river to catch little fish by hand. He remembered picking up a spotted blue feather that a jay had dropped beneath the summer trees. He remembered the caterpillars on the chestnut trees. He remembered stepping on them and squashing them, picking up the thread out of the greenish blood and soaking it in vinegar before stretching it out and drying it to use for fish lines. He remembered catching frogs, skinning them and putting them on sticks to attract wasps so that he could trace them to their nests. He had enjoyed eating not only the wasp larvae, something that city children knew nothing about, but also the succulent leaves of the *suikogi* tree that drooped into the rice paddies, and of the knotweed and the *suiha*.

Dormant images from his childhood returned to life. He remembered, as he had not done for many years, how he had watched the fox fires in the skies beyond the distant mountains around his old home.[10] He remembered how the nighthawks would fly about so unnervingly close overhead in the evenings. He remembered seeing, in the village school he had first attended, a student who was said to have been possessed by a fox . . .

Bachelor of Science Hirooka came over to the window.

"Where were you born?" Takase asked him.

"Echigo," he replied.

About to leave the school at noon, Takase suddenly heard a shout outside the gate.

"You bum! I'm going to smash you!" Otokichi's younger brother had picked up a big stone and was making threatening motions toward someone.

"He's just joking," Hirooka said as he came out, giving Takase a reassuring smile.

Takase was taken aback at such rough behavior. Yet at the same time he took pleasure in the discovery that he found such boorish playfulness much preferable to the etiolated wit of the city. He wanted to stay here a while, working with these congenial colleagues and getting to know the simple lives of the farmers much better. His heart reached out to the valleys and to the mountains beyond them.

Two more years had passed. His original commitment had been fulfilled, but Takase showed no inclination to leave. "The country is a better place for study," he would say, settling in more firmly than ever.

Another two years passed. Another classroom building had been added to the school and there were more teachers now. The faithful and punctilious Kusakabe had joined them and the foreign-style painter Izumi was coming over once or twice a week from Chiisagata. Yet the cheerful laughter that had once been so much a part of life gradually became rarer and rarer. Everyone now worked in silence.

There were too many teachers for them all to use the manager's office and they moved to a former classroom on the corner of the second floor. A huge brazier was brought in and a cast-iron teakettle constantly boiled away on it. Captain Masaki would sometimes come over to roll a cigarette of imported tobacco, but now he seldom joined the conversations as he had before and he usually stayed in the manager's office, making use of his spare time to practice calligraphy. The headmaster would come only when he had business to discuss; he would drink a cup of tea prepared by Otokichi and then return to his office next door. As soon as he finished his teaching assignments he would put on a cloth hat such as hermits wear, walk out through the schoolyard with its now oppressively overgrown cherry trees—young no longer—and set out, not for his home, but for his villa at Nakadana.

Koyasu too fell silent. He had married the daughter of a physician in the town and he now commuted from his new home in the samurai quarter. Kusakabe, the latecomer, seemed to be quiet by nature.

The air of the faculty room was usually filled with the smoke from Bachelor of Science Hirooka's old-fashioned engraved silver pipe.[11] Takase too would shift his shoulders in a habitual gesture and take a luxurious puff on his cigarette before going downstairs to teach the students.

One day after Takase had finished his own classes, he happened to pass by Hirooka's classroom. The bachelor of science, at the point of ending his class, was still standing in front of his desk explaining something to the students. On the desk were a bottle of hydrochloric acid, some marble chips, a drinking glass with a glass cover, glass tubing, and various other objects. There was also a lighted candle. The teacher picked up the drinking glass and tilted it a bit, releasing carbon dioxide from under the cover. The candle went out just as if he had poured water over it.

The students were gathered wide-eyed around his desk, some smiling, some standing with arms folded, some with their chins cupped in their hands. When they were told that a mouse or a bird would die if placed in the glass, one student immediately piped up.

"Wouldn't a bug do, sir?"

"No, bugs don't have quite the same need for oxygen as birds and mammals."

The student who had asked the question suddenly vanished from the classroom only to reappear beside the peach tree outside the window. One of the students looked out and exclaimed, "Oh! He's going to get a bug!" The boy in the garden searched under the cherry trees, picked something up, and came back. He handed it to the teacher.

"A bee?" said the teacher, with some alarm.

"Hey! He's really mad! Look out! He'll sting you!"

The excited students chattered on as the teacher bent himself backward as far out of danger as possible. As the bee went into the drinking glass the students laughed nervously.

"It's dying! Its dying!" one of them cried, while another observed that it must be a weakling. As if to prove his point, the bee buzzed around inside the drinking glass, writhed a bit, and died.

"Well, I guess he's a goner all right," the teacher said, joining in the laughter.

The bachelor of science joined Takase soon afterward. When they got back to the faculty room, no one was there. The door of Headmaster Sakurai's office was also closed. Captain Masaki had gone home as well. Hirooka stepped into his office to retrieve the bow he kept there and came back to where Takase was.

"How about some archery? We haven't been getting much in these days."

Takase accepted the invitation and the two went down the stone steps in front of the school building.

Most of the students had already left. All was still except for the sound of Otokichi industriously cleaning the classrooms. His wife, a child strapped to her back, had come to help him and they were working in the classroom closest to the gate.

Hirooka spoke to Takase in a familiar manner.

"They say that Otokichi's wife was once in service at Masaki-sensei's house. They got together while Oto-san was going over there to tend the garden. I suppose you could say that he got the two of them together."

As they marched out to the beat of a vigorously applied duster they looked back and caught a glimpse, through the window, of a woman's face, ruddy and sparkling as a quince blooming among the stones.

The new foliage was just out and the leaves of the acacias in front of the school buildings glistened in the sun. Their slender branches had become a dense cover overhead.

Takase and Hirooka walked off toward the Kaikoen, the older man carrying a bag containing his bow, a quiver of arrows, and another small bag containing rosin and the like. On their way to the old castle grounds they passed along the stone walls edging the mulberry fields that had once been the site of impressive samurai residences. The railroad had greatly changed the neighborhood and they could see places where leftover sand and stones remained heaped up.

A physician mounted on horseback greeted them as he passed by. Hirooka gazed after him.

"That doctor will try raising anything—chickens, herbs, birds, morning glories. When chrysanthemums are in season, he'll try chrysanthemums. He's a strange one, even for a country doctor. He's quite opinionated too. 'Those other guys,' he'll say, 'they're no doctors! They're just a bunch of medicine peddlers!' But he's a good sort. He'll go way out to isolated farms and if they have no money to pay him, he'll say that any produce they might have on hand will do. 'Just give me a few leeks when they're ready,' he'll say. The farmers think highly of him."

The bachelor of science himself had been in the wars of the Restoration, and he often spoke of his first campaign at age nineteen. Both Captain Masaki and Headmaster Sakurai were former Tokugawa bannermen who had enjoyed the privilege of direct audience with the shōgun.

They passed through the great gate with the plaque marking it as the entrance to the Kaikoen. To their right stood a high stone wall that was black with moss and lichens.

A former foot soldier bowed to them as he came past carrying two buckets of water.

Captain Masaki and Headmaster Sakurai had built the archery range, putting up a small building in a quiet spot hidden away among the greenery of the maple and zelkova trees at the foot of the foundations of the old keep. They met the captain and the physical education instructor there, along with a few other members of the group. There had been a time when the entire staff of the school would come down together but Koyasu had gradually dropped out and Headmaster Sakurai seldom put in an appearance anymore. Takase went over to pick up the archery equipment that he kept at the teahouse. When he came back he stayed closer to the bachelor of science than he usually did.

"Tomorrow it will be a full year since I took up the big bow," said the physical education instructor, the most recent recruit to the group.

"Even after a year's practice, if you stop for even a little while you can't hit a thing. I can't believe it!" laughed the captain, who pulled the strongest bow.

Stillness prevailed in the now somehow cheerless archery range, its air of desolation augmented by the hushed quiet of the pine forest. The vast slope of Mt. Asama was visible through the young foliage of an ancient zelkova tree that lacked much of its bark. The sound of farmers digging furrows in the mulberry field behind the range came to them. The captain's house was just on the other side, across a swale densely grown with shrubbery.

The bachelor of science pulled the weakest bow, but he worked hard and hit the target regularly. He picked up a target that he had made up himself and went out to change it.

"This is awful! And the target is fifteen inches! I've got to get myself together!" said the captain as he shot at the new target.

"TWANG!" came the mocking exclamation of the physical education instructor.

"That just won't do!"

The captain snapped the bowstring against the inside of his arm, laughed nervously, and lapsed once more into a melancholy silence.

Takase remained with the group until the farmers working in the mulberry fields began to head home. As long as Bachelor of Science Hirooka was releasing his beloved hawk-feathered arrows to the target, he seemed like one who had found a good hiding place where he could forget all his troubles.

Takase and Hirooka headed back the way they had come, toward the castle gate, leaving the captain and the others behind.

Suddenly the bachelor of science began to talk as though he had just recalled something.

". . . my boy Isamu is getting to be pretty good at children's sumō. Just the other day he came back with a bowstring he had won. They really give out strange names in sumō. I asked him what his was and he said 'Oka no shika,' the stag of the hill!"

The bachelor of science put out his tongue playfully and Takase laughed like a small boy.

"His older brother has a sumō name too, so I asked him what it was and he replied that since his father is fond of archery he is called 'Ya-atari,' arrow strike or bull's-eye, so that he might win often. Children are really funny."

When they reached the castle gate they met an archery acquaintance of Hirooka's, one of the old local samurai, carrying a fishing net. He was on his way back from the Chikuma River.

"I've given up the bow," he said in a cheerful voice and proceeded to expand on the subject. "They say we samurai are all finished. About the only one of us in Komoro with any guts left is Masaki from the school."

The bachelor of science and Takase stood and talked with him for a while.

"Just look. Everything around the castle is going downhill. Until two or three years ago I could get fish whenever I went down to the river. People say they were already gone but they were still there two or three years ago. Now there aren't any fish at all. . . . And those pine forests—they've all passed into other people's hands."

He spoke rapidly, then left abruptly. The two gazed after him for a moment and then set out once more for home. Hirooka walked very slowly.

When he came into Komoro from his home at the foot of Mt. Eboshi, Izumi would catch the train at Tanaka or else walk all the way, sketching as he went. In the afternoons of the two or three days a week that he came to school he would still have the energy to engage Takase in conversation. Immediately after returning from study in Europe, Izumi had set up a studio in a mountain village where there was fine scenery but he had also joined the faculty at the school, explaining that he couldn't simply shut himself in and do nothing but study.

Takase enjoyed listening to Izumi's stories about the French countryside and would frequently draw him out on the subject of the farmer-artist Millet. Eventually he borrowed some critical biographies of Millet that Izumi had brought back with him, sometimes asking Izumi to translate a difficult passage for him.[12]

They also spoke about other matters. "Have you read Yamada's translation of Tolstoy's *The Cossacks?*[13] It tells of Russian youths going off to the Caucasus. At the end the protagonist reflects that 'peasants are peasants and I am I,' and we have that feeling sometimes too. I am very fond of the farmers here. I go to spend the night in students' homes—I talk with them—I've gone over to Oto's place and eaten *konnyaku* stew[14] with his father—but I still have the feeling that I really cannot see things their way."

Leaving the school where everyone now worked in silence, Takase walked homeward along the sandy road. He came out in front of the railway station. Along both sides of the street advertisements for special noodles, banners for beef and horsemeat, and placards for pilgrimages to Zenkōji were fluttering in the spring breeze. In one of the storefronts he suddenly caught sight of the smiling face of Hirooka among the timetables, the advertisements for beer and sake, and the smoke from the cookfire.

Hirooka nodded in recognition, then stepped across the room to address the very businesslike lady of the shop.

"Have you got anything for me today?" he asked, sitting down among the people waiting for the train. Takase joined him.

Careless though he usually was about his appearance, Hirooka sported a stylish necktie today. He began talking to Takase in great high spirits. From time to time a phrase of light and fluent French would flow from his lips.

"There's too much traffic out here. Please come inside . . ."

It was the master of the shop speaking now, and Hirooka looked around him. There was a farmer from a nearby village tieing his horse up at the entrance. A succession of anonymous passersby, some incongruously dressed in formal kimono with crested jackets but with straw sandals on their feet, looked in the door before walking on down the street.

"Well, Hirooka-sensei, we've been able to make the place a bit larger than when you were commuting from Ueda," the master's wife said as she welcomed them.

The flask of warmed sake that Hirooka had ordered soon came. He sat face to face with Takase on the floor of the newly added back room. A small footed tray laden with a neat arrangement of simple dishes was set between them. Takase asked about the couple's children as he poured himself a drink.

"Tell the others about this place, Takase. It's pleasant here and you can see what a congenial person she is. And it's gotten this big just in the time since I was coming in from Ueda."

"I've learned to drink a bit myself since coming to Komoro."

"I'm sure you have. The people around here are good drinkers. I suppose it's because this is cold-weather country. Who's the best drinker at school? Masaki's certainly good."

Explaining that he did not want to drink more, Takase added that he would be happy to stay and talk. He took a country-style tobacco pouch out of the pocket of the suit he now wore to school. His hair was longer and his expression sadder than when he had come from the city, but he sat contentedly smoking as he listened to the bachelor of science.

"Well now, Takase, it's about my son, the one who's just applied for entrance at the school. He's not like his little brother; he's a good boy. He's always liked drawing, ever since he was in grade school, and he's always received top grades. When I asked him what he wanted to be when he grew up, he said he wanted to be like Izumi-sensei. Do you think he has any future at that?"

The bachelor of science drank steadily as he went on.

"It's a strange thing. My wife is still much fonder of the younger one. She'll do anything he says. If I object we invariably have a quarrel. She says I always take Shigeru's part and that is because I don't see through him; that's why nobody pays any attention to me anymore. That's what she says. . . . But the older boy's weaker and I try to protect the weak one . . .''

He mopped his face with his hand towel.

"But, Takase, why do I get so concerned about him? You've got a couple of children of your own, haven't you? It's hard, bringing children up. It's still not too bad when you've just got two, but look at us—we've got them swarming all over. And every last one of them is a big eater."

Hirooka laughed as if he had just thought of something. "But really, to tell your children not to eat so much; to make do with three bowls of rice . . . A parent just can't say such a thing!"

The frankness of his talk made Takase laugh. Hirooka started off on another tack.

"Now after Isamu we've got a girl. She was born in Ueda. She doesn't listen to a thing we say. It must be because she was born at such a difficult time. . . . We really haven't been able to give her the proper attention—there just hasn't been time to consider the children. But come to think of it, my wife has really done wonders. She bears up under hardship much better than I do."

He fell silent as a stone for a time. The sake began to show in his face, his long gray-flecked scholar's eyebrows standing out still more sharply against the flushed skin. He grew so excited that he began shifting about, now sitting cross-legged, now shifting back to a formal kneeling position as he looked across at Takase. Then his tone changed.

"Now the French language is extraordinarily sophisticated in some ways," he said, skillfully pronouncing two or three words.

"Maybe I should study with you," said Takase.

"Why don't you?"

"There's a lot of French in the novel I'm reading right now and it's giving me trouble."

"Well then, what we should do seems clear."

Hirooka's eyes always lit up with a special light when he was speaking French.

Later Takase saw the bachelor of science home and then made his way back to Aioichō. As he walked along the street he received a constant stream of rustic greetings from the people he met. Some of them were still wearing their hair long in the old style.

A day of rest.

Takase had been living in the house at Baba'ura for so long that it could no longer be said to be a temporary residence. He decided to use the day as free time.

He went over to the shōji facing south. There was a hedge of larch just beyond the veranda that had been heavily damaged by the winter's snows and winds. Each year the lonely voices of the frogs could be heard from this shōji. He went next to the northern veranda. There he saw the trunk of the apple tree standing near the eaves of the decrepit thatched roof. It was growing weaker year by year under the onslaughts of insects, but the short, ill-formed limbs had put out leaves once again. A faint perfume came to his nostrils. He leaned against the veranda, gazing at the leaves of the apple tree under the April sun. When his wife, Oshima, happened to come out and stand beside him, she found him with a strange, obsessed expression on his face.

"I feel like I'm going crazy," he said, trying to make a joke of it. Oshima looked up at the sky from the veranda and replied casually.

"Maybe you should try getting a haircut."

A huge bumble bee suddenly came buzzing into the room. Oshima rushed over to where one of the children was taking a nap. The bee, which had come in from the garden, continued on out the front door.

"Where's Maa-chan?" Takase said, asking about the elder of the daughters who had been born in that house.

"Outside, playing."

"She's playing with the carpenter's daughter again, isn't she? That girl really worries me. I don't think we should let her play with such a rough child."

"I agree, but she insists on playing with her even though she keeps coming home in tears."

"Just refuse the next time she comes over to ask her out—don't even let her into the house. I'm serious."

It was the kind of bright sunny day when no healthy young person can possibly sit still. Takase had not been visiting the samurai quarter as often as he should recently, but he felt more inclined that day to walk out among the fields wherever his feet happened to take him than to make duty calls on colleagues. He left the house in the afternoon.

Little streams tumbled down among the stones everywhere. He walked along a path that he never tired of. When he came out behind Akasaka, green barley fields lay before his eyes. The heads of the barley were once again showing pale on the stems; he was now seeing them ripen for the fifth time. He entered the fields on the back side of Aramachi with its earthen walls and its white stucco walls, emerging presently behind Yoramachi at the southeastern edge of town where huge stones lay buried in the cropland. There he met a youth from the town, hard at work in the fields.

He was, in fact, not really a youth any longer. He had already married and established his own household. Takase sat on a stone beside the field for a while and watched the young man as he grubbed in the soil.

The man kept up a stream of talk as he leaned over and struck from the hips, breaking up the clods. With the wind that came blowing over the barley, the sound of flowing water, and the voices of the frogs, the two could only make out bits of each other's speech.

"I really think we should at least have houses built for Sakurai-sensei and Hirooka-sensei," said the man in the field. "I've been asking about it for the sake of the town . . ."

The frogs began to sing very loudly as Takase was taking his leave to return home. The broad, deep Chikuma River valley overflowed with their voices. White clouds were still riding the distant mountain ranges of the Japan Alps off toward Hida, but Takase did not stop to enjoy the view. An uncanny feeling of loneliness rose up out of the valley on the sound of the frogs. He grew uneasy and half fled back to his wife and children.

"Father!"

The child's voice brought Takase back to himself. He was standing by the hedge in front of his house in the company of his daughter Mariko.

"Let's go home, Maa-chan."

He spoke in a soothing voice as they entered the front garden. The mattock and other implements for tilling the soil stood in a corner. Oshima was sitting in the entry nursing their second girl.

"The maid took Maa-chan to play in the Kaikoen," Oshima told her husband as she looked back at her nursing child. The baby was now old enough to seize the nipple for herself.

"Give me some too!" begged Mariko.

Oshima had been chewing on some dried squid. Now she put down the nursing child, got up, and went to the cupboard by the hearth.

"I'll give you some bread! Come over here!"

"No! I don't want bread! I want dried squid!"

A smiling Takase had been watching this scene. Mariko came to him.

"Don't be naughty now!" he said to her.

"I'm not. Not at all," she contradicted him, but in the most matter-of-fact voice.

Takase sighed and went in. He was sitting alone in his study when Oshima brought him his tea. He was doing nothing—just sitting there.

"I'm feeling uneasy all of a sudden. I can't seem to do anything about it so I decided to just sit here."

Evening came. There was the sound of a rock striking against the shutter box on the south side of the house. Someone outside had thrown it.

"Who's there?" Takase called, running over to the shōji and looking out beyond the veranda. "Throwing rocks against the house! Who is it? —You'd better watch what you're doing! I mean it!"

He spoke angrily as he peered out beyond the hedge. The mischievous little neighbor girl, with a look on her face that would bring tears even to a parent's eyes—but very pretty in spite of it—ran and hid behind the wall across the street.

"Why are the girls around here so rough? You can't tell if they are girls or boys!" Takase said from the veranda to Oshima, who was also looking out beyond the hedge.

"You told me not to let her play with the carpenter's daughter, and when she came over to invite her out I refused. But Maa-chan went out on her own. . . . I'm sure they had a fight. . . . But throwing rocks! Even the maids and the girls taking care of their brothers or sisters—all of them around here are tough."

Looking up at the evening sky, Oshima spoke as though she were at her wit's end.

"Come on home, Maa-chan!" she called to the little girl who was once again out playing.

"The bogeyman'll get you! Come on in!" added the maid, who had been out at the well getting water.

Mariko was getting to be more and more like a mountain girl but she was not always a nuisance to her parents. After dinner she came carrying a doll to show her mother.

"Come on now, smile," she told it. Then she carried it throughout the house, dancing and singing a lullaby. No one had taught Mariko this bedtime routine; she had developed it all by herself.

The April night gradually deepened in the back streets of Komoro. The neighborhood girls had come for their calligraphy lesson with Oshima and then gone home by the light of their paper lanterns. Most of the houses around were already closed up and their occupants fast asleep. Then an unidentifiable voice called out of the stillness outside.

"Takase!"

"Takase! Are you in?"

The voice drew nearer to the hedge.

"Ah!" Takase strained his ears and went to his trembling, frightened wife.

Oshima went down and opened the front door. The bachelor of science Hirooka and the physical education instructor Koyama came reeling in.

Takase brought the lamp out to the entry where it illuminated the red, impudent face of Hirooka, apparently out to give Baba'ura a little surprise. He and his companion were both wearing leggings and straw sandals.

"Give them some water," Takase said to his wife.

Now somewhat reassured, Oshima brought water from the kitchen. Hirooka was so drunk he could hardly control his movements but, apparently determined to remain conscious, he opened his bloodshot eyes wide to stare into the faces of the couple and at the lamplight reflected in the water in the drinking glass.

His hand trembled as he reached for the glass. Oshima held it out to him.

"We are being rude. The two of us went out into the mountains today . . . got drunk . . . I am truly sorry, madam."

Hirooka placed both hands on the sill of the entry, bowed his head to the floor, and made an honest, well-intentioned apology.

Koyama burst into drunken laughter. He placed his hand on his companion's shoulder as if offering assistance but he too was quite far gone.

The two went reeling out once more on unsteady legs. Takase took the lamp out into the street to light the dark road for them, but when he returned to the house he was struck by the unexpected dreariness of the night they had left behind them.

That night Takase went to bed late under the roof of a house that somehow seemed to be falling apart. From time to time he opened his eyes to the sight of the hungry rats that came into the room to disappear and reappear around their bedding. He slept fitfully, overcome by a fearful panic at the thought that they might climb up on him. He roused his wife in the wee hours and they scraped around the kitchen to get a rat trap set up.

All kinds of unexpected things occurred during the summer and autumn of that year. The bachelor of science Hirooka lay ill for three months in his house behind Aramachi. His case had looked hopeless for a while but then, just as he was beginning to recover, Captain Masaki fell ill and died, leaving his children for his wife to bring up, his work at the school unfinished. His body was buried in the graveyard of the samurai quarter. After a family conference, the collection of Japanese and Chinese books he had left to his children was sold at auction to settle his debts.

Headmaster Sakurai's long white beard grew noticeably whiter. Day after day Takase would go off to the school, watching the snows that seemed to pile up on the headmaster's beard, and then return home. Bachelor of Science Hirooka, who had barely survived his illness, was staying completely away from sake now. By the time he had finished his winter preparations for the potted morning glories that his wife had taken care of all summer and brought their seeds in, there was already a heavy frost on the roof of Takase's house and on the fields in back. A cold wind stripped the trees bare. Everything turned an ashen gray—the soil, the stones, even human skin. There were days when the very sunlight took on an ashen hue. An unexpectedly heavy snow fell. The doorway was buried and more than a foot of snow remained clinging to the north side of the roof. The crowing of the roosters sounded distant and the entire land seemed to be covered over and muffled. When the sun shone out of ashen skies onto the south shōji the light-gorged snow glittered. The dismal sound of meltwater dripping from the eaves went on endlessly, monotonously, day after day.

Shut in for the winter, Takase huddled over the brazier while Oshima went to the *kotatsu* to warm the children's icy hands. Outside the house, snows once melted were replaced by new snows, ground once uncovered was buried again, and as the sunlight grew distant and feeble, they found themselves in the midst of a half-frozen world. Threads of vapor scarcely worthy of being called clouds banded together in the cold skies. They struggled through to another new year, staring at the swordlike icicles hanging from the eaves on the north side of the house.

It grew still colder. The snow froze solid on the north side of the house and in the garden, and day after day went by with no sign of thawing. The icicles reached two and three feet in length. When Oshima went to the hearth to prepare warm milk for the children she sometimes found it frozen into a pale greenish ice and there would be nothing for them to drink. The water from the kitchen sink froze into a solid mass beneath it. Most of the vegetables they had stored away were frozen. When the maid went out to the well for water she would wrap a cloth about her head and put on gloves before setting off, bucket in hand, looking very cold. She would return with the skin of her hands cracked. Blood would ooze out here and there. Oshima now had time only for one concern: how to keep her children from freezing. On evenings when Takase sat reading to the accompaniment of the resounding cracks from the freezing timbers of the house, he would feel the cold penetrating to his very bones. Beside him, Oshima would be warming one of the children by holding it against her bare skin.

To pass through that long, long season of cold, huddled in on oneself, living as though buried in the ground throughout the winter, was no easy thing. Takase and his wife longed for spring.

When the worst of the cold began to relax its grip on the mountains, Takase started to rouse himself out of dormancy. He crawled out like a hibernating insect to survey his surroundings. The cold of that winter had led to the loss of one of the students at school.

On a day when a warm rain suddenly began to bring life back to the land, Izumi came over by train all the way from Chiisagata to mourn the dead youth. That youth had also been a student of Takase's for four years and he accompanied Izumi to the student's house.

They caught up with Bachelor of Science Hirooka as they were going down the slope in Akasaka.

"It hasn't been this cold for ten years. I thought we were all going to freeze to death. Even the young ones couldn't stand such cold," he said, staring out through the rain that was soaking into the dirty snow.

The soil, reappearing at last, yellow bamboo groves, bare trunks and branches, the leafless persimmon, damson, and other trees that the three saw—everything presented a soiled and drowsy face.

Talking together under a huge, foreign-style umbrella as they descended the slope came Koyasu and Kusakabe. All the teachers from the school gathered in the rain.

It was the loss of a promising student, only eighteen years old, that had brought them all together. He had gone to help his older brother, the tailor, repaper his shōji at the end of the year and then took to his bed soon afterward. The fever had advanced from his lungs to his heart and the three attending physicians had drawn more than a pint of fluid from around his heart. The bachelor of science stood talking about this while the botanist Kusakabe told of how the student, whom he had known since childhood, had begun taking care of his invalid mother when he was only about ten years old, cooking breakfast in the mornings and even arranging her hair before going off to grade school. Even during his illness he had had his own bedding put out where he could keep an eye on his mother.

The funeral was at the student's home. Headmaster Sakurai and his wife attended. Captain Masaki's widow sat in a corner of the room, her head down. The boy's classmates from Komoro Gijuku sat on the veranda or stood under umbrellas in the tiny garden.

That day Takase learned for the first time that the dead student had been a Christian. Headmaster Sakurai presided, standing beside the black-draped coffin. A cross and a bouquet of artificial peonies had been placed on top of it. A hymn was sung by the believers in the gathering. The widow of Captain Masaki had turned to religion and she now stood beside the headmaster's wife, holding a hymnal. The headmaster read the first verse of the fifth chapter of II

Corinthians. As he gave the elegy for the dead student, the mother bowed her head over the Bible in her hands and wept.

Takase and his colleagues followed the casket out to the samurai cemetery through the driving rain. The body was buried in a peaceful stand of pine trees at the top of a small rise. Another hymn was sung at the gravesite. The boy's classmates stood watching the scene from under the pine trees that stood among the grave markers.[15]

One day a lady from the city came calling at the house in Baba'ura. This stylish lady carrying a pastel-colored umbrella was a friend of Oshima's who had come up from Tokyo. Even here in the mountains the snow was all melted by now and a warm spring sun shone on the moss-grown thatched roof and on the racks along the wall where *daikon* were hung out to dry each year.[16]

She found Oshima in a sunlit corner of the front garden, her hair wrapped in a hand towel, completely absorbed in the task of starching some laundered clothes and stretching them out on boards to dry. When her friend first caught sight of her she stood absolutely still, staring as if unable to believe this was really Oshima.

Oshima hurriedly put the stretching board down, took the hand towel off her head, and greeted her friend whom she had not seen for six years.

"Okamoto-san!" her friend exclaimed, nostalgically calling her by her maiden name.

Oshima's friend stayed and talked until it was time to take the next train for Nagano. It had been a Sunday. Takase arrived back home wearing pale yellow drawers, the skirt of his kimono tucked up in his sash, a hand towel dangling at his waist, and a melancholy light in his eyes.

Oshima brought some of her best pickled vegetables from the kitchen to go with the tea she served her husband at the hearthside, laughing as she told him about her friend's visit.

"I must have looked a fright, out stretching the laundry. She had the most astonished expression on her face . . ."

"I guess that shows how we've all turned into country bumpkins," laughed Takase as he looked around him. Illustrated calendars given out by businesses in town hung on the soot-stained walls to please the eyes of the children—this year's, last year's, even one from the year before.

"But you're beginning to use Komoro speech without realizing it. When I listen to you talking with other people it's all *yō gowasu* and *meta meta*," said Oshima.

"You're not far behind yourself."

The two laughed without constraint.

"What else did your friend say?"

" 'My husband's away in Europe right now, so tell Takase-san to come down for a visit!' "

"Me? I could understand it if she asked me to come for a visit when her husband's at home but isn't it a little bit odd to invite me for a visit because her husband's away?"

The two laughed again.

Mariko had become just as naughty as the carpenter's daughter.

She ran out to join her playmates, tossing her head and shouting, "Damn you! I'll get you!" in a voice like the north wind howling through the leaves of an oak.

Notes

"Bifū" (1912); *Tōson Zenshū* 5:241–280.

1. See *Chikuma River Sketchbooks,* note 40.

2. Note that the map puts these two houses on opposite sides of the street.

3. The traditional desk for reading or writing, shaped something like an oversize wooden footstool, was intended for use while kneeling on the floor. Its presence speaks of ways of using the space in a room and of a way of life that are completely different from those implied by the European-style desk and bookshelves in the headmaster's office at school which appear a little later.

4. Tōson, who was born in the mountains of western Shinano, is in a sense once again inhaling his native air in this still strange and new place.

5. English word used in the original text; see note 3 above.

6. See *Chikuma River Sketchbooks,* note 24. Its spacious side chambers and loft were briefly used by the Komoro Gijuku in 1884, the first floor serving as a dormitory, the headmaster living on the second floor, and the third floor being used as a classroom.

7. See *Chikuma River Sketchbooks,* note 19.

8. His kimono had tubular sleeves like those of European garments rather than the deep, flowing sleeves with pocketlike lower corners normal in elegant Japanese wear.

9. Koyasu uses the English-based neologism *chiamunesu,* improvised out of "charm" plus "-ness."

10. This description seems inconsistent with the usual sense of *kitsunebi,* which is the same as that of "fox fire," its literal English equivalent.

11. The old-fashioned Japanese pipe consisted of a wooden or bamboo tube with a metal mouthpiece on one end and on the other a tiny metal bowl holding only enough finely shredded tobacco for a few puffs. The tobacco, lit with a coal from the brazier, would be smoked, the ashes tapped out, and the pipe refilled and relit from the remaining coals of the previous pipeful in a rhythmic and comforting ritual.

12. Tōson seems to have acquired his interest in French language and culture in the early 1890s while studying Chinese with Kurimoto Jō'un, a former shogunal commissioner of foreign affairs and special envoy to France. His knowledge of French advanced under the tutelage of Father Jacquet in Sendai; see "At the Foot of Mt. Asama II," p. 137. Perhaps Samejima Shin, the model for Hirooka, was also an effective teacher, but there is little evidence one way or the other.

13. See "Afterword to *Chikuma River Sketchbooks*," note 15.

14. See *Chikuma River Sketchbooks,* note 50.

15. See Sketchbook XII, "The Death of a Student."

16. The *daikon* is a giant white radish that may be eaten raw, dried, pickled, or cooked.

An Impoverished
Bachelor of Science

One of the members of the Asama Society[1] visited me just last month and talked about Saitō-sensei.

Since his death there had been no occasion for an exchange of visits and I had been virtually out of touch with Sensei's household. Although I wondered how his wife and family had been getting along, I had never called. It appeared to be the same with the other members of the Asama Society; I got no news about Sensei's survivors from them.

I had encountered Sensei's widow just once, on a streetcar bound for Edogawa. She was with her daughter Oiku. I did not even make the conventional inquiries about where they were bound, but they had the air about them of people out on some business occasioned by Sensei's death. It was, after all, just the seventh day after his death. We were standing next to the door of the streetcar and it was crowded. I couldn't really hear what she was saying to me nor was I successful in making myself clear to her. I simply gazed at her face and tried to remember how many years it had been since I last saw her. And Oiku, whom I had not seen for even longer, had grown into a person on whom an adult hairstyle looked appropriate. I recalled hearing from Sensei that she had gotten married to someone in Osaka. She had apparently come up from Osaka for the funeral and was staying on for a few days afterward. I could discern in her mother's face the knowledge that they could only hope to get together on such unhappy occasions. In the meantime a pair of seats became empty on the streetcar and the two sat down side by side. I continued to stand but I could see in the widow's glances toward me that she was recalling old times. She was wiping away her tears with the sleeve of her underrobe.

That was the last time I encountered anyone from Sensei's family. Even though the news of Sensei's death had reached me at my house in Koishikawa my intestinal problem had acted up again on the very day of his funeral, making it impossible for me to attend. I sent someone in my place but he came back reporting that he had arrived just after the coffin had been borne away and had only been able to burn a stick of incense at the house. Later inquiries among the members of the Asama Society suggested that most of his former students had also failed to attend the funeral. It was Yakata who behaved most admirably; I heard that he was the only former student of Sensei's to see him off. So in the end I did not even make my farewells to Sensei. Nor did I gaze upon his dead face. I don't even know if the body was taken straight to the cemetery for burial or if it was cremated instead.

Even though he was in no way connected with Sensei, I was reminded of what a friend had said about the funeral of a person named Shōda:[2] that there had never been a funeral as dismal and poorly attended as Shōda's. Sensei and Shōda differed in the conditions of their final years and so their deaths were different, but they resembled each other in the feelings that were left in those who saw them off.

No one had expected Sensei to die so suddenly. In fact the members of the Asama Society had even gotten together to discuss the possibility that Sensei might have to be hospitalized some day, agreeing that we would all go to see him and help out in any way possible. It had only been a few days since Sensei had dropped by my place on his way back from picking up some medicine at the hospital, and he had sat before me drinking the hot tea I set out for him.

I don't remember exactly when it was that Shiina and Tsuchiya from the Asama Society called on me. Shiina was teaching at the Marine Products Institute and also seemed to be doing something at the Botanical Gardens. Tsuchiya appeared to be in good enough health but he still seemed to be a drifter, living out the hardships of the artist in training. When Sensei taught physics and chemistry, and I English, Shiina and Tsuchiya had been children in short pants. It was a shock to see them again at their present ages.

"When I was teaching you two, I was younger than you are right now," I said.

Tsuchiya, trying to recall those times, said, "Were you really that young?" He turned toward Shiina, saying, "It's really impossible to imagine him younger than we are now, isn't it?"

"I can't imagine it either. It seems to me that the people who were teaching us then haven't changed a bit since," Shiina replied with a laugh.

When I think of it now, I was so very young when I went off to be a country teacher. I did not yet know that such a person as Sensei existed, or even Captain Masaki. It was only because I had studied English and become indebted in many ways to Headmaster Sakurai during my youth that I accepted his invitation to come and help out at the school for three years. I had set out for the provinces with high hopes at the time.

Awaiting me on the lower slopes of Mt. Asama was the modest building of the Asama Gijuku. It must have been in the second-story room that then doubled as the manager's office and the faculty room that I met Sensei for the first time, and it must have been Headmaster Sakurai who introduced us.

Headmaster Sakurai had later explained to me that "Saitō has a school of mathematics in Ueda, but it hasn't been going at all well. We felt sorry for him and asked him to give us a hand here. And besides we need to have someone with the proper credentials in order to be accredited as a middle school."

It was only then that I realized Sensei was commuting by train from Ueda and that I understood how important your credentials as a bachelor of science were.[3] That was why when the headmaster held a dinner for those in the town connected with the school he introduced me as a teacher newly arrived from Tokyo, but before he did that he got up and went around to pour sake for all the influential local people.

"The character of the school is still not clearly defined. This is no easy spot I've put myself into," I thought.

But from the very moment I took my seat in the Naoetsu train in Tokyo there was something in the speech and dress of the other passengers that gave me a strong sense of being on the Shin'etsu line.[4] I felt that I was leaving home. And, once I had climbed to the second-floor window of the school and looked out toward the distant Tateshina range and the highlands of Minami Saku, I felt that I had at last arrived at a place in the country where I could carry on my studies in peace and quiet. The thatched roofs of a section of the samurai quarter were also visible from that window and the boughs of the scattered willows were faintly touched with green; the late-arriving spring was at last putting in an appearance. Even though the school was small I found it pleasant to be working with my new colleagues. It was intriguing that a person like Headmaster Sakurai should have hidden himself away in Komoro to spend the rest of his life in teaching. I also found it interesting that such a self-assertive man as he should also have a side to him that would find satisfaction in planting flowers near the mineral spring in Nakadana in preparation for a quiet old age. It was interesting, too, that a soldier like Captain Masaki should have retired to his old home district to devote himself to tilling the soil and reading and that he should have been willing to assist Headmaster Sakurai in the post of business manager.

In those days I hadn't yet become well acquainted with Sensei, but one day when I was talking about him with Headmaster Sakurai and Captain Masaki I said, "Saitō-sensei certainly pays little attention to his appearance."

"It's not that he doesn't pay attention; it's that he is incapable of paying attention," Captain Masaki responded with a laugh.

Sensei would come over from Ueda dressed in the most extraordinary way. Utterly nonchalant, he would appear in an old suit, trousers held up by a long Japanese sash dangling down below his vest, and wearing low shoes of ragged canvas. If it happened that no blackboard eraser was handy while he was teaching mathematics, he would do the job with the sleeve of his jacket and, upon returning to the faculty room, would take out his pipe and tobacco completely oblivious to the chalk dust covering his hands and clothing and even his face. Observing him, I found I could not agree with Captain Masaki that he was incapable of paying attention to his appearance. It seemed to me rather a measure of the indifference into which he had fallen. It was impossible to think that he had always been so indifferent. The things that told of Sensei's past—the sparkling French phrases scattered here and there in his conversation, the engraved gingko-leaf pattern on the silver portions of his old-fashioned pipe—were inconsistent with his present situation.

One day Sensei held out his left hand, showing me the ring finger that was partially missing.

"How about that finger?" he said. "You didn't notice it, did you? There's a history behind it." He went on to explain that it was his memento from baseball, showing me how he had failed to handle a hard-driven ball properly. Even that finger seemed to me to speak of his silent past. Of course no one up in those mountains really under-stood Sensei.

It was about a year later when Sensei moved his family over from Ueda.

"I'm here to become Komoro soil."

At the time, the new addition to the school was being built and Koyasu had come up from Tokyo to join the faculty. The school was only just beginning to establish itself. Headmaster Sakurai taught everything from ethics to history and geography, and the business manager Masaki taught classical Chinese and calligraphy. Upon Koyasu's arrival the responsibility for history and geography was transferred to him, but I seem to recall that he adamantly insisted that English was not his field. Sensei covered all the mathematical subjects and physics and chemistry as well. He worked very hard, but everyone was in good spirits then. It was the kind of time when Captain Masaki would come to school dressed in a skimpily cut, narrow-sleeved kimono and jacket[5] and the students all wore straw sandals—not just those from the town but also those from Kawabe, Kashiwagi, and Chiisagata—from four or five miles around. Some-how the family feeling in the school made us forget the shortage of teachers, the inadequacy of the facilities, and everything else. We would stay in the faculty room until the bell marking the end of classes and then I would walk down toward Nakadana with Sensei and Koyasu.

It was quite often that I walked with Sensei along the path leading from Headmaster Sakurai's neighborhood in the samurai quarter through that old part of town with its high garden walls and down the steep cliff toward Nakadana. Headmaster Sakurai would already have preceded us as far as the small villa that he had built in Naka-dana and he would come out the door to join us, carrying his dingy yellowish hand towel. Sometimes, just when we were reaching the bathhouse, we would catch sight of Captain Masaki, accompanied by his wife and children, coming down from above to join us, all wreathed in smiles.

As we soaked ourselves in the sulfurous waters and listened to the roar of the Chikuma River out beyond the apple orchard in front of the bathhouse, we seemed like one big family. It was at such times that Sensei would speak of his family back in Echigo. Then, having been invited by Headmaster Sakurai to stop by the villa for some tea, we would make our way back up along the steep path through the swale planted with azaleas to that room whose splendid view added such zest to our conversations.

"I grew a lot of morning glories in Ueda. I'm giving them a try here too. I don't know how well they're going to do this year, but why don't you come by and see in a little while? I've heard there are people who grow morning glories in Komoro too—people who really fancy them. But I still don't know this place very well . . ."

It would have been on the way back from the bathhouse that Sensei said this, getting at last to his favorite subject of morning glories.

During the following two years things gradually changed around the brazier in the faculty room.

"Is Masaki trying to take over the school?"

When I heard those words coming from Headmaster Sakurai's lips it seemed to me that I was at last witnessing what was obviously bound to happen between the two of them sooner or later.

Sensei never knew about this but I had already encountered it when I first arrived in Komoro. That was when Headmaster Sakurai had hinted to me about leaving Komoro and moving to Minami Saku. I had only just accepted the job from him and moved out from Tokyo and his words came as no small surprise. Further inquiries revealed that Sakurai, the headmaster of the school, was receiving a smaller salary than I, who had just come. It seemed to me that things just couldn't go on that way. I suggested that if Headmaster Sakurai's inclination to desert, against his true feelings, the school he had established after such effort—this child of his, to which he had literally given birth—if this was due solely to his difficulty in making ends meet, then I would intercede with Captain Masaki for him.

"I would not want the people of the town to think that I had inveigled you into that," was Headmaster Sakurai's prompt response, but I set it down to a simple reluctance to impose the duty on me and I went straight to Captain Masaki.

That was the first time I ever set foot in his study with its stacks of Chinese books and rubbings of samples of calligraphy. Captain Masaki looked me in the face for a time. The most extraordinary expression of despair passed over his face and then he replied that if that was the case we should consult with the people of the town about more suitable compensation for the headmaster's labors. The implication was that there was a deliberate intent to give better pay to those teachers invited in from outside and for him and the headmaster to accept lesser compensation. A passionate determination to work together with the headmaster in educating the youth of the region was reflected in his words. There was also a hint that simply having to listen to such talk was damaging to the collegiality of the school. That was when I came to understand the economic condition of the school and just what low salaries those two men were accepting. Yet I simply couldn't stand by when Headmaster Sakurai was feeling so discontented. Captain Masaki could draw on his pension as a retired army officer, but the headmaster had nothing to fall back on. Captain Masaki seemed to appreciate this and he undertook to pursue the matter. I succeeded in keeping Headmaster Sakurai with the school but I have come to realize that the seeds for what happened later had already been planted at that time.

The headmaster had come to Komoro from elsewhere, just as Sensei, Koyasu, and I had. Captain Masaki, on the other hand, was a local person of samurai background with deep attachments in Komoro. I believe that this fact alone created difficulties for the headmaster. In addition to the work which the headmaster alone had carried out for the school, it was also assisted by grants from the town of Komoro and from Saku county and this meant that the local people watched it very closely. What's more, at that time the town offices in Komoro were still filled with a group from the old samurai class and the people behind them had very grand ideas.

Whenever I went out through the gate of the school and set out toward the Kaikoen, passing alongside the stone walls of the mulberry fields, I would invariably meet people who lived in the samurai quarter, which was in that area. Sometimes I would meet the physician, returning on horseback from his rounds. He was another of the old samurai who had stayed in Komoro. Watching him ride away, Sensei said one day:

"That doctor will try raising anything—chickens, herbs, birds, morning glories—and when chrysanthemums are in season, he tries chrysanthemums. You'll always find a doctor like him in a country town. He's quite opinionated too. 'Those other guys,' he'll say, 'they're no doctors! They're just a bunch of medicine peddlers!' But he's a good sort. He'll go way out to farms in nearby villages and if they have no money to pay him, he'll say that any produce they might have on hand will do. 'Just give me a few leeks when they're ready,' he'll say. The farmers think highly of him."

We often had such conversations. But I had to wonder how people like this physician, who lived right next to the school although he had no direct connection with it, viewed Headmaster Sakurai. Did they see him as an outsider, almost as a person from another country?

And how slowly Sensei walked! "They say that fellow who lives beside the gate to the Kaikoen was a foot soldier in the old days." I recall talking about that at some time or other.

The stone memorial in front of the Kaikoen, the slender stream, the vacant land overgrown with railroad weed—all of this lay beside our path. Whenever I stood in that place still redolent with ancient history and looked back across the railroad line to the forest around the Kashima Shrine, and beyond to the flourishing town, it seemed beyond question that I was seeing the very footprints of "time." Our archery range was located where we could look up through the great zelkova trees at the stone foundations on which the main keep had once stood. The place was dominated by the sense of ruin that emanated from the old castle and by the quiet of the pine forests, in which we could hear the sound of mattocks hilling up the plants in the mulberry field behind the archery range. The backyard of Captain Masaki's home lay just across a heavily forested swale. Everyone from Headmaster Sakurai, Masaki, and Koyasu to Tsukui the physical education instructor would gather there. Tsukui, a local man and a former sergeant, was the type who would often preface his remarks with the statement "When I was in the army . . ." As I stood observing them there at the archery range, Headmaster Sakurai and Masaki struck me as a pair of distinguished seniors against whom I could never hope to measure up. Masaki could not stand to be beaten at anything and his inept but intense character showed even in his archery practice.

"This is awful! And the target is fifteen inches! I've got to get myself together!"

As Masaki fitted his next arrow to the bowstring, it was Tsukui who mocked him with a loud "TWANG!"

"That just won't do!"

Masaki gave a nervous laugh; he could not permit himself to be amused even by something this trivial.

Unable to stand the thought of being outdone, Masaki pulled an even stronger bow than Headmaster Sakurai. Saitō-sensei always pulled the weakest bow but he was very consistent. Whenever I was ready to leave the archery range it was always Sensei who walked homeward with me, since we lived in the same district.

". . . my boy Jirō is getting to be pretty good at children's sumō. Just the other day he came back with a bowstring he had won. They really give out strange names in sumō. I asked him what his was and he said 'Oka no shika,' the stag of the hill!"

Sensei put out his tongue playfully; he always talked to me without the slightest restraint.

"The older brother has a sumō name too, so I asked him what it was and he replied that since his father is fond of archery he is called 'Ya-atari,' arrow strike or bull's-eye, so that he might win often. Children are really funny."

Talking in this vein, we reached the castle gate where the bachelor of science met an archery acquaintance of his, a former samurai, now on his way back from the Chikuma River. He was carrying a fishing net.

"I've given up the bow," he announced. Then, in a manner befitting a member of the old local samurai, he added, "They say we samurai are all finished. About the only one of us in Komoro with any guts left is Masaki from the school."

Casting net in hand, he stood there talking with us.

"Just look. Everything around the castle is going downhill. Until two or three years ago I could get fish whenever I went down to the river. People say they were already gone but they were still there two or three years ago. Now there aren't any fish at all. . . . And those pine forests—they've all passed into other people's hands."

I still can't forget what these companions in archery said to each other and their expressions as they spoke. Sensei, a former retainer of a domain in Echigo, had taken part in the wars of the Restoration, seeing his first action around Nagaoka at the age of nineteen. How would he have seen those ivy-grown walls of Komoro castle? Surely he must have realized that people burning with the fiercest partisan sentiments had dwelled at the foot of this volcano, and that the mulberry fields around our school, Headmaster Sakurai's house, and those other places where only crumbling gates and walls and foundation stones remained were the former dwellings of those people. I've heard it said that the reason so few of the promising people of the old

domains managed to live through the changes was that they
destroyed each other during the Restoration.

Sensei, when I think about the Asama Gijuku now, it seems like
the recollection of a dream. Just when was it that Headmaster Sakurai's wife started the girls' school, which they called the Jishūsha?[6] It
was only right that in addition to the Gijuku itself, which taught the
boys of the region, there should be a school to teach the girls as well.
You certainly were in agreement with that, Sensei. The headmaster's wife was a very capable woman and she had the firm backing of
some influential local people who happened to have daughters: the
owner of the vinegar shop, the owner of the Kadoya,[7] and the
banker Yamada. You, Sensei, and Koyasu and I—indeed, each of
the teachers at the Gijuku with the exception of Masaki and Tsukui
—gave a bit of our time to help,[8] but whenever the subject of the
girls' school came up, displeasure would show on Masaki's face.
Headmaster Sakurai, being the gentle and accommodating kind of
person he was, must also have seen that he could not simply exclude
his wife. At any rate, whenever the fact that the students at the girls'
school did better than those at the boys' school came up in the conversations around the brazier in the faculty room, Masaki would put
his hand to his forehead and give out a forced laugh. Occasionally,
when only Masaki and I were in the faculty room, I would see him
get up in his baggy black trousers, march over to the window in
grave and serious military style, and gaze out over the roof of Headmaster Sakurai's house, where the classroom for the girls' school had
been set up. Looking toward the branches of the plum tree, he would
mutter to himself.

"I'm going to keep the school going no matter what."

Just how tenacious and stubborn Masaki was could be seen in his
efforts to master a style of calligraphy that was totally lacking in any
pleasing or interesting qualities. Yet the degree to which he suffered
in his unceasing struggle to win out over others showed only around
the edges of his conversation.

"Just try on these glasses, Masaki," Headmaster Sakurai would
say and Masaki would laugh.

"I don't need reading glasses yet," he would reply. He was the
kind of person for whom it was impossible not to say something like
that. But then when he actually tried the glasses on, his tone would
change. "Say! This is amazing! You can see even better at a little

distance than you can close up. How about it, Saitō-sensei?'' he would say, passing the glasses on to him.

''Yes, I really can see better!''

''You're *really* bad off!''

Even when he did not go that far, Masaki was nevertheless unable to defer to his elders among the faculty. A silent struggle between Headmaster Sakurai and Masaki gradually began to manifest itself. Back when the headmaster was constantly saying ''Masaki, Masaki,'' he had placed full trust in him, tears even coming to his eyes when he told me, ''When I was developing that mineral spring in Nakadana, Masaki came down, shovel on his shoulder, dressed just like a farmer.'' Now there was no more ''Masaki'' coming from the headmaster's lips, and Masaki himself no longer indulged in the hearty laugh that had formerly been so much a part of him. Sometimes he would tell the headmaster that he was ''like a full-fledged king.'' It pained even me to hear this.

As you know very well, Sensei, the headmaster was a very articulate speaker. The sparks seemed to fly when he got into his subject. I don't think Masaki was any match for him. The headmaster also possessed an exceptionally imposing physique. I would sometimes find myself utterly entranced by the ineffable elegance of his manly presence. I believe that Masaki looked on him with a mixture of envy and infatuation. And then, while the headmaster's wife was very competent, Masaki's wife was competent too. I sensed that something was coming out of their most profound depths, augmenting the silence between them. Whatever its sources, the silence was difficult to bear.

I believe it was around the time when the new classroom building was finished that we moved from the room serving both the faculty and the business manager up to that second-floor corner room that had such a fine view. Yakata must have already started coming over from Nezu to teach art. It must also have been around then that the highly respected Kusakabe was added to our staff to teach botany. There was a huge brazier in the faculty room and the teakettle on it was always boiling. Masaki would sometimes come over to it to roll a cigarette filled with his fragrant imported tobacco, but he no longer joined in the conversations as he used to. He was spending all his time in his office, practicing calligraphy when he had nothing else to do. The headmaster would make an appearance only when he had some business to conduct, and on those occasions he would drink the tea that the janitor poured for him and then go back to his own room. As soon as his classes were over he would don his mendicant-style headgear and walk around the back of the school on his way home or to his villa in Nakadana. When things had reached this pass between the two, the rest of us also gradually lapsed into silence. Koyasu virtually stopped talking altogether, growing even more silent once he had married the daughter of a local physician and established a new home of his own. As for Kusakabe, he was quiet by nature.

I often escaped from the silence by joining the students. Also, since I had regarded trees as friends ever since childhood, I was able to draw strength just from going to see the young cherry trees planted along the walls and on the top of the embankment around the school. By the time the three years of my initial commitment had slipped by, these cherry trees could no longer be called young; they had in fact grown to an almost oppressive size, with some of the branches hanging down within easy reach. The students would sit on the stones in their shade. Others would play at sumō, while still others would be running and playing at nothing in particular, shouting in their somehow innocent voices. Shiina and Tsuchiya are now members of the Asama Society, but they still had rosy, childish cheeks in those days and they would often come to me for a friendly, companionable talk between teacher and student.

It was around that time that Sensei came to be a source of strength to me and I came to be on close terms with him. Thinking one day that I would like to observe Sensei teaching his students, I went over to his classroom. He was at the point of ending his class, but as I watched from the door he was still standing in front of his desk explaining something to the students. On the desk were a bottle of hydrochloric acid, some marble chips, a drinking glass with a glass cover, glass tubing, and various other objects. There was also a lighted candle. He picked up the glass and tilted it a bit, releasing carbon dioxide from under the cover. The candle went out just as if he had poured water over it.

The students were gathered wide-eyed around his desk, some smiling, some standing with arms folded, some with their chins cupped in their hands. When they were told that a mouse or a bird would die if placed in the glass, one student immediately piped up.

"Wouldn't a bug do, sir?"

"No, bugs don't have quite the same need for oxygen as birds and mammals."

The student who asked the question, apparently wishing to resolve his doubts, abruptly left the classroom only to reappear beside the peach tree outside the window. One of the other students looked out and exclaimed,"Oh! He's going to get a bug!" The boy in the garden searched under the cherry trees, picked something up, and came back. He handed it to the teacher.

"A bee?" said the teacher, with some alarm.

"He's gonna sting you! He's gonna sting you!"

The excited students chattered on as the teacher bent himself backward as far out of danger as possible. As the bee went into the drinking glass the students laughed nervously.

"It's dying! It's dying!" one of them cried, while another observed that it must be a weakling. As if to prove his point, the bee buzzed around inside the drinking glass, writhed a bit, and died.

"Well, I guess he's a goner all right."

Saitō-sensei, a bachelor of science, habitually went about looking just like a local farmer. Since it was obvious from the expression on his face that he couldn't have cared less about his appearance, I couldn't help but laugh at the sight of him.

But while laughing I also felt a deep despair, realizing that here was a declassé scholar come to this mountaintop where there was no one for him to talk to.

I think Sensei and I grew close because there were so many things that brought us together. First of all, we lived near each other. Sensei lived behind a grade school near Aramachi and I was in Baba'ura, close to Honmachi. Leaving Baba'ura, my route cut across the main street in Aioichō into a path with mulberry fields and stone walls on either side, crossed over a small bridge, and went past the place where a girl with reddish hair often stood watching beside the road; then it continued through a poor street below a warehouse before climbing up to the railroad crossing. Sensei would come shuffling along, dragging his stick, and meet up with me somewhere around there. The two of us would then walk the rest of the way to school together. Also, since we were both fond of travel we would always go together on the school outings.

Once we walked with the students all the way from Komoro to

Shimonita, a distance of some forty-five miles, in one day. I'm certain that in my whole life I had never walked like that before. When we crossed over Uchiyama Pass and began our descent into Jōshū, we saw wisteria blossoms hanging from the eaves of every house. It was amazing that such an elegant custom should be followed in such a rustic place.[9] Darkness fell at the Kanra River and it was nine o'clock in the evening before we reached our lodgings in Shimonita. I had injured my leg when crossing the mountains and by the time we reached the banks of the Kanra River I was so tired I wanted to sit down in the middle of the road under the starlight. I think that trip brought us even closer together.

Sensei had already become very fond of country things when I first met him, and I too was fond of the farmers. It wasn't just the farmers either—I enjoyed calling at the homes of people around Komoro who lived at or below the average level. That was where Headmaster Sakurai and I differed. He associated only with people of some local distinction while I would visit the homes of the tailor in Baba'ura and the dyer in Ōte-machi. I even got a warning once from Mrs. Sakurai when they thought I was getting too familiar with the tailor's family.

But it was people like the couple who ran the candy shop called the Kansendō that I wanted to know. There was another shop lady who was famous in the town for her slovenly ways; her place was known as the "Lousy Tōfu Shop."[10] When her son began to go out to make deliveries he would regularly stop in front of my house, put down his load, and make a fine noise cutting up the tōfu for "eight-cup" or anything else we might want.[11] I became extremely fond of that "Lousy Tōfu Shop" and I would go over to the family shop with its "penny lunch" sign, warm myself around the fire with the local teamsters and laborers, and enjoy listening to their mountain talk. Sensei and I shared this taste for earthy things.

Yakata, who was coming over from Nezu once or twice a week to teach art, would invariably drop by my place for a long talk on his way home afterward, saying that he couldn't simply stay shut up in his mountain village studio. Sensei, Yakata, and I—the three of us got together often. Yakata and I would playfully call Sensei "the déclassé bachelor of science" in such a context of intimacy that it did not seem in the least rude. Sensei—that Sensei who had said, "I am here to become Komoro soil"—must have found allies in us in spite of the differences in our ages.

Even now I have the feeling that I can say anything to Sensei. There was one reason and one reason alone that I allied myself with him. He was old and he was poor. I have already mentioned Shōda. It was after Shōda died that I found myself frequently unburdening myself before him. Shōda seemed to me to have become far more confiding after his death than he had been when still in good health. Just what would happen if he should return living to this world? There's no doubt that I would not be able to speak with him face-to-face as I've been speaking with him since his death. It some-times seemed to me that this was because he was such a very sarcas-tic person: I wouldn't have wanted any more of his wit that could enslave others, make sport of them, and eat its way right into their core.

I feel the same way about Sensei. If he were restored to health again, I would not be able to talk to him like this. Face-to-face I wouldn't be able to say to him that he was poor because he drank. When he still commuted by train from Ueda to the school, it was the Momonjiya in front of the station where he would take his ease. And at the worst times, it was said that he had been seen drunk and fallen in the snow beside the main street in Aioichō. But I would not be able to talk with him about such things face-to-face. Sensei always had his own sad stories to tell. He may have heard very little of what I said to him.

And so it is that I find it so satisfying to speak without restraint to the departed Sensei. Just when was it that I drank with Sensei in that shop in front of the station?

"Won't you stay and talk with me a little while? This is a pleasant place. And the lady who runs it is very understanding. Every time I pass by I end up like this," he said with a laugh.

But before that we had sat with the other passengers waiting for the train in the front of the shop. Advertisements for special noodles, banners for beef and horsemeat, placards for pilgrimages to Zenkōji —there was no way to sort out all of the things that were crammed together in that earthen floored storefront. A railroad schedule hung on the wall among the advertisements for beer and sake. Smoke from the cookfire also came drifting through. Sensei made his way through the confusion to the woman who ran the shop and asked, "Anything special today?"

"There's too much traffic out here. Please come inside," said her husband. We were conducted to an inner room that had recently been constructed. The local farmers tieing up their horses outside, the travelers passing through, the tradesmen carrying their wares, the men dressed in formal coats marked with family crests but wearing straw sandals on their feet—everything we saw marked this as a provincial station.

"We've been able to make the place a bit larger than when you were commuting from Ueda, Saitō-sensei," the wife said as she worked.

I had drunk once before, with Kusakabe, in that place in front of the station. I was amazed that day by Kusakabe's ability to hold his sake.

"I usually don't drink very much but I've become a bit more practiced since coming to Komoro."

"I'm sure you have," replied Sensei. "The people around here are good drinkers. I suppose it's because this is cold-weather country. Who's the best drinker at school? Masaki's certainly good."

Once he'd had a bit to drink, Sensei began to talk about himself. It was the nature of what he said that drew me into his talk.

"Well now, Takase, it's about my son, the one who's just applied for entrance at the school. He's not like his little brother; he's a good boy. He's always liked drawing, ever since he was in grade school, and he's always received top grades. When I asked him what he wanted to be when he grew up, he said that when he got big he wanted to be like Yakata-sensei. . . . Do you think he has any future at that?

"It's a strange thing. My wife is still much fonder of the younger one. She'll do anything he says. If I object we invariably have a quarrel. She says I always take Tarō's part and that is because I don't see through him; that's why nobody pays any attention to me any more. That's what she says. . . . But the older boy's weaker and I try to protect the weak one . . ."

I began to think that was all he was going to say about the matter. But he went on, pouring himself drink after drink, seeming to relish each sip. He mopped his face with his hand towel.

"But why do I get so concerned about him? You've got a couple of children of your own, haven't you? It's hard, bringing children up. It's still not too bad when you've just got two, but look at us—we've got them swarming all over. And what's more, every one of them is a big eater. But really—to tell your children not to eat so much; to make do with three bowls of rice . . . A parent just can't say such a thing!

"Now after Isamu we've got a girl. She was born in Ueda. She doesn't listen to a thing we say. It must be because she was born at such a difficult time. . . . We really haven't been able to give her the proper attention—there just hasn't been time to consider the children. But come to think of it, my wife has really done wonders. She bears up under hardship much better than I do."

Recalling his wife's strength in the face of adversity brought all kinds of thoughts to his mind. But the mere scent of sake had the power to make Sensei forget all his troubles.

None of us knew much about his past. As I watched Sensei's face that day I was astonished once again that such a person should have buried himself in this place and I wondered how, even if he had buried himself, he could have fallen so far. If I had asked him about this, surely he would have just laughed at me. He had first relied on the owner of a dye shop on the edge of the town of Ueda through whose good offices he was able to rent an old temple[12] or something of the sort and set up a small school of mathematics; I'm sure he would have said no more than that.

On another occasion the flush on Sensei's face went beyond a sunset glow to turn an alarming shade of purple, making me wonder if alcohol poisoning might have been the cause. Was Sensei poor because he drank or did he drink because he was poor? In the end I found myself unable to make the distinction.

"We would like at the very least to build houses for Headmaster Sakurai and Saitō-sensei. They have done so much for the town . . ." Someone in the town said this to me one day. Although they generally kept quiet about it, there were people in Komoro who were concerned about them.

For all his poverty, Sensei once held a drinking party at his place. Invitations had apparently gone out as far as Nezu, since I recall that it was Yakata who came by to invite me and that I went over with him.

"Saitō-sensei is really crazy about morning glories. They say there was a fire in the neighborhood once and he went on talking about his morning glories while watching the fire!"

Yakata laughed as he told me about this on the way over to Sensei's place. Sensei's morning glories were famous in Komoro.

"But when Saitō-sensei is having a drink with his morning glories in front of him he seems to forget all his troubles."

I wondered what kind of people had originally lived in the house next to the grade school that Sensei rented. They seemed to have been very hard on the place. The road to Akasaka passed directly in front. Behind was a sushi restaurant situated on high ground commanding a view of the castle. The slope below its white rear wall was retained by a stone embankment and Sensei's house lay at the foot of that embankment, looking as though it had just fallen there. In front hung a signboard Sensei had brought over from Ueda and in the time he could spare from the school he would give students who came to his house tutoring in mathematics. The house was extremely humid, being right next to the paddy fields. Sensei had transformed his yard with its bamboo and its running water into something like a nurseryman's garden and pots of morning glories were everywhere. Yakata and I went around to the garden first to see all the morning glories.

Sensei's wife stepped out of the kitchen to welcome us.

"He's so crazy about morning glories that he filled the whole garden with those pots as soon as he got to Komoro. The janitor from the school came over and made the benching—such fine benching!"

It seemed to me that I had heard the same thing from her any number of times but today she was not talking to me; she was telling Yakata about it. Yakata immediately took out his sketchpad and pencil. He never went anywhere without them.

"Oh! Please come around this way!" came Sensei's voice, speaking very formally, but Yakata continued to stand in front of a bench of morning glories, intent upon his sketch of the *tenaga,* a variety that one could scarcely believe was a morning glory.

It appeared that Sensei had canceled all his lessons that day for our sake. To welcome us, the alcove of his living room had been decorated with an old hawk-feather arrow and a morning glory in its pot. From that room we could see the plaque hanging in the next room on which Sensei had mounted his diploma from Rika University. The signature was that of a president who had served long ago.

"Hey, Jirō! The teachers from the school are here! Won't you come out and give them a bow?" his wife said as she came in. "Tarō! What are you doing just standing there?" Her hospitable scolding of the children reached as far as Oiku, who was serving tea.

Oiku was still quite childish and she blushed furiously when we spoke to her.

"I've always wanted to invite the teachers from the school over and to have all of you join me in a drink before a well-trained morning glory. . . . That's what I have been planning."

Sensei spoke as though a long-held wish was now being fulfilled. Tsukui arrived. It was only about fifty yards to Sensei's place from the house where Tsukui's father had his blacksmith's shop. It seems to me that a townsman from over toward Yora had also been invited.

Sensei tasted each dish that was brought out to us, scolding his wife in our presence by saying that this one was a bit too salty and that one a bit too sweet. He asked her to bring out his treasured sake cups and when she had washed and set them out before us, he took up each of the cups in turn to wipe it with his hand towel before serving us with sake.

"Well now, this is it! Here is today's biggest treat!" he said, going into the next room and bringing back a trained morning glory plant.

"The round and the peony types have already gone by. The lions and the *tenaga* are always a little later. Just look at this! I grew this lion myself. Now that's a real lion!"

Sensei put the morning glory down beside him and turned to an exchange of sake cups with Tsukui. Since Yakata wasn't much of a drinker either, there was only Tsukui to keep company with Sensei at this. I recall that there was talk about how unfortunate it was that the plants which Sensei most wanted to show us that day were only just beginning to break their big, solid buds, so that Sensei could not share with us his pleasure in their coloring, a red that went far beyond the possibility of artifice.

"This year I've become a disciple of Saitō-sensei and I am beginning to learn about morning glories," said Tsukui.

"That made me happy! So very happy! I've never been so happy in all my life!" Sensei said. "Now let me show you," he went on, bringing out a photograph of his college graduation. Among the nine classmates—who were some of the very first college graduates in Japan—could be seen a youthful portrait of the present head of the Tokyo observatory. There were others among the nine who had not lived up to expectations. Sensei was one of these.

It was at such times that Sensei would drop into French. Among those of us gathered together there, no one other than Sensei knew any French, but he went on like an aged songbird with fond memories of its song.

"The French language has some extraordinarily sophisticated things about it," he remarked, pronouncing for us with the greatest skill a phrase of two or three words. It was then that I began to think of studying French with Sensei.

"You really think you would like to?" Sensei said. "Well then, let's work together at it!" His eyes never sparkled as they did when he was speaking French.

"I'm afraid that speaking French to me is like reciting the Nembutsu in a horse's ear," said Tsukui, humoring the old man as he went on drinking cup after cup of sake.

"This is nothing to be taken lightly. We even have an Italian coffee cup in our house," Sensei said in good humor, and, as if foreign pottery would surely be a treat for his guests, he brought out a treasured old coffee cup and showed it to us. It had apparently been given to him long ago by a foreign lady as a memento of her trip to Italy. Yakata praised the floral designs on the cup and saucer. I must have drunk tea from that coffee cup at some time or other. Sensei was happily shifting from a formal kneeling posture to sitting cross-legged and back again. His face grew faintly flushed and his long eyebrows appeared to be even more heavily flecked with white.

I still remember what his wife said as we were leaving the party.

"I'm so delighted that you could all come over and enjoy a quiet, leisurely time with him. There aren't many happy times in a house like this one. My husband and I are always quarreling over his drinking. I never really intend to be such a scold. There's plenty about me to make him want to drink—really, I'm getting terribly short-tempered as I grow older."

Gazing at me with her large eyes, she spoke in the tones of one who had been brought up in a good family.

"Oiku! What are you doing standing there? Tarō! Aren't you going to say good-bye? You should say, 'I am so pleased that you could come over today.' Honestly, my children have no manners at all," she continued, but then Sensei gave her a look that meant "Don't scold them so!" Drunk as he was, he still took Tarō's part. It seems to me that the children who had been born in Ueda, Oiku and her little brother and sister, were still very young at the time.

I believe it was shortly afterward that Sensei's sixth child, a girl, was born in Komoro. "Just when we thought there would be no more children—not only that, but twins in the bargain!" It was no laughing matter the way Sensei spoke of it. One of the twins died shortly after birth and Sensei named his last daughter Otomi. He had to admit that she was a lovable little girl after all. And wasn't it Otomi, born after he had grown old, that Sensei favored second only to the weakly Tarō?

I remember another incident in connection with Sensei's drinking. It was while I was living in the house in Baba'ura. It was a solitary place even in the daytime and at night the distant, menacing roar of the Chikuma River sounded very close. There under that thatched roof I suddenly heard Sensei's drunken voice. Of course at first I had no idea that it was Sensei. Everyone closed up their doors quite early in that neighborhood and so when the silence beyond the hedge was broken by a voice calling my name, I did not know what was happening.

"Anybody home?"

"Anybody . . . home?"

We sat there trembling at the sound, with no idea what to do. We were all still in good health at the time and so I finally had my wife go and open the garden gate. Sensei and Tsukui came reeling in out of the darkness.

I brought the lamp from the back room out to the entryway where it illuminated the flushed faces of Sensei and his companion, who seemed to have dropped by for the express purpose of giving us a scare. Both were wearing leggings and straw sandals. I had never seen Sensei as drunk as he was that evening. He was so drunk that he couldn't control his movements but he attempted to look us in the face as though there was nothing in the least unusual going on. I'd had a new hearth cut into the floor of the front room. There was a cupboard beside the hearth and just beyond the cupboard was a spacious, wooden floored country kitchen. Sensei seemed to be in great discomfort, so I asked my wife to get him some water. Reassured at last, she brought a glass of water out from the kitchen and offered it to Sensei. He opened his glazed eyes wide in the lamplight, trying to focus on the water in the glass with the same expression as when he had been staring at us. His hands shook terribly as he reached for the glass.

"We are being rude. . . . The two of us went out into the moun-

tains today . . . got drunk." Sensei bowed before us. I somehow
had the feeling that this drunken bow of Sensei's was no ordinary bow.

"I am truly sorry, madam," Sensei said, turning to my wife as he
apologized to her, both hands on the sill of the entry.

Tsukui burst into drunken laughter at the sight. He placed a hand
on Sensei's shoulder as if offering to help him leave, but he was quite
far gone himself. Then he and Sensei went reeling out of our place
on unsteady legs. I took the lamp out into the street and watched
Sensei, supported by Tsukui, take his leave. I was less worried that
night about the dark road ahead of them than about what awaited
Sensei once he got home, where his wife would be waiting up for his
return.

"Sometimes I really feel sorry when I look at the face of my husband," his wife said to me once. "I wonder if he could survive without his beloved sake . . ."

During the five years I worked with Sensei and the others, all
kinds of unexpected things happened at the school. It was in the
spring of the fifth year that Sensei himself fell gravely ill. A frightful
amount of black blood burst forth from his bowels. Everyone who
saw him said that he was beyond help, but he had barely escaped
with his life when Masaki passed away.

It was a great loss to the school when Masaki died, leaving his wife
to bring up their children and his educational enterprise unfinished.
I believe that even Headmaster Sakurai recognized that fact. The
silence between the two of them had grown ever deeper and the
headmaster's attention had seemed to be turning more and more
toward the girls' school. Just before his death, Masaki had once
again taken up going to the Kaikoen to practice archery all alone. I
remember that he had begun to come red-faced to his afternoon
duties. Sometimes when I went into his office on business I would
find him smelling of sake even in the morning. That sort of thing
had never happened earlier on. And yet I believe that, once he was
dead and we had all paid our respects to his remains in the samurai
cemetery and had seen all the books and calligraphy specimens and
fencing gear that he had left to his children sold off at auction, everyone was aware of what a loss the school had suffered.

I wonder which of Masaki's mementoes Sensei bought. As for
myself, I bought a sample of the calligraphy of Huai-su.[13] As I've

said before, I was always on Sensei's side, but Sensei, old and poor, had not the slightest interest in forming his own little cabal in the school. I had been quite close to Headmaster Sakurai during the years when I was passing from childhood into adolescence; I had even lived in his Tokyo house for a time while I was going to school. So strong was that connection that when I came to Komoro and found that some of the things he'd done during his long years as headmaster had invited the criticism of some of the local people, I could not think of him as they did. What he had been to me during my childhood glowed within me like a lamp. To me he was one who had sowed the seed. There are no words to describe the unseen struggles that he had undergone during his ten years of sowing the seed up in those mountains. The benefits of the seeds sown by this aged sower of seed were reflected not only in the youth of the Saku region but also in the peach orchards in Moriyama, in the mineral spring at Nakadana, in the households of many of the local people, and ultimately in the town hall of Komoro itself. The headmaster was not, however, suited to the labors of bringing in the harvest. From that perspective, I realize that by the time of Masaki's death Headmaster Sakurai must already have grown tired of the work at the school.

Sensei, having barely escaped with his life, promised to be careful with his drinking and began putting his morning glories, which had been left to his wife for a whole summer, back in order. I believe it was around the time for gathering the seeds when he began to come over to my place to speak of his concerns about the school. Whenever Sensei, a bachelor of science who no longer had the heart to carry his investigations to their logical conclusion, would waylay me and try to win me over, I would find myself growing uneasy. His endless complaints depressed me. He gave himself the name of "The Indomitable" and he took up as his creed the ideal of never losing control. But yet, every time he had some little idea, he would come over to my place and show it to me. Once it was a chart to teach geometry through a system of patterns and I believe he had the idea that if some publisher put this out it might help him with his living expenses, but only a glance at his plan was enough to convince me of its hopelessness. Sensei laughed as he told me about a famous European mathematician, a man who was able to make great discoveries but who could not keep his own personal account book in order. He returned home, leaving behind him as always the miasma of the almost unbearable misery of his poverty.

At school, Sensei was inevitably drawn into the conflicts that arose after the death of Masaki. Although it wasn't generally known, Headmaster Sakurai intended, as part of his plan to reorganize the school, to keep Kusakabe and me and discharge Sensei and Koyasu. It was I who took Sensei's part at that time in full awareness that it might cause the headmaster to doubt my good faith.

Sensei seemed to have been particularly concerned about the speech the headmaster had given in the grade school auditorium, which he saw as a disaster. That Headmaster Sakurai was a fighter was clear from the mere fact that he went to the auditorium to attack the ineffectuality of the local physicians. I did not hear this speech myself and so I had no idea if the physicians' outrage was justified or even if the attack had been made in manly fashion. It was my opinion that we should just forget about it. After all, if the physicians possessed some weakness that had called for the headmaster's attack, then it could not be helped that they were attacked. But Sensei's concern for the welfare of the school would not permit him to observe all this in silence. He asked the chief of police to mediate in the interests of peace in the town. Sensei and the chief of police appeared to have expended a great deal of energy over the affair. Headmaster Sakurai became angry in his own right and whenever I called on him at his villa in Nakadana he spoke of the matter as though it had been some juvenile escapade.

One day I received a totally unexpected letter from the chief of police requesting my presence at a nearby restaurant in Baba'ura. I immediately understood what it was about, but felt that if Headmaster Sakurai had really gone too far in what he had said, then he was the one who should be asked to make a retraction. I had no intention of making a bow of apology in his place. For one thing, I had no idea of what it was that I was being asked to take back. Yet I couldn't help being aware of the efforts that the chief of police had made on behalf of both parties and so I set off reluctantly for the restaurant. Almost every one of the physicians with whom I was acquainted were assembled there on the second floor. Among them I saw the physician who lived in front of the headmaster's house in the samurai quarter. The chief of police suddenly turned toward the corner of the room where the physicians, all dressed in their best formal attire, were muttering among themselves. He made a deep bow. Once he had done that there was no way I could avoid bowing myself regardless of my wishes.[14] I was left with a feeling of the utmost distaste for some of the duties of a country teacher.

I had come with a commitment to stay for three years but I ended up spending seven years in those mountains. Although I was concerned about what might happen to Sensei when I was gone, I had reached that time of life when I wanted to get a piece of work done and, unlike Sensei, I had not come with the intention of becoming Komoro soil.

"You're leaving too?"

As I gazed into Sensei's aged face and saw how his strength seemed to be failing, I felt that I simply couldn't go away and leave the school. Yet at the same time I felt that this was not a time when I could allow myself to be completely absorbed by what was going on around me.

When it became known among the townsmen that my intention to leave Komoro was serious, all kinds of people came by to try to dissuade me. Perhaps I had already stayed too long; when it came time actually to resign, it seemed to me that my life had taken root in those mountains. The master of the vinegar shop, who also operated a silk mill and was a member of the town council and whose children attended the school, called upon me any number of times, doing his best to get me to change my mind. He felt that Headmaster Sakurai was making no effort to keep me and was simply standing by in silence. His indignation was so fierce that he seemed on the verge of a breach with the headmaster. He did everything short of clinging to my sleeve to keep me there.

"If people keep trying to keep me here this way, I'll have to sneak off in the middle of the night," I sometimes said half-jokingly to my wife.

I believe the reluctance of the local people to let me leave caused further resentment on the part of Headmaster Sakurai. It could be said that I was a mere common soldier while the headmaster was the general. However, even though he should have been pleased that the people did not want to part with me, I had angered him and his wife so many times that he could no longer take any pleasure at all in my popularity. By the time I was ready to leave Komoro I regretted my having gotten so close to that gentleman whom I had once looked upon almost as a parent. I do not fault him for this. It was simply something that could not be helped.

On the day when Sensei, along with Kusakabe and Koyasu and the young men of the town, held a small farewell gathering for me, I joined them in Nunobiki.[15] I believe that Yakata also came over from Nezu on that day. We spent half a day talking together in a room of that old temple high on the bank. I seem to recall that the little river fish known as *haya* were especially delicious.

"Saitō-sensei, are you able to drink again like you used to?" someone asked, and Sensei seemed to be recalling his grave illness as he replied, "A little . . . ," and gave a sad little laugh. It must have been about then that he started drinking again.

When I came as a teacher to the Asama Gijuku I was still an unmarried youth, but when I returned to Tokyo I was accompanied by three of Sensei's students. I remember that Sensei brought flowers and tossed them through the window as the train pulled out.

Azuma naru	In the East
Miyako no sora wa	The capital skies are
Tōkeredo,	Distant but
Chikatsu no mori ni	In Chikatsu/nearby forest
Kokoro todomeyo.	Let your heart remain behind.[16]

I was overwhelmed when I read Sensei's poem. He had written it on the underside of the writing desk that the teachers and students had given me as a going-away present.[17] I believe Sensei told me that the desk had been made from a single pine board that had been brought from a place called Chikatsu in Saku.

I left Komoro with the feeling that I had somehow made a cold parting with Headmaster Sakurai. Yet I have any number of things for which I am grateful to him, and I became all the more aware of them after I had left Komoro. If Headmaster Sakurai had not invited me there I would never have been able to learn what I did from the farmers who live in the highlands in Saku. In truth, from the time on that first morning in Komoro when I gazed out upon the mountains like a famished traveler—those distant, snow-capped peaks—Mt. Asama, and the range shaped like fangs, the deep-shadowed valleys, the ruins of the old castle, the clouds clustered like wisps of smoke over the mountain peaks—from the time I first caught sight of them bathed in morning light, I felt that I was no longer the same person as before. I went out as a teacher; I came back as a student.

Sensei occasionally sent news from the mountains down to me in Tokyo. It must have been about a year after I left that I received his letter telling me of the decision to close the school. I learned how terribly concerned Sensei and Koyasu were. They had even gone so far as to express their dismay before the students gathered in the school. And it was in a letter from a graduate of the school living in Nishihara, near Komoro, that I learned how Headmaster Sakurai, having made all his farewells, had taken down the tablet before the gate of the school as a memento of Captain Masaki's calligraphy.

It was after that that I received those visits from Sensei in my home in Tokyo. He brought his family down from Komoro to Tokyo and he left them there temporarily while he taught in a school in Maebashi. Things seemed to have become even more difficult for him after he left Maebashi. Sometimes when I entertained him I would find it impossible to decide just where my troubles ended and his miseries began. I recall receiving from him a pot of morning glories that he had grown in his desolate Tokyo home. It must have been around then that an old friend of mine from grade school days made an effort to build up the membership of a morning glory society for Sensei's sake.

"To go off on a hot day to some distant place, sweating all the way, just to deliver a single pot of morning glories, only to be told that there is no one at home, really gets me down—" he would say, looking especially tired and run down at such times. Sometimes he wolfed down the pastries and refreshments I set before him without thought of restraint or propriety. I nearly burst into tears as I watched him, wondering how it was that a person like Sensei could have sunk to this. At the same time, I would find that even when I had money to go out drinking with friends I had none to give to Sensei.

One day I was on the train returning from a call I had made on an acquaintance living on the seashore at Inage. It was time for the autumn harvest and a golden sun poured down its light over the fields. Men and women were hard at work. The richness of the harvest gave me a powerful sense of the bounty of nature. Such harvest times are indeed nature's gift to man. I returned home, still in that mood, and the very next day Sensei came by to tell me about his plan to go to Hiroshima. Thinking that a late autumnal calm had at last come to Sensei's life, I treated him to a dinner of loach. I recall that as a parting gift I set out before him an old jacket whose seams had been undone in preparation for sending it out to the laundry but which had not yet gone out. I apologized for the quality of the gift, but Sensei replied in good spirits that he would have his wife sew it back up and send it on to Hiroshima.

"Really? That would be fine."

Sensei and I both caught our breaths at the same time. I left the house with him to see him off and we walked together for two or three blocks.

Sensei did a lot of traveling after he came down from the mountains. He went to Maebashi, to Hiroshima, and then to some other distant school, working a year or two at each. He would go off, saying that his credentials were given even more respect in public schools than at a place like Asama Gijuku. Each time I welcomed him back to Tokyo he would look older. His complaining reached the point where it depressed me. I cannot recall just when it was that his beloved Tarō died. Yakata had also left his studio in the mountains and come down to Tokyo to set up a home at about the same time as Sensei, and it was under his sponsorship that Tarō, up until his death, had been working in the lithograph department of a printing shop. When Tarō died of lung disease, Sensei seemed to lose heart. He blamed his son's lung troubles on the close quarters and the bad ventilation of the workers' dormitory at the print shop. I believe that this son had been very kind to his father, but didn't one of his daughters also die of the same lung disorder?

"Enough! When even your children start dying of lung disease, that's enough of poverty!" he must have said.

Wasn't that really what Sensei, when he caught hold of me, was always trying to tell me as long as he lived? He always had with him that old silver-mounted pipe that he had brought from Ueda to Komoro and from Komoro to Tokyo. He had been using it for so long that the gingko leaves engraved on the bowl were half worn away. He would tap his pipe, delightedly puffing away whenever I put some of my own tobacco in his pouch. Or else he would smoke one of my cigarettes and talk about almost nothing but his family. When the daughter born in Ueda went to work in a factory making watch chains, she was making eight *yen* all by herself; Sensei told me how she brought the money home and showed it to her mother.

"She really put on airs. Little slip of a girl that she was, she started talking about taking us all out for a treat . . ."

I could almost see the smiling faces that filled Sensei's impoverished life. It was much later when his second daughter married, only to have her husband take to his bed with lung disease, at the point of death. The two had nothing to eat in the house when Sensei came to confer with me about whether he should call his daughter back home.

"Let's go out for some net fishing!"

I once invited Sensei out onto the water. He too seemed to want to go out and heaved a deep sigh. He got himself up in an extraordinary costume to join me and the boatman we engaged, one who was skilled at casting nets. We set out from the Kanda River and I rowed down to Eitai Bridge. We went out as far as the deep green waters off Shinagawa, where we listened to the lonely but pleasant sound of the nets being cast and talked about Headmaster Sakurai and Kusakabe and Koyasu. Our old friends from the Asama Gijuku were now scattered to the four winds. I understood that Sensei had clashed quite bitterly with the headmaster when he left Komoro but now that he was far away we both missed him and we exchanged stories of bygone days. I subsequently learned that Koyasu, who went to America after the school closed, had sent for his wife and the two of them were living together abroad; they must already have been in America that day when we talked about them on the boat.

I think it was shortly afterward when Sensei went to take up a position in Nara prefecture. It seemed that he found that half day on the boat unforgettable, for he wrote from Yamato about how delicious the fish caught off Shinagawa had been that day. From that time on I only saw Sensei once a year. And when I was off on a trip myself, three whole years might go by without my seeing him, but I often got letters from him. He once wrote of the customs and mores in the mountains along the upper reaches of the Totsu River,[18] and of the history of the school that had been established in that rustic setting. It seemed to be frightfully far back in the mountains; one had to walk more than forty miles from the railway station to get there. I assume communications between the school and the rest of humanity were cut off whenever there were floods. I imagine, too, that the children, accustomed to eating only sorghum and millet, must have been astonished by the luxury of eating rice at the school. Sensei wrote that it was like a land of mountain spirits but whenever I thought of him in that country, I felt that this time he had really gone to a place deep into the mountains to teach.

When Sensei and I next got together in Tokyo, he seemed still older. It wasn't surprising—it was already some nineteen years since we had first met, and neither my wife nor my children whom Sensei had known in Komoro were with us anymore.

From that time on in Tokyo, Sensei would say, "All I want for my final memory is to go and work in just one more school. I just don't get along with Jirō. I'd like to make what money I can, without being burdened with children. But then I remember Tarō. If only he were still alive, I'd be able to talk with him. That's what I think . . ."

Sensei and I often talked about such things. When he came calling with Jirō, who was by then working in a pencil factory, we would talk about members of the Asama Society; Sensei relied on the students he had taught at the school as though they were his own children. However, they did not seem to play the role quite as he had expected them to; it just didn't go over well for him to take his money problems to those young people.

"No matter how much we give Saitō-sensei, it's like dripping water on a hot stone. He drinks up everything we give him. It would be better for us all to get together and give him something for some special purpose."

Shiina and Tsuchiya came to my place once to say that. But even they quietly worried about Sensei.

In his final years, Sensei complained every time he caught hold of me. On rare occasions a light would come to his eyes and he would seem about to listen to what I was saying, but such times were very rare and it seemed that he never talked about anything but his own complaints. I think now that this need to complain was an indication that he was getting ready to leave the world.

Sensei, you were never one to reply to anything I said. Now you will never speak again. Just as one might wish to worship even the leaves of grass that have been offered to the dead, I now find precious my memories of his old hat and his old stick. I've recently moved to a house that Sensei never knew but whenever I am alone in my room it somehow seems that Sensei is sitting across from me.

Rather than the days before his death when with a sniffle he would say, ". . . and we went out netting fish off Shinagawa," it is only now, after his death, that he speaks to me, of all kinds of things.

Notes

Tōson Zenshū 10:169–205.

1. The Asama Society was the actual name of the alumni association of the Komoro Gijuku (Asama Gijuku in this story).

2. The model for Shoda is Saitō Ryoku; see the "Afterword to the *Chikuma River Sketchbooks*," note 5.

3. In the generation of Samejima Shin (b. 1852), the model for Saitō-sensei, graduates in science were still a rare and precious commodity in Japan. The social recognition and career opportunities normally enjoyed by such a person would have been analogous to those of the holder of a doctorate in nuclear physics in the 1950s or in computer science in the United States during the 1980s. Note that this piece is sometimes voiced as direct address to the departed Saitō-sensei and that in these passages Tōson makes use of the polite third person.

4. The Shin'etsu line, completed in 1893, runs from Tokyo northwestward across the widest portion of the island of Honshū to the town of Naoetsu on the Japan Sea coast between Niigata and Toyama. It passes through Karuizawa and Komoro well before the halfway point. The line provides access from Tokyo to Shinano province (modern Nagano prefecture) and to the Japan Sea coast.

5. See "Among the Boulders," note 8.

6. The allusion here is to Kimura's third wife, Takako, whom he married after his second marriage had ended in circumstances similar to those described in Tōson's "Former Master" (*Kyūshujin,* 1902). Although the husband in that story was described as a banker, the resemblance to Kimura and his domestic problems was so transparent that the magazine in which it was published was withdrawn from circulation. The episode appears to have been one cause of the growing estrangement between Tōson and Kimura.

7. One of the largest establishments in Honmachi, the Kadoya was located on the corner on the north side of Honmachi. The exact line of business is unclear.

8. Morimoto Teiko, in *Fuyu no Ie* [Fuyu's Family] (Tokyo: Bungei Shunjū, 1987), p. 179, also lists Tōson's wife, Fuyuko, as a member of the staff of the girls' school, but nothing is said about her duties.

9. A direct echoing of Bashō's travel journals. Tōson shared the great poet's delight in such juxtapositions of the elegant with the bucolic.

10. In a discussion of the Agehaya in *Shimazaki Tōson to Saku* [Shimazaki Tōson and Saku], ed. Saku Kyōikukai Tōson Iinkai, 2nd printing (Saku, Nagano prefecture: Saku Kyōikukai, 1978), pp. 76–84, the name "Shirami no Tōfuya" is said to be of Tōson's coinage. The unidentified writer writes *shirami*

phonetically in *kana,* explaining that the common tendency to write this word with the Chinese character for "lice" is based on a misreading and that Tōson was in fact referring to the fact that the operators of the shop started work each day in the earliest light of the dawn (*shirami* 'whitening,' a word which can have this meaning but which often means "faded" or "washed out," in all the senses of those English expressions). Neither the Shinchōsha *Shimazaki Tōson Zenshū* (11:184) nor the Chikuma Shobō *Tōson Zenshū* (10:178), both of which give the Chinese character for "lice" in this passage, admit of any such ambiguity. The context seems to support this choice of characters.

11. *Hachi-hai-dōfu,* a dish consisting of tōfu cut in thin strips and boiled in four cups of water, two cups of soy sauce, and two cups of sake, a total of eight cups (*hachi-hai*).

12. Yet another reminder that after the anti-Buddhist campaigns of early Meiji, empty temples were a drag on the market all over the country.

13. Huai-su (fl. ca. 760), a priest from Ch'angsha who came to the T'ang capital, Ch'ang-an, at an early age, eventually established himself as one of the outstanding calligraphers of the age.

14. See *Chikuma River Sketchbooks,* note 58.

15. The Nunobiki Kannon is a fourteenth-century temple of the Tendai sect spectacularly sited on the face of a cliff across the river from Komoro. Its veranda affords a panoramic view of the town with Mt. Asama in the background.

16. Ikeda Yoshitaka, in *Shimazaki Tōson no Shōgai* [A Life of Shimazaki Tōson] (Tokyo: Kadokawa Shoten, 1961), p. 260, gives the fourth line as "Chikatsu no koto ni" (Of Chikatsu/Of nearby things), but both the Shinchōsha and the Chikuma Shobō *Zenshū* print the fourth line, with its richer and more graceful play on the place name, as I have given it here.

17. Tōson gave his own desk to Kōzu Takeshi, after writing the following inscription on the underside:

> Companion of seven years, helper in my reading on mornings of greenery-filled windows, on evenings of snow-filled gardens, made still closer to me by serving as a cutting board for rice cakes on a New Year's morning of longing for spring. Now you go to a new master to be bathed in as yet unknown warm feelings. Fare well! May you serve as an unchanging souvenir of those days.

> April 1905

> On the day I moved out of Baba'ura to return to the capital

> Tō

18. The Totsu River flows northward into the Ki River after draining the extreme southern edge of Nara prefecture. Although relatively close to the ancient metropolitan area of Japan, the ruggedness of the country has always made it seem remote. A generation earlier, the region had suffered such severe flooding that a large part of the population moved to Hokkaido.

Production Notes

This book was designed by Roger Eggers.
Composition and paging were done on the
Quadex Composing System and typesetting
on the Compugraphic 8400 by the design
and production staff of University of
Hawaii Press.

The text typeface is Baskerville and
the display typeface is Schneidler.

Offset presswork and binding were done by
The Maple-Vail Book Manufacturing Group.
Text paper is Glatfelter Offset Smooth,
basis 60.

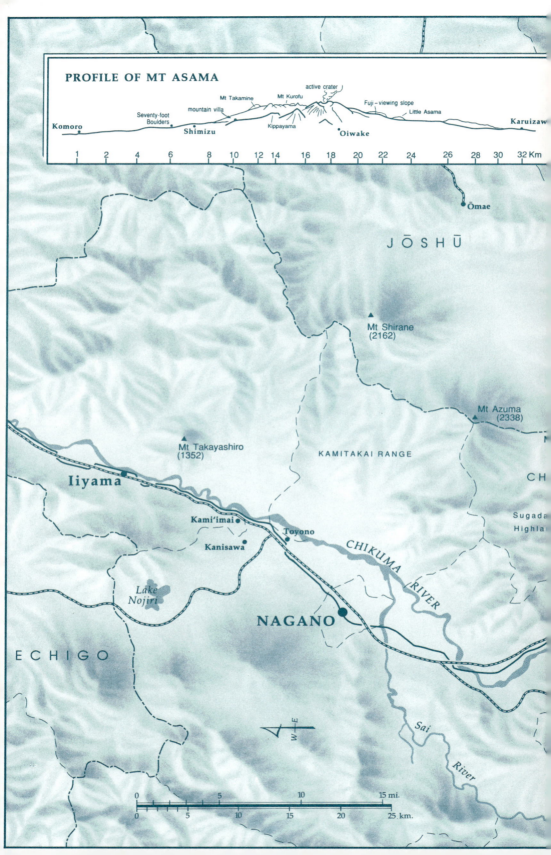

active crater
Mt Takamine
Mt Kurofu
mountain villa
Fuji – viewing slope
Little Asama
Komoro
Seventy-foot Boulders
Shimizu
Kippayama
Oiwake
Karuizaw

| 1 | 2 | 4 | 6 | 8 | 10 | 12 | 14 | 16 | 18 | 20 | 22 | 24 | 26 | 28 | 30 | 32 Km |

Ōmae

J Ō S H Ū

Mt Shirane
(2162)

Mt Azuma
(2338)

Mt Takayashiro
(1352)

KAMITAKAI RANGE

CH

Iiyama

Sugada
Highla

Kami'imai

Toyono

Kanisawa

CHIKUMA RIVER

Lake
Nojiri

NAGANO

E C H I G O

Sai
River

W—E

| 0 | 5 | 10 | 15 mi. |
| 0 | 5 | 10 | 15 | 20 | 25 km. |